Note to Self

Note to Self

ALINA SIMONE

FOURTH ESTATE • London

First published in Great Britain in 2013 by
Fourth Estate
An imprint of HarperCollins*Publishers*
77–85 Fulham Palace Road
London W6 8JB
www.4thestate.co.uk

First published in the United States in 2013 by
Faber and Faber, Inc.
An affiliate of Farrar, Straus and Giroux

1

Designed by Jonathan D. Lippincott

A catalogue record for this book
is available from the British Library

ISBN 978-0-00-750939-3

Printed and bound in Great Britain by
Clays Ltd, St Ives plc

For Joshua

Note to Self

Time theft. This was Anna's first thought when she found out she was being let go. Everyone was doing it—Brandon was practically webcasting gay porn from his cube—but for some reason management had decided to unleash the mailbox scrubbers and digital hounds on her. Worse, she couldn't deny it. The Internet had draped itself, kudzu-like, over her brain. There were disturbing signs. Or rather, signs that Leslie later pointed out were disturbing. Like the spam collection. "Spam's not a collectible," Leslie had said when Anna laid her confession on the table. "That's not a thing, Anna." And Anna had to explain because Leslie didn't know what it was like out there—her floors were cleaned by tiny robots with cute names. Market brinksmanship had driven spammers to new poetic heights. *Someone* should be saving it, studying it, sorting it according to some matrix of desperation, even.

"'Tiny bubbles of discontent surround me because I'm as lonely as a shark in the deep blue ocean.'" Anna quoted from a Ukrainian escort's solicitation she'd rescued from the filters. "Don't you think that's kind of beautiful?"

"Don't you have better things to do than read spam?" Leslie countered.

That assumption, Anna had to admit, was debatable.

Of course, when Anna was called into Mr. Brohaurt's office, she felt ill at the thought he'd discovered her little *Kunstkammer* of spam. Only four years older, Chad Brohaurt made forty times her annual salary and could cleave the Earth with his jawline. There was some incredibly filthy stuff in there, things she'd felt obligated to include for the sake of completeness. Sitting on his couch of real leather, she had the urge to confess, explain that she always started off clicking on something perfectly reasonable. Then one thing led to another and before she knew it, *whoops!* down the rabbit hole. Only it wasn't a "rabbit hole" was it? "Rabbit hole" implied someplace whimsical and fun, an enchanting place where you could enjoy weapons-grade cocktails with a well-dressed rodent. The Internet was more like an asshole. An asshole whispering of African fruits with miraculous weight-loss properties and discounted mani-pedis in some forlorn section of Queens.

It turned out her dismissal from Pinter, Chinski and Harms had nothing to do with time theft, though. Mr. Brohaurt had sat down by the window, put a sad hand on the knee of his expensive pants. "This has nothing to do with you, Anna," he'd said. "Everyone's getting a haircut." And Anna had stupidly looked out at Madison Avenue, curious about the new haircut. Of course, he'd meant budget cuts and the other white-shoe law firms. The new austerity. The end of everything.

But that was five weeks ago, and now here was Leslie's voice calling her back to their "sesh" like the gentle chime of a laptop rebooting.

"Thirty-seven is not the end," she was saying. "It's really just the middle."

Anna had taken Leslie up on her offer reluctantly. In general, she felt pretty ambivalent about time spent offline. With other people she always ended up pretending to be someone else, someone more like them. Whereas alone with the Internet, she was totally herself. There were no vagaries. She clicked on exactly what she felt like clicking on and each click defined her. Even the spam. Especially the spam. Besides, what kind of person needed a life coach? Of course, Leslie wasn't a real Life Coach, but she was a consultant at McKinsey, which trafficked in all the same theories, or so she had assured her. But to her surprise, Anna found herself looking forward to the ritual. They met on Sundays at Café Gowanus, which she liked even though it was built on a Superfund site. The café was as clean and bright as the Apple store it might well have been, full of ambitious people with hyphenated jobs and nice clothes, hunched over their MacBooks. It was as though the sugar packets had all been secretly filled with Adderall; just being in the room gave her a charge. Each week, Leslie armed Anna with a variety of motivational sayings—Reposition Your Disposition, Negativity Is a Self-Fulfilling Prophecy—cranks to power her way toward a new life. It hadn't exactly worked out that way. For now, her weeks were still powered by Triscuits and the Web, but she enjoyed the security of Leslie's firm hand on the rudder.

"Did you think about what we talked about last time?" Leslie said.

"Yes," Anna said, remembering only that last time they had talked about what to talk about this time. "I'm thinking of taking a class."

She waited, but Leslie's expression did not change. The pen stayed where it was, next to the half-eaten scone and the egg timer.

"You already have a master's," Leslie said.

"This is different."

"Taking a class isn't strategic, Anna. That's operational."

"It depends—" Anna began, because she already had a theory about this, but Leslie cut her off again.

"Remember: a goal without a plan is just a wish."

"Yes, but—"

"And I'm sure you've already asked yourself this, so let's pretend I'm not asking, but is this really what you need to be spending your severance on?" Leslie set her latte down inside Anna's Core

Competencies as if it were nothing more than a cocktail napkin. Which, of course, it was. They were sitting by an open window, the air off the canal as fresh as a newborn fart, with Anna's Life Map on the table between them. "Your Core Competencies still look thin," Leslie said, prodding the moist napkin. "Let's go back to your experience at grad school, mine it for some strengths."

"That was years ago," Anna began. If anything, shouldn't they be talking about Pinter, Chinski and Harms, where the wounds were still fresh, Google-searchable? "Why rehash that stuff now?"

"Because you can't know where you're going if you don't know where you've been," Leslie said, possibly for the second time. "Start with the dissertation."

Anna's stomach plunged. *Dissertation* had the same effect on her as the word *sarcoma*.

How she had missed graduate student life at first! Her amorphous days tethered to an illusory sense of purpose. Setting off for a bright café like this one each morning to not write her thesis. How she missed lunches with Sveta and Evgeni (the Slavic Studies department was stuffed with Slavs perfecting their Slavism). Of course, a month after the department kicked her out the pendulum had swung hard the other way. Academia, she realized, was a sham. An intellectual sports club where she could walk the treadmills of her pointless arguments for years, mesmerized by the illusion of progress. Suddenly she wanted nothing more than to rise early each morning, get on the subway with her lunch in a bag, disgorge at the foot of some gleaming mass of glass and steel, serve as the filling in a capitalism cannoli. She had taken the job at Pinter, Chinski and Harms because it was a name that made people say "Oh!" They hadn't heard of it, just felt as though they should have. In truth, it didn't pay that much—not enough to live without a roommate—but there were benefits, including, Anna remembered with a twinge, tuition reimbursement. Six years later and what did she have to show for it? Aside from the cubital

tunnel syndrome she'd developed dragging files from one subdi-
rectory to another for hour after useless hour. No, she didn't
want to talk about the past, she wanted to talk about the future.

"Criminology," Anna said. The idea had come to her while
watching a TiVoed episode of *True Crime*.

"Huh?" Leslie said, looking up from the Venn diagram she'd
begun drawing.

"The class. I know it sounds random, but in a crazy kind of
way, it's perfect. Look, it's got something for each of my Spheres."
And to Anna's surprise, Leslie allowed her to take the pen from
her hand. "Criminology. It's about figuring things out. It's about
writing and analysis. And when you think about it, it's all about
people." Leslie continued to say nothing, which Anna found encouraging. "The other thing I like is how it's sort of, you know,
provocative. Because—let's admit it—murder is interesting. 'Ab-
normal personalities,' " Anna air-quoted. "Psychopaths, rapists,
pedophiles." Leslie looked around in alarm at the word *pedophiles*, but Anna kept going. "So even if you're just moving a bunch
of papers around on a desk, the serial killers still keep things
jumping on a certain level—"

"*If*," Leslie cut her off, "you are *really* serious about criminology and you're *sure* that's what you want to do, we'll put it on the
map. It's *your* map, Anna. Honestly, do whatever you want. You
can be a criminologist. You can be a unicorn. It's all you. But know
that this is major. OK? Something like that changes your entire
Vision Statement. It's a campaign, not something you can just
stick in your Spheres." Leslie took the pen back from Anna, who
had waved it decisively all around the map without daring to make
an actual mark. And as it slipped from her hand, Anna couldn't
help but notice that Leslie's pen, which was heavy and silver and
probably had her initials engraved on it somewhere, was, let's
face it, kind of obnoxious. It was—how hadn't she noticed this
earlier?—a fuck-you pen. Despite herself, Anna suddenly hated
Leslie all over again. Leslie, who could sit there looking so very

Whole Foods, with her curator husband and three-bedroom condo at the Emory, her job at McKinsey, those Selima Optique sunglasses—telling Anna exactly what she could and couldn't stick in her Spheres. Anna couldn't help but wonder if Leslie and Josh were still trying to have another baby or if things had gotten dire. She imagined Leslie wouldn't let it go lightly. There would be egg donors, sperm spinning, even surrogacy. Wouldn't it be just like Leslie to outsource?

"Of course, if you feel like you've given criminology the proper amount of consideration," Leslie continued, "and you're ready for Process and Learning, then let's do it. Go ahead. Put it down."

They both knew that Anna was not ready for Process and Learning.

And criminology wasn't even the worst of it. Anna had spent last night jotting down ideas in the margins of *The New Yorker* that she'd gotten from ads—the Middle Monterey Language Academy (Make a language breakthrough!), Voyages to Antiquity (Experience the extraordinary cultures of ancient civilizations!), Vantage Press (Publish your book now!)—opportunities that had seemed so alluring, with their elegant font and refracted *New Yorker* glory, when she'd perused them alone at her kitchen table.

"You think I'm mean," Leslie sighed.

"No!"

"I just want you to weigh your options before jumping into something," she said, rising from the table. "Again. Honestly, Anna. You have a nice life. Is this the kind of thing you really want in your head before you go to sleep at night? Murder? Pedophiles?" She shook her head, shook out the pedophiles. "I'm going to run to the *loo*, and when I get back, I think we should start all over with some To-From statements. Stop worrying about the big picture, OK? Better to have some low-hanging fruit at this stage. Makes the whole thing look doable. Start without me and think about the 'From.'" Leslie gave Anna a light squeeze on the shoulder and smiled. "Carpe diem, right?"

Leslie's eyes were so clear and calm, so reassuringly full of goodwill that all Anna could do was smile back. And as Anna smiled, she hated herself for hating Leslie, who had, after all, sacrificed her Sunday afternoon to help Anna. Leslie was, in fact, always volunteering to help Anna, forwarding e-mail about secret sample sales, reminders about daylight saving time, status updates from people they'd both gone to high school with, whom Anna had deliberately (and at no small emotional cost) managed to ice out of her life. Leslie had canceled her Pilates class to make Anna's whole thing look doable, but what had Anna ever done for Leslie? And on the heels of this self-doubt came another panicky thought: had these laptop people been sitting here the whole time, listening to her and Leslie? The tables at Café Gowanus were jammed right up against one another, practically overlapping. Anna turned to the couple at the neighboring table, and was relieved to find them both too deep into their screenplays to notice much else.

"What's with the Celtx?" the man was saying. "I thought I told you to buy Final Draft."

"It does the same exact thing," said the woman, who looked gaunt and *Vice* magazinish, her cheekbones holding up her face like tent poles. "The only difference is one's free."

"If you think producers won't see the glitches when you convert to PDF, you're wrong. They're definitely gonna think you belong in the slush if you won't even cough up two-fifty for professional screenwriting software."

The woman stared morosely into the screen, not saying anything as the guy retreated to his cell phone.

"I'm telling you," he said, jabbing apps with one finger, "you send it in like that, you'll hear crickets."

"Whatever, MFA timewaster."

And in that moment, with their undrunk drinks, shadows tattooed to the wall, the man's hat struggling to contain his hair—there was something so oddly familiar about the scene. Suddenly, she had it. *L'Absinthe*! Only it was the modern-day equivalent of the Degas painting: *L'iPad*. Feeling pleased with herself, Anna took a fresh sheet of paper and wrote the words *Pinter, Chinski and Harms* under the word *From*. She underlined the words twice, stared down at the page. But a minute later, it was still blank and she couldn't help thinking this whole exercise begged the question How many fresh starts can a person reasonably expect to make in life? Unironically, that is.

Now here was Leslie again, looking somehow refreshed. She had done something to herself in the bathroom. What was it? A fresh coat of lipstick? Or blush, the invisible kind that looks like you aren't even trying? No. Maybe she'd *removed* a coat of something? Was that the trick? You refresh by stripping back, like peeling away the generic wall-to-wall carpeting to reveal the charming hardwood below? Suddenly, more than anything, more than solving the riddle of her future, all Anna wanted to know was what Leslie had done to herself in the bathroom.

"What?" Leslie said. "Is there something on my face?"

"No." Anna pressed a glass of ice water to her cheek. "I just like your hair more the other way."

Leslie glanced at the piece of paper, flipped it over. "You're taking things too literally. What do both of these things have in common? Grad school and Pinter?"

"The B line?" Anna ventured.

"Stasis," said Leslie. "I want you to stop worrying. Stop thinking."

"OK."

"Don't take it as criticism." Leslie drew a line down the middle of the page, wrote "Definitional Present" at the top of one column, and "Aspirational Future" at the top of the other.

"I know."

"And don't drift off on me again. This whole process will go so much better if you clear your mind."

"OK."

"Remember, there's no need to rush into Implementation."

Anna was about to agree again. To agree as many times, in fact, and for however long, as Leslie wanted her to, when a man balancing two lattes bumped into the table, spilling his coffee. They both looked up. He wore the standard hipster uniform—a T-shirt featuring a bleak water tower and skinny jeans—yet somehow radiated the unmistakable air of a cherry picker. *There's unread e-mail in that man's in-box*, Anna thought. His cell phone was probably vibrating against his balls at this very moment. Lately it had become hard to separate what Anna really wanted from the things she felt obligated to manufacture for Leslie's consent, but now she experienced a moment of clarity. The thing she wanted more than anything else, the answer to every To statement, was simply: *e-mail*. More e-mail, better e-mail. Looking up at the man, she lost herself to a fantasy of his in-box: booty calls, exclusive invites, jokey messages from intelligent colleagues about inspired, time-sensitive projects. E-mail like that one she'd received from Columbia years ago informing her she'd been accepted to the Department of Slavic Languages. Con-gratu-fucking-lations. Her heart beat faster now, just thinking about that e-mail. What she wouldn't give to feel the adrenaline rush of that first virgin click again.

Since leaving Pinter, Chinski and Harms, Anna had kept a solitary unread e-mail in her in-box. It sat there like a goldfish in its parenthetical bowl, keeping her from feeling lonely. When she went to lunch, she turned off her phone just to ride the high of withdrawal, and while she ate tried to guess the number of messages that would be waiting for her back home. Often the number was still one. She would then sit in front of Gmail for a minute or ten, willing the 1 to change to a 2. And sometimes, as if by sheer magic, it did.

"Excuse me," the man said, executing a deft, Zumba-like move to prevent more spillage.

"No problem," Anna said, wondering how many Google search results there were for his name. Ten thousand? A hundred thousand? More? She looked back down at her Life Map, watching as the slow latte river blurred the word *objective*, coming menacingly close to the little star-shaped icon. The one representing her.

2

Thirty-seven is *not* the end, Anna decided. No, forty-three is more like the end. Strike that. Forty . . . six. Or maybe the end just kept zooming away from you the older you got, like the outer bounds of the universe expanding from the blastula where hope was first born? Of course, there were always exceptions; she'd read once that the Marquis de Sade didn't really get his perv on until he was fifty-one. Still, ignoring the outliers, Anna had only, let's face it, ten years max to get her shit together. The clock was ticking. Many different clocks were ticking, in fact, if she really stopped to consider it. But stopping to consider the orchestra of ticking clocks was pointless and only paralyzed her. Still, there was a reason that store was called Forever 21, not Forever 37. Maybe she had already pissed away her quotient of potential. Who else was a late bloomer? Well, there was always Grandma Moses. And some people said Jesus didn't do his best work until after he was dead.

Anna and Leslie had decided to wrap up their life-coaching session early. Anna had made enough progress for one day, and besides, Leslie had to pick Dora up somewhere or drop Dora off somewhere, and everyone knows that as soon as someone mentions their child that's the end of it. They absolve you of all social responsibility, children do. Like cancer, or church. But Anna hadn't particularly wanted to go right back to Sunset Park after Café Gowanus, to the back issues of *InStyle* scattered on the sofa where she'd fallen asleep last night and the refrigerator full of dubious bodega produce. The walk back to the subway was a dismal one—Third Avenue wasn't much to look at—yet surprisingly it was here, in the long shadow of a Dunkin Donuts that simultaneously managed to be a Pizza Hut and also a Taco Bell, that the idea struck her: *What if I wrote a book about women who were late bloomers?*

From there, the plan unfolded quickly. If she used the rest of her savings, the severance, the money from Aunt Clara, her tax refund, she could take a trip around the country, or even the world. She would find and interview the heroic women late of bloom— unlikely political candidates, entrepreneurs, madams, all those makers of organic kimchi and knitters of artisanal tampons fleeing unhappy jobs at hedge funds. She could picture herself sharing confidences with these women in taxicabs, on Vermont porches, in ashrams, touring a factory floor in matching hard hats. They would remain friends after that first initial interview, so touched and flattered would the women be at having been elevated to exemplar status. And, of course, as a late-blooming woman herself (nowhere near *forty-six*, of course, but still . . .), there was a beautifully seamless logic to Anna taking on such a project. She would bloom late while documenting late bloomers. It would be so *meta*. This fit her Core Competencies perfectly, and if Leslie were still here, Anna would tell her, yeah, go for it, change her Vision Statement or stick it in her fucking Spheres, whatever. She was ready for Process and Learning!

The feeling lasted until Anna got home and checked Amazon only to find there was already a book about women who were late bloomers. It was called *Late Bloomers* and—this killed her—it was written by a *man*. A man who was clearly already in full bloom (this was his fifth book) and could just as easily have written about human beatboxers or ironic leitmotifs in London street art or heirloom fucking melons. This man, whose name was Lars Stråtchuk, with a little circle above the *a* (he wasn't even

American!), had quite literally stolen her future. A future Anna had already inhabited for two sparkling hours, where she moved purposely through each day and her work had weight and meaning. She did not want to go back. Already she felt the apartment closing in on her, the late-afternoon light muddying the corners, the drapes and the stained IKEA carpet letting go of the day's heat, filling the air with their stale breath, making her tired. But first there would be a comfort snack. A tub of Sabra hummus and pita chips. Or a pint of blueberries with cottage cheese. She would eat with her mother's familiar remonstrations ping-ponging around her head.

Eating that will only make you hungry.
Fruit has more calories than chocolate.
I guarantee those nuts will taste better if you eat just one.
Anything you eat after six o'clock turns right to fat.

No, Anna decided, she wasn't going to do it. No couch. No snacks. Since Pinter, Chinski and Harms let her go five weeks ago, she'd spent the bulk of her time couching and snacking. Surfing the Web, actually. Presumably looking for jobs, but not really. Occasionally looking for love. Mostly just reading stuff. The day began with the refreshing of three tabs: *The Daily Beast*, *New York* magazine, and *Gawker*. From there, a kaleidoscope of options opened up, like snowmelt cutting innumerable channels down the side of a mountain. Hours later, she could end up anywhere: *Deadline Hollywood*, *Art Fag City*, or just somebody's Tumblr, reading about that new underwear that prevents cameltoe. Meanwhile, she couldn't help but notice, the things she always said she would do once she finally left Pinter weren't getting done. They'd been crushed by freedom. Her freedom. The sheer quantity of time at her disposal and the weighty responsibility of her own untapped potential made doing any one thing impossible.

She woke up in the mornings already exhausted by the possibilities. And, of course, the question arose of whether it was depression or merely situational. Leslie didn't think it was depression. Leslie's own postpartum depression had been serious, life-threatening. She knew all about the drugs and the research, the ins and outs of serotonin uptake, the interaction effects of different kinds of therapy, and she'd discussed all these things with Anna. Admittedly, Anna was kind of into the idea of it being depression. Then none of it would be her fault. She remembered something about her gap insurance covering mental health, and, of course, there would be the reassuring routine of regular appointments someplace uptown, which would get her out of the house. But gap insurance probably covered only a few months of sessions. Plus the medicine made you fat, didn't it? It destroyed your sex drive. One was faced with a miserable choice between sad, sexed up, and thin or fat, sexless, and happy. Of course, Anna was already fat, definitely sexless, and probably sad. But taking the drugs would rob her of hope. They would slap a cruel ceiling on her Aspirational Future. If she could never be thin, and would always be sexless, how could she ever be happy? It was a thicket of catch-22 situations. But if the two hours she had spent in the future, working on late bloomers, had taught her anything, it was that living in hope is a beautiful thing. There was no better feeling. In fact, the feeling was even better than the doing, because when she stopped to think about it, Anna had to admit she didn't much like to write. Ergo the unwritten thesis. And the thought of writing an entire book, ass-to-chair, day after day, sounded lonely. Worse than lonely, actually. It sounded fucking miserable. But being *on the cusp* of writing a book—or, better still, having already written a book—was something else. She'd gotten such a charge picturing herself telling Leslie, changing her Facebook status, moderating her lively new blog on LateBloomers.com as she crowdsourced suggestions for *Late Bloomers, Volume II* . . .

Without quite realizing it, Anna was surfing. She had sorted the Amazon comments for Stråtchuk's *Late Bloomers* so that the one-star reviews came up first, and a link in one of those comments had led her to another website about late bloomers, which was called Kurinji, after (the header announced) a rare Indian shrub that takes up to twelve years to bloom. Now Anna started reading the home page Q&A with Paul Gilman, a filmmaker from Los Angeles, who, at age forty-six(!), had become an impresario of the microcinema scene before going on to bigger and better things. Anna read through his bio and—no surprise—learned that the first forty-five years of Gilman's life had been noticeably devoid of promise: a ho-hum upbringing in the exurbs of Kansas City (he didn't even bother to clarify which one), a so-so college career, a drift from one forgettable white-collar job to another, an unsurprising failure to start a family. Now Gilman had a house in Brentwood. He had recently married a young actress (they'd met during his fellowship at Cannes) and was expecting twins.

K: You are known for your improvisational style.

GILMAN: I never use scripts. A script only imposes moral constraints on the actor. What I'm interested in is the uninhibited id. I take the actors and put them in a box. Then it's up to them to break out of the box. Sometimes literally.

K: Up until recently, you didn't exactly work with *actors* in the technical sense.

GILMAN: Right. Nonprofessionals.

K: How did you find them?

GILMAN: Craigslist. I would put up an ad for actors, no experience needed. I didn't care about age or size or race. I didn't ask for headshots. This was back when I still lived in Kansas City. It's not like Los Angeles, where you put something like that out and—

K: Everyone's straight from the Formica factory.

GILMAN (laughs): Right. These were real people. Actuaries. Teachers. Cooks. Whatever. People who needed the extra cash. I paid fifty a session. Sometimes I'd go to their house. Sometimes I'd tell them to meet me somewhere. The pay phone in front of the Cash America pawn. Or the loading dock behind the rug warehouse downtown. I'd drive over with my camera and see them waiting for me on the street. Then I'd drive around the block a couple of times, figuring out how they'd fit into the scene. After that, I'd make up a story on the spot.

K: Both *Calista at the Cum 'n' Go* and *Rurik, Rurik, Traffic Cop* have this really visceral, really frenetic quality. How did you edit those movies?

GILMAN: I edited all of my films in-camera.

K: Just record, then stop?

GILMAN: Exactly. Stop or pause. It is what it is. And since I'd never met the actors before, anything could happen. My one rule is that while I'm shooting, I won't talk. This one woman I hired, she worked at the hospital and came to meet me straight from work, still in her scrubs. I told her, "Here's the story: you're an EMT and you just responded to a call about a car accident that involved your husband. His back was broken in two places. He sustained internal injuries and the doctors have no idea whether he's going to live. You leave the hospital. You're on your way back to your car and you can't remember where you left it. You're lost in the parking lot"—we were in a parking lot— "and you call your mother on your cell to tell her what happened. Action!"

K: This sounds like *Clean Rite Meltdown*.

GILMAN: It ended up that way—

K: Spoiler alert.

GILMAN (laughs): Right. The woman wouldn't do the scene. She wouldn't do any of it. She just started screaming at me that she didn't know what the fuck I was talking about. Her face right up in the camera, calling me every kind of name. Went on about how she knew "the scam I was running" and her boyfriend had my license plate number, blah blah. Amazing stuff. The whole movie turned out to be just that one continuous shot of her face—

K: *Clean Rite* showed at Sundance?

GILMAN: It did. It's in MoMA's permanent collection now.

K: You've certainly come a long way. Can you say something about working with Johnny Depp?

GILMAN: Johnny is just an amazingly brilliant guy. Amazingly brilliant.

K: Any last words for aspiring filmmakers?

GILMAN: Get a camera. Let the rest take care of itself.

When Anna finished reading, she noticed it was dark. It was dark and now she was hungry. She got herself a bag of rice cakes and a tub of salsa and went back to the computer, where she searched Gilman on IMDb, and read the *Variety* reviews for *Calista at the Cum 'n' Go* and *Rurik, Rurik, Traffic Cop* and *Clean Rite Meltdown.* When the rice cakes were gone, Anna switched to vegetable chips (baked, not fried) and googled Gilman's wife for no reason. And when her roommate, Brie, came home from kickball practice, it was well after six and Anna's food was turning into fat. She was watching *Can't They Always Make More?* on YouTube and still hadn't turned the lights on.

"Hey," Brie said. She threw her cleats in the corner, setting off a small dirt-clod explosion. "Can you believe all I had for dinner was a glass of Merlot?"

"Good practice?" Anna said.

"Gotta poop."

"The postkickball poop!" Anna said, laughing nervously as though this were a perfectly normal thing for her to say. Something one of Brie's much-younger friends might say.

"Uh-huh," Brie said, breezing past Anna on her way to the bathroom.

Anna hit pause, got up, and turned the lights on. She threw away the plastic bag from the rice cakes and wiped the salsa ring on the table. She checked inside the bag of veggie chips. How many had she eaten? From the hallway, she could hear a flush and the sound of running water. Then Brie was back, wiping her hands on the butt of her shorts.

"What are you watching?" Brie said, head already in the refrigerator.

"This movie, *Can't They Always Make More?*"

"I didn't know you were into Gilman."

"I love Gilman," Anna found herself saying, unsure of whether she really loved Gilman or whether she was just happy to have something to talk about with Brie.

"You know that one, *Rurik at the Drive-In?*"

"*Rurik, Rurik, Traffic Cop?*"

"Yeah. Totally craptastic!"

"I know, right?" Anna said uncertainly. She always had trouble getting a read on Brie. Even when she wanted to kiss her ass, she could never predict where exactly Brie's ass was going to be. It's like she was always running around the room, lips at ass level, chasing after her. Maybe it was just the fact that Brie was still young enough to make declarative statements. She could still put periods, even exclamation marks, at the end of a sentence, whereas Anna had already changed her mind so many times about so many things it was all question marks and ellipses for her from here on in.

"But in a good way," Brie said, reaching into the refrigerator for a cold quesadilla. "I love how he's not afraid to just, like, let his movies be bad, you know?"

"It's a style," Anna said, pushing the bag of chips toward Brie.

"I love that one with the candy hearts. Oh, wait. I think I'm thinking of the girl." She dipped the edge of the stiff quesadilla into Anna's salsa. "You know, the other one? Who makes the movies on her cell phone?"

"I don't think so."

"They all hang out together," Brie said. "God, what's their name?"

Anna didn't know.

"Shit. I feel like I just read about them on *Daily Intel* the other day. This is going to kill me," Brie said. "I should text Rishi." Brie went over to her bag and started unzipping various pockets.

"I just love the way, with his movies, it just is what it is, you know?" Anna said, feeling like she was finally finding her groove in this conversation. "He just lets things *happen*."

But Brie wasn't listening. "Shit," she said, zipping and unzipping. "Where's my cell phone?"

"Did you bring a jacket?" Anna said, standing up.

"Shit." Brie was pulling things out of her bag, throwing them on the floor.

Anna made an effort to look concerned. "Should I check the bathroom?" she said.

"No. Fuck. It's either on the bus or back at the park."

"You'll find it . . . ," Anna said, hoping she wouldn't have to offer to go back to McCarren Park with Brie to hunt around in the dark grass for her cell phone.

"I can't believe this," Brie said, shaking her bag empty over the floor. Crumbs, bobby pins, pennies, receipts, pen caps, one of those inexplicable plastic Japanese toys with a head that was all teeth, a chewed-off thumbnail. Chinese fortunes—too many to count—drifted down like parade streamers.

"I'll be back," Brie said, standing up. She grabbed her wallet from the pile on the floor. "Can you stick this back in the fridge for me?" She nodded at the half-eaten quesadilla she'd set down on the couch.

Anna took the quesadilla, opening the door for Brie.

"If Rishi calls the landline, tell him what happened," said Brie. Before the door eased shut behind her, she passed a reflexive hand over the light switch, leaving Anna in the dark once more.

3

Anna felt her way back across the room toward the laptop glow. She yanked the cord out of the wall, letting it drag behind her as she made her way down the hall. Even though Brie was gone, Anna still made sure the bedroom door was closed before pulling off her pants. She slid her bra out from under her T-shirt and dropped it on the pile on the floor. The bra didn't have far to fall; the pile was almost as high as the bureau. Taking care of the pile was "on the list," though the list itself was a kind of bureau-high pile, wasn't it? Anna lay down on top of the comforter, pulled the laptop onto her bare thighs, and finger-typed *Gilman* into Hulu. Of course, *Clean Rite Meltdown* came up first, followed by *Rurik* and the film she'd just seen. But here was another one she hadn't watched yet, *Age of Consent*.

Anna clicked on the title. And as the movie loaded, she wondered how Gilman made any money when everything was always free, right here, on the Internet. How did anyone make any money on the Internet when even Anna had never clicked on a banner ad in her life? Except that one time, for the free pair of Uggs. And in return for filling out some endless form about her customer preferences, what did she get? Nothing but aggressive, filter-eluding spam—not the kind worth collecting—for mortgage refinancing and "authentic quality pharmaceuticals." *Never again*, she thought, and hit PLAY.

There were no credits. No theme music. A black screen with the title faded in and faded out too fast. Then there was a man, sitting on a bed, with a paper bag over his head. The man had on khaki shorts and a bright blue T-shirt. The words *Sun Microsystems* stretched across the roll of fat in his lap in huge white letters. Daylight struggled against the shades, which were pulled all the way down. A lamp with a crooked shade tossed a warped football of light across the wall. The room reminded Anna of one of those shabby motor inns where you drive right up to the door and all the windows face the parking lot. Other than the lamp, the only decorations were the radiator and a potted ivy on the windowsill that may have been plastic.

"This is where I keep my collection," the man said. Two eyeholes had been punched into the bag, also a slit for the mouth, through which wet lips and a swatch of mustache were visible. "Under the bed." He bent down, felt around, and pulled out a large plastic bag.

"Does it matter which one we start with? No? OK, so this one is *Penthouse Forum*," he began, taking out a magazine and laying it on the bedspread. "It's, like, just letters about celebrity fantasies and shit like that. It's not that interesting, actually. It's kind of a joke. Look at this. Every letter always starts out with the same horseshit line. 'I never thought these letters were real, until I decided to write one myself,'" the man mimicked in a low, husky voice, then laughed from inside the bag. "Almost like parodies of letters, you know? And the celebrities are . . . where is it . . ." The man started flipping through the magazine. "Yeah, man, check this one out," he held up a page and the camera zoomed in on a photo of Andie MacDowell wearing a red dress, smiling hard. "Who's gonna jerk off to some has-been MILF that's not even showing her vah jay jay, right? Who's gonna jerk off to Andie MacDowell? Would *you*, man?" he snorted. "I think I saw this same photo later, too, in a Campari ad. I guess it doesn't matter, though. If I'm already horny almost anything will work. It's like

I'm just looking for that final, uh, you know, *push*." The man put
the magazine back in the bag. "So that's *Forum*. But they have ads
for these nine-hundred numbers, too," he said. "Sometimes I use
those. OK, next." The man reached in and grabbed a bunch more
magazines. "So then I got some of these multipacks. Why? Because
they're cheaper. They're, like, old issues of things that're combined
into different groupings. Like, 'butts' or 'dildos' or whatever. And
I have a thing for, you know, the young ones. I mean, you can't sell
any images of girls under eighteen, but these girls are total jail-
bait, I bet. I like this one." He held up the cover of a magazine
with a young girl whose mouth had the permanently doughnuted
look of a blow-up doll. "*L'age légal.*" The man began turning the
pages, this time slowly and deliberately, and the camera moved in
close. There were pictures of hairless girls, wearing an inch of lipstick, their lingerie pulled to one side so their tits could pop out.
Page after page, they kept moving their panties aside and looking
perpetually shocked at the discovery of their own business. It was
kind of amazing. Anna couldn't help but think, *I mean, don't they
get bored?* It could be, like, their eighteenth shoot of the day and
they still have to be all, *Whoa! What's this . . . ? Well, hello! Look
who's here?* Unbelievable. *I would make the crappiest porn star
ever*, Anna thought, as she shifted the laptop, which was now
burning the tops of her thighs, to the pillow next to her head.

"I'll be your tampon any day," the man said to a cherubic
blonde who happened to be going down on another blonde, who
was busy plunging a dildo into a brunette whose entire face had
been swallowed in the gutter of the two-page spread. He flipped
through the rest of the magazine quickly, until it was done, then
tossed it aside.

"*Purely Anal*," the man announced, shaking his head with
what might have been delight. His head made a loud rustling
sound inside the bag.

"This one's kind of embarrassing. See this lady?" The man
flipped the page. There was a picture of a disembodied white

cock squirting onto the face of a black woman. "She's always wearing sunglasses. See? Every picture." The man turned the page and there was the same lady, giving a blow job, indeed wearing the same sunglasses. "It's kind of cool, though. Almost a cult thing. This is a good one, actually, this issue. I think this is the one that, uh, deserves a reading." The man hesitated. He stuck one of his hands up the bag to scratch his face, then reached down and readjusted himself. "Now I'm supposed to read this, right?" He stood up on the bed. For a second the camera zoomed in on his athletic socks, which had blue and white stripes at the top, then tilted queasily upward. The man was shifting uncertainly from foot to foot on top of the bed, his head close to the low ceiling, holding *L'age légal* away from his face at arm's length with one hand.

"Halt!" he bellowed suddenly, in a labored Shakespearean baritone. "In this enseamed Greyhound station bathroom? But it is so dirty here, dear lass! Nay? Perchance, you cannot wait? My hot throbbing cock is bursting its seams and your loins cannot withstand it! Kneel then, by the porcelain throne yonder, as my hands caress your rock-hard nipples, as you take me unto yourself and my hot foaming jizz rushes like a cresting wave over your fair brow. Forsooth, your knees be raw, but thou art fucking me like a crazy bitch, a deeper and harder banging I hath ne'er imagined. Thy pussy, so wet, so fucking wet and—" The man, overcome with laughter, sat back down and bounced awkwardly a few times on the bed.

"Sorry, man. I couldn't help it. I know I promised, but the writing in these things is pretty ridic, you know? Porn mags aren't really about the writing. Sometimes I'll be reading and, like, notice that I'm going along, correcting the grammar in my head? I'll be like, 'What the fuck?' Psht." He crossed his legs and went back to flipping through *L'age légal*. "Anyway, the other weird thing about this magazine? It totally isn't *purely* anal. Look. Blow job. Fucking. Head. Head. Three-way." The man kept flipping. "Anal.

Only *now* we get to anal. The whole thing's supposed to be anal and there's, like, barely any butt action at all! But I kind of like the weirdness of it, like they're tricking you into thinking it's all anal. Even though," he added, sotto voce, "I am really into anal sex.

"God, we have a lot to get through, man. This is a lot." He paused, pulling another handful of porn out of the bag. "This bag is totally gonna rip soon, too. Want to know something weird? I bet my mom knows I have this stuff. She cleans in here. She must have found them by now. When my brother still lived at home, he kept his pornos under the bed, too. He's the one who showed me. I could move them, I guess. Hide them better. But I like to be able to just reach under the bed, you know? It's all about the easy access. And, OK, this is gonna sound really fucked up, but some-times? Sometimes I think about my mom finding this stuff as I'm jerking off. Like, I *picture* my mom finding it and it gets me off that she *pictures* me getting off or something. Isn't that fucking sick? You should bleep that out, dude. I can't even believe I told you that. OK, but here are two more: *Tight* and *Young and Tight*. *Young and Tight* sounds like it would be good, right? But I actu-ally like *Tight* better. It's pretty disgusting." He opened up an issue of *Tight* and flipped through it in silent contemplation. "I haven't actually bought porn for a couple months, so these are all getting kinda stale. I mean, it's not like I've squeezed everything I can out of every picture or anything. But I definitely could use another hit, you know? Whoa—I love this one. Check this out, man." He held the magazine out to the camera, reading the title out loud. " 'The fragile beauty of young anal lesbians.' " He shook his head laughing again. "Hilarious."

Then the man stood up but the camera stayed where it was and Anna could see only his midriff, his khaki shorts, and a roll of fat.

"Hey, do you want some cheese?" a voice asked from above. Then the midriff walked off camera and there was just the bed, the pile of porn, a lonely tentacle of ivy snaking down the wall.

The sun hacked at the edges of the shades. The camera jumped to the ceiling, then cut out with a stab of static.

The scene reopened with the man's ass backlit by the refrigerator. *Asslit*, Anna couldn't help but think. He emerged holding a wedge of cheese on a plate, then made his way over to the sink to grab a cutting board. As the man rummaged in a drawer, the camera drifted around the room until it settled on a milk crate of empty beer bottles in the corner. The milk crate was set on top of another milk crate, also full of empties.

"Hey, you want some of this, man?" The camera swung back to the man, who was holding out a piece of cheese stuck to the flat end of a knife. "It's Emmentaler. Good shit, seriously. I got it at the farmers' market fresh. These two guys have, like, some kind of artisanal cheese farm out in Ashby and they truck it in on the weekends. Try it, man. It's straight outta the sheep or whatever." He waved the knife in front of the camera again. "Come on, man. It's been all day, you must be hungry. At least have a glass of water or something . . . ? OK, right. I forgot your whole thing." The man snorted. "Who's gonna watch this movie anyways? Me and cheese and butt fucking. Not exactly *Avatar*, man. You gonna have this in 3-D, too? Charge like sixteen bucks?" The man stuck the cheese into his mouth hole and chewed. "That's not a bad name, by the way. *Me and Cheese and Butt Fucking*. You should remember that."

He started walking back to his room and the camera followed.

"I was thinking of getting one of those pictures of the black lady in the sunglasses custom framed," the man called over his shoulder. "With, like, a backing and glass and a really, really nice wood frame? Just as a joke. That's only for when I get my own place, though," he added. "Not while I'm still living here."

Back in his room, he sat down on the bed and crossed his legs. "Back to work, right? OK. This one's just, like, a catalog. They have a lot of ads for, you know, toys and videos. The place I go is basically a video store, by the way. Sugar's. I remember

going in there for the first time. It's actually not far from here.
You probably drove past it. Right after that Sunoco station at the
exit? I was kind of scared. I walked in, looked around, and was
like—whoa, these people are *gross*. Every time I go in, I'm thinking to myself, I'm definitely the least gross guy in here." The man
paused for a moment. "I almost got a toy for Kylie. But that was
right before things got weird with us. We had butt sex once. Well,
kind of . . ." The man trailed off. "Anyway, if you want to see that
other stuff, it's up in the closet. I've got some vintage, too, where
it's not all girls with Barbie doll parts—"

Then the camera suddenly swung to the door. A voice was
calling from just outside.

"Snickers just left skid marks on the kitchen floor again," a
little girl yelled. "You better clean it before Mom gets home."

"You clean it," the guy barked from inside the bag. Then, to
the camera, "Fucking cat."

"I'm gonna tell Mom you told me to walk to my lesson—"
the girl's voice called back.

"Get outta here, Kay. I'm busy doing something."

"—and she won't let you have the car on weekends anymore." The door opened and a girl who looked maybe eight or
nine walked in. She had lank brown hair and was wearing a long
black robe, plastic glasses, and a maroon tie over a flowered tank
top. A Harry Potter costume, Anna realized. The girl held a wand
in one hand; the other hand stayed on the doorknob.

"Shit, Kay. I told you, don't come in here." The man began
frantically pushing the magazines off the bed and into the crack
between the wall and the radiator. Kay's eyes went wide.

"Why are you wearing that thing?" she asked, stepping into
the room.

"It's just a game, Kay. Get out."

"Who is that man?"

There was the metallic *clung* sound of magazine spines hitting
the radiator on their way to the floor. Kay turned and pointed her

wand at the camera. "Are you the one who called last night and hung up?"

"Leave him alone, Kay."

"I could hear you breathing, you know," she said to the camera, moving the wand in slow circles. "I command you—answer me!"

Having finished with the magazines, the man now stood and walked over to Kay.

"Answer me." Her voice edged up, high and shrill. "What are you doing? You're in my house. What are you doing in *my house?*"

"Hey, movie over, man. Movie's over. Cut!" The bag was crooked on the man's head, slanted to one side so that only one eye lined up with its hole.

"*Silencio!*" Kay screamed, whirling around to face the man with the bag on his head. She was crying now.

"Hey, turn that thing off, man," the man said to the camera. "C'mon, Kay." He got up and went over to the girl. "It's just a friend."

"W-what's the bag on y-your head for?" Kay was really sobbing now. The man kneeled down. He put a hand on Kay's shoulder, then twisted around to face the camera again.

"I said turn it the fuck off, man. *Now.* Can't you see it's fucking scaring her? C'mere, Kay," the man said. He pulled Kay stiffly into his arms and the camera zoomed in on Kay's face, tears leaking from her eyes, which were squeezed shut. It zoomed in on her mouth as she licked the tears and snot from her upper lip.

"Why wond ee s-say s-someting?" Kay sobbed. But her face was invisible as the camera jerked over to the man's fingers on Kay's shoulder. You could see the hair on his knuckles and the back of his hand. He squeezed her shoulder. And then the camera moved to Kay's flowered top. To a single purple flower with a yellow dot inside. Closer and closer, until its pixilated center filled the screen. Until the whole screen was just one raw, hideous, quivering pixel sun.

"It's just a friend," came the man's voice from somewhere, a little hoarse. "It's just a friend."

Then the screen went dark and the word *FIN* appeared. As if from a great distance, the sad strains of an acoustic guitar struggling to stay in tune could be heard. A Will Oldham song. Anna realized that she was crying. She read the credits, which were short and consisted mainly of Gilman. Later she would try many times to explain this Road-to-Damascus moment to herself, but would always come up short. All she knew was it felt as though she'd slipped a hand between the sofa cushions to find a new world among the lost coins and the unsightly crumbs. An underworld you could traverse unencumbered by the opinions of anyone else, where you could just be yourself. The opposite of pop culture. *Unpopular culture.* A place she might just belong.

It felt like a significant discovery, even though she didn't really know what it meant. And she was suddenly very tired. The lights were already off. The cars going by on the street below sounded like rain, like waves, like the soundtrack to some Gilman movie about the impossibility of sleep. She pushed the computer out of kicking distance, off to one side, then turned around and shut her eyes.

The laptop battery would die overnight, but she didn't even care.

4

Anna emerged from the subway to find that a new public art exhibit had been installed in City Hall Park. A tourist stopped in front of the same sculpture that stopped Anna. He was wearing flip-flops and holding a bag from the 9/11 memorial gift shop.

"What kind of fucking shit is this?" the man said, more to himself than anyone else, as he held up his iPhone and took a picture. It was an inadvertently accurate question—the sculpture honestly did look like shit. Anna found a plaque over by the water fountain that explained the installation, which was called *Seiri, Seiton, Seiso, Seiketsu, and Shitsuke*. The artist was a Japanese sculptor by the name of Mitsuri Yagihashi.

"I have always been fascinated by rituals of hygiene," Yagihashi was quoted as saying, "and the relationship between purity and paranoia. In Japan, one's cleanliness is considered a reflection of one's inner state. These five shrines were cast from the dung of macaque monkeys indigenous to Japan, then covered in gold leaf. I consider them 'taboo' structures." Yagihashi's quote was followed by a lengthy paragraph by Joseph Fierhoff, the director of the New Museum and chairman of the city's Arts in the Parks Fund, who described Yagihashi's work as "drawing on his country's rich folk art traditions" and "a response to Japan's famous 'toilet culture.'"

On the whole, Anna had to admit, the sculptures didn't seem to really transcend the raw materials they came from. They didn't look much like shrines to her. They looked like enormous gold-colored turd balls grouped in random clusters. Which wasn't to say that the park didn't seem kind of cheerful, improbably strewn with golden turd-ball clusters. But what was most impressive here, Anna couldn't help thinking, was the fact that they had been installed in City Hall Park at all. The sculptures sucked, true, but Joseph Fierhoff found the shitty shrines or whatever impressive and so did the Arts in the Parks commission and a number of other top-tier cultural institutions. They almost became, in a sense, monuments to artistic ambition. Monuments to themselves. This was Gilman and Yagihashi's great trick, Anna realized. They had figured out how to make a job out of simply being themselves, turned their perverse, narcissistic, possibly enlightened selves into marketable commodities. Maybe this was all art really was—being yourself. Seen in this new light, the turd balls lifted Anna's spirits considerably as she cut through the park toward J&R, dispelling any final misgivings she still had about buying the camera.

Brandon, had told her it didn't matter what camera Gilman used, that nowadays it didn't make sense to invest in anything but HD.

"Why hamstring yourself with technology?" he'd asked. "You think your Gilman guy doesn't convert all his crap footage to HD before he screens it at Cannes or whatever? Everyone does. That's why I'm right, right? Look, if you want to go analog, then go all the way. Real film. Super 8. But for fuck's sake, don't half-ass it."

Anna didn't want to half-ass it. And she trusted Brandon, who had studied film for a year at USC before transferring to Hunter. So she got back online right away after talking to him. The cheapest HD camera she could find on CNET reviews was a Panasonic HDC-TM700 for $794.29, but when she sent the link to Brandon, he'd immediately shot that option down as well.

"A big NO on the HDC-TM700!" Brandon replied in an

e-mail. "It does have some nice features. But mostly it's just a cheap piece of junk. It lacks external audio inputs and all you really need (are you paying attention?) is GOOD AUDIO. It's amazing what a professional soundtrack can do even for shit footage like Gilman's. In your case, I would actually recommend a camera with two mic inputs: one for a boom and one for a lavalier. You might try the VIXIA HF S10 or JVC GZ-HD6."

It made sense. She remembered the jarring sound of the bag rustling whenever the guy in *Age of Consent* moved his head, how real it sounded and how it seemed to bring you right into the scene. But when Anna went back to CNET, she found that even the VIXIA HF S10 and the JVC GZ-HD6 had only one mic input; all the cameras with two mic inputs were in a different price range altogether. Plus, boom mic and lavalier units were, of course, sold separately, and together added about seven hundred to the total cost. When Anna finished pricing everything out and sent the links to Brandon, he agreed that even with a minimally acceptable package, she was looking at close to $3,200. Or "thirty-two bucks," as he had put it.

B&H, Brandon had assured her, would give Anna a better deal than J&R, but all the clerks at B&H were Hasids and Anna found this too distracting. The last time she'd gone there (two Christmases ago, to buy a digital camera for her mother) she could think of little else but the Hasids, who seemed so happy and prosperous living under such terrible constraints. The Hasid who had helped her that day had red hair and blue eyes, and, of course, Anna couldn't help but thinking this was unusual for a Jew. She couldn't stop herself from wondering how many children he had, or from staring overmuch at his yarmulke. And the salesman's benign comparison of wide-angle focal lengths did nothing to camouflage his contempt for her lifestyle. She was sure of it, that if all the Hasids at B&H had any say, they would agree that Anna, a woman, shouldn't be there discussing megapixels and LCD screen resolution in the first place. That her hair should not be dyed. That her dress should not be so low-cut and should instead remind men of Soviet architecture. That she should be at home, making things nice for the husband and children she didn't (but should) have. She knew Hasids didn't have sex until they were married, until after they'd *had* children even, and could only imagine what the red-haired Hasid would think if he knew that she'd had phone sex—regular phone sex, not even the brave video-chat kind—with a man she'd met on the Internet.

No, the winner of this double-consonant-ampersand contest could only be J&R. Even if it was cheaper, B&H was out of the question.

The salesman who ended up helping her at J&R was named Khuleh. He was from Oman and, unlike the Hasids of B&H, who spoke with the clear diction and authoritative tones of asylum attendants, Anna understood none of what Khuleh said. She did understand that he was trying to sell her a different camera, because he had picked up the box for a Kodak Zi8 and started waving it slowly in front of her face.

"Goolex!" Khuleh insisted. "Goolex." Whatever that meant.

This only made Anna angry, because she knew all about the Kodak Zi8, which didn't have *any* mic inputs whatsoever and was just an overpriced pocket cam for tourists. Anna pointed instead at the box for the Panasonic 3MOX AVCCAM.

"I want this one," she said.

But Khuleh kept waving the Zi8 at her, so she picked up the AVCCAM box and waved it at Khuleh, realizing that now they had become two people waving boxes at each other, executing some complex, consumer form of Butoh in the camcorder aisle of J&R. Finally, Khuleh, conceding which side his bread was buttered on, stopped waving the Zi8 and took the AVCCAM box from Anna. He filled out an order form and Anna went downstairs to the cashiers. With New York sales tax everything came to almost thirty-five hundred. And when Anna handed half of

Aunt Clara's money over to the cashier, she kept reminding herself of the little things she skimped on. *I don't have cable*, Anna
thought. *I've never downloaded a ringtone*. After running the
card, the cashier made a big thing of explaining J&R's return
policy, which was sternly worded and seemed to indict Anna as a
money launderer or a pedophile before her goods were even in
the bag.

She made it as far as the park, as far as the smiling Chinese
family posing for a snapshot in front of *Seiso*, the tottering turd
sculpture that looked not unlike a man on a horse, when she realized the box was too heavy and flagged a cab back to Brooklyn.
An additional thirty dollars, Anna could not help but notice.

When she got home, she set the box down in front of the hallway
closet and went to fix herself lunch. Brie wouldn't be home until
past seven—on Tuesdays she worked as an intern at Condé Nast's
ad sales department. The rest of the week, Brie had a different
internship, at a small music management company downtown.
Anna did not really understand how Brie survived when her per
diems barely covered lunch and didn't include a Metrocard. But
Brie had told her these internships were highly competitive. They
took only *five* people at Condé Nast per semester, and had it not
been for Brie's prior internship at *Women's Wear Daily*, she could
never have snagged this one. The music management position was
even more exclusive; Brie had to wrangle that one through inside
connections. It was amazing to Anna that Brie worked so hard
just for the privilege of working hard. But what did Anna know?
She was, after all, ten years older than Brie. In her day, people had
simply gone out and gotten jobs after college or some kind of
paid fellowship. Still, Anna was willing to concede that those were
simpler times—before 2007 and the collapse of hope.

She put a frozen saag paneer dinner in the microwave for four
minutes on high, and while that was cooking, ate half an avocado.

But with a minute and a half still left to go, the avocado was already gone, so Anna got herself a bowl of seedless grapes and sat down to check her Gmail. She had eleven messages, which was good for a Tuesday. But then, heart sinking, she realized only one was real—from Brandon—and the rest were just Flavorpill bulletins, auto reminders about various depressing things she'd pay to forget, and a bulk-mailed greeting from a woman in the contracts department of Pinter, Chinski and Harms, smugly enjoying her overseas "vacay."

The microwave pinged and Anna, feeling already full, looked over at the box, still sitting by the door. J&R didn't have a bag big enough for it, so the AVCCAM box sat naked on the floor, its sides splattered with pictures of itself, its features announcing themselves in garish cartoon letters. Next to the AVCCAM box lay a large plastic bag that contained the two smaller boxes with her sound gear: an AV-JEFE CM520 professional lavalier mic with Shure mini 4-pin XLR connector and a Sennheiser MKE 400 compact video camera shotgun microphone.

The microwave pinged again, and Anna got up to fetch the saag paneer. This one didn't come with rice, so she got herself a roll of sourdough bread. She ate straight from the plastic container while reading The Daily Beast's "Cheat Sheet" on her laptop. When she finished eating, she clicked over to Daily Intel, then Fishbowl NY, then back over to her e-mail, where there were no new messages in her in-box. She considered checking Newser (though she didn't much trust Michael Wolff), or PopEater (even though it always made her feel guilty afterward). Then Anna wondered whether The Daily Beast's "Cheat Sheet" had refreshed in the past half hour, whether it was worth maybe checking back in. But then she caught herself and remembered the box.

She had cleared her entire day for that camera, so why was it that now, after all the hassle and money spent, with the camera finally home, she did not want to open the box? It was because, Anna knew, inside the box, the camera would be broken into its many subcomponents. And each component would have to be assembled according to very specific instructions that would be meticulously outlined in an instructional booklet divided into eight chapters, and translated into French, Japanese, German, and Russian. Annoyingly, there would also be a separate disk with software that might or might not be compatible with her operating system. There would be many small plastic bags inside the box, with little coiled cables inside each bag. Each cable would look exactly the same, but of course their inputs and outputs, their minute, electronic genitalia, would differ ever so slightly. The cables would be molded into perfect little bows and held in place with a single twist tie. Unwrapping them would make Anna feel guilty. Ripping the small plastic bags open would make her feel guilty. Throwing away the cardboard backings would make her feel guilty. She pictured herself with the components and the bags and the cables all spread out in a big, guilt-inducing, Earth-destroying pile before her, and she pictured the tiny font of the instructional booklet, which she would dutifully struggle to follow before tossing it aside to just follow her instincts instead. Inevitably, she would unpack everything only to find that something was missing. Or that she had an extra component left over. She would turn on the camera to find that it wouldn't turn on. Or that a little red light wouldn't stop blinking. There would be visits to the "troubleshooting" section of the AVCCAM website, and calls to an 800 call center in Tehran where a man insisting his name was Pierce would walk her through the installation process in lightly accented and unfailingly polite English. And Anna would think overmuch about his fate, and life under an oppressive regime where female circumcision might still be allowed and people were put to death for stealing soccer balls. And she would find herself wondering whether "Pierce" might be able to use his connections at Panasonic to perhaps secure an HIB visa, and bring his family over to the States, so his kids could excel at math and science and brainy sports like squash, and eventually get accepted to an Ivy or at least a good tier-two school like Tufts. But all the while, even as she planned Pierce's immigration, Anna would be cursing his ineptitude, his inability to figure out why the fucking red light kept blinking and how to please, please, please, *just make it stop.*

5

From very, very far away, like the tremor of the subway running down Fourth Avenue four stories below her apartment, Anna sensed it. The box, the bags, the responsibility the things inside them imposed upon her, had begun to feel oppressive. Her enthusiasm was already waning. And, realizing this, Anna felt three things at once. The first was an overpowering urge to do nothing, to sit at her computer and surf and surf and surf until she ended up somewhere truly well and gone. Somewhere deep in the eighteenth century, learning about religious motifs in Sorbian military garb or laser-guided excavation techniques used to unearth Pygmy artifacts. The second was to go back to J&R, endure their enhanced interrogation techniques, return the camera, return the mics, and put Aunt Clara's money back in the bank. And last, of course, was to beat back the weak-willed default of quitting. To at least *try* to try.

Anna got up and busied herself with the apartment, which was something. She watered the ten-dollar plants from IKEA and shook the crumbs from the fleece blanket covering the couch. She swept the crumbs off the floor, then swept the other parts of the floor that didn't require moving any furniture. And as she moved her little pile of dirt around the table legs, then around the apartment, Anna considered the Middle Way. This was her thing lately—taking China as an example. She had learned about it while reading an article on Chinese economic reform. The philosophy, as far as Anna understood it, was based on precepts of Buddhism and the idea of "paradoxical integration," which posited that two completely opposite-seeming states might, in fact, be interdependent. And even though Anna was not in any way endorsing China, which *Mediabistro* often pointed out was evilly suppressing bloggers, this idea resonated with her on many levels. She considered her own life and decided maybe embracing limitless potential—like being a good drunk—required first building tolerance. Not everyone could be Obama, she reminded herself. Come to think of it, not everyone could even be Gilman. She couldn't instantly vault to these heights, would instead have to shuffle toward her goals, crab-like. Maybe this is what Leslie meant by Process and Learning?

And it suddenly occurred to Anna that she could solve this problem, the problem of the camera in the box, and what to do now, the same way she had solved so many other problems: on craigslist. Craigslist! Where Anna had found a rare Fiesta teapot in Burnt Caramel and Brie. Where she hadn't found Ray from Arizona (she preferred OkCupid for that kind of thing) but where she had admittedly, on her horniest days, scrolled through the "casual encounters" section and given herself over to the (surprisingly compelling) fantasy of an anonymous fuck in the back of a Chase ATM lobby. Now that she considered craigslist, it all seemed so obvious. Wouldn't there be filmmakers there, looking for other filmmakers? *Of course the filmmakers will be there*, Anna thought. *Everyone's there.*

Once Anna was on craigslist, things fell into place. Immediately, she sized up her options and realized there were a number of ways to go. She could start with "tv/film/video" under "jobs" or she could start with "talent" under "gigs." The pragmatist in her knew it was probably better to dip a toe in the water with a "gig," but Anna couldn't help thinking that money wouldn't hurt. That—hello?—she didn't have a *job*. Alternatively, she could get the lay of the land in the "film" section under "discussion forums." Follow some threads, get a sense for the lingo, and come off sounding more like a pro. Then again, meh? Why waste her time in some pointless forum for loser filmmaker wannabes? Who had time for that stuff, anyway? Anna clicked into the jobs sections and felt that familiar high. The ads fanned down the page in a long, reassuring list.

Right away she got distracted by something that shouldn't have even been there in the first place. "Pretty Girls Needed for Thursday Foot Fetish Event." OK, she had to click on that one. Just out of curiosity. "We are looking for very attractive girls with pretty feet," the ad said, "to have their feet massaged and kissed at our weekly foot fetish events." Anna looked down at her feet. She slipped off a shoe and, without even thinking about it, began considering her biggish veins. *Crap*, she thought, jamming her shoe back on. What did that ad even have to do with film? This was how the hours flew by like panicked zebras on the African savanna, how craigslist sucked you in. Then again, these ads were unbelievable. "Tap-Dancing Vagina Needed for Vaudeville Comedy Show"? Shouldn't someone in Craig's vast empire be screening these things, weeding out the total nut jobs? Jesus, Brie would love this. And wouldn't it be funny if she just started texting Brandon these subject lines without any explanation? Anna got up and nuked some frozen spanakopita triangles, which she spent some time arranging on a plate around a crescent of sour cream. She poured herself a glass of Tropicana, and suddenly, as she was putting the carton back in the refrigerator, it struck her that she was doing it again.

OK, when I sit back down, Anna told herself, *I will stay on topic. I will only click on entries that relate to film. I will start a separate Word file. I will contact at least five people today.* She thought about actually writing these instructions down for herself on a Post-it note. Better yet, she could form an Intention Statement. But even with the helpful list of "continuous action verbs" that Leslie had e-mailed her, Anna somehow balked at forming an Intention Statement without Leslie there.

Once she redoubled her efforts, the obvious problem confronting her was that most of these ads requested that people have very specific skills. People who could "disseminate encoding protocols," had a "basic understanding of UNIX," and knew their way around an "MPEG-2 Transport Stream." What Anna had to offer was a bit more vague. Not many people, admittedly, were looking for an unemployed woman with an AVCCAM in a box who happened to be conversant in the nuances of real estate tax law. But then Anna stumbled on an ad for a "producing partner" that required no professional experience, only a "passion for cinema." She wrote that one down. And when she extended her search back a few weeks, she found some other possibilities. "Indie Filmmaker Seeks Non-Union Crew." "Assistant for Film Distribution Company." "Film Intern—Production/Postproduction." (Who knows, maybe Brie had the right idea about internships?) She had promised herself five contacts, true, but come to think of it, four was good enough. Anna actually felt kind of invigorated. Not quite ready to tackle the AVCCAM box, perhaps, but ready to at least start unpacking the microphones. She was just about to close the craigslist tab when she saw it:

ARE YOU A REAL PERSON?

Anna had to admit, that was a good one. And hadn't she admirably resisted clicking on that other funny ad, the one with the subject line "Do you eat chalk?" She deserved a freebie, so she clicked.

As you live life, you film it. Your mind's eye is a camera. Your life experience is your demo reel. You are full of patience and open to everything. You are any sex or several. You are any ethnicity. You are 19 or 99. Above all else, YOU ARE NOT AFRAID.

You are a creative partner whom I can trust and build a lasting professional relationship with.

I know Craig's List is an unlikely place to seek communion. You don't belong here and neither do I.

(Unfortunately, due to the nature of this operation, there is no pay. With that in mind, please only serious inquiries.)

There was no phone number or website listed, just an automatically generated e-mail address: Reply To: job-xrtrtp-13588541609 @craigslist.org.

OK, Anna thought as she opened up Gmail, *this will be funny*.

Dear 13588etcetera, she typed. *This is Anna Krestler writing to you. And I am a real person.*

6

The phone rang while Anna was eating breakfast in front of the computer, but it was only Leslie.

"Where do you go for a bikini wax?" she asked as soon as Anna picked up.

"Lucky Nails on Fifth Ave. at Fifty-Eighth. Out in Sunset Park."

"Ugh. Don't you know any place in the city?"

"Nope."

"Last time I went to my place? They tore my skin off."

"Ew," Anna said, opening another tab for Salon.com. She clicked back to Facebook and left a comment on a friend of a friend's wall, because yes, last night's episode of *Real Housewives of Dallas* was total bullshit. *That lady's boobs were for sure fake. Cassandra was right :)* Anna typed as she spoke. "Well, Lucky Nails uses this special hard wax. I think it's from France? Plus they *really* get in there with the tweezers."

"At my place, they skip the tweezer part," said Leslie.

"No way!"

"Way. I think I'm just going to shave. I have to go to one of Josh's things tonight."

"Don't," Anna said, scrolling through her twitfeed. "It'll only grow back thicker."

Waxing, Anna had to admit, was something that had crossed her mind careerwise. Not the inhaling-crotch-musk-all-day part, not the really-getting-in-there-with-the-tweezers part, but the personal part. Anna always ended up telling Wendi, the Chinese lady who groomed her crotch, everything. And without even meaning to, Anna began to wonder how Leslie styled. Wendi once told her that crotch-styling preferences said a lot about a person. So what was it, a Brazilian? A perfect little St. Moritz landing strip? She wouldn't even put it past Leslie to try vajazzling. And this line of thinking served only to remind Anna that she was getting a little overgrown herself down there. She should give Wendi a call—her pubes were probably hanging down around her knees.

Leslie was still talking about something. Her fertility treatments? But cars were honking in the background and for half a minute a loud siren drowned her out. Anna noticed *Gawker* had an article about candy cigarettes being banned by a smoking-prevention law.

"—zen person's pants?"

"Huh?" Anna said, clicking on something.

"—ess than a *ten percent chance*. That's what the doctor said. After that it's pointless. I told Josh we should switch clinics, but can't decide between Columbia or Cornell."

"Isn't Cornell in Ithaca?" Anna said. She forgot what came next after IUI. IVF? Or was IVF first? All the *I*s confused her. So many *I*s engaged to create yet another *I*.

"They have a center in the city, too, but the thing is—I'm sorry this is so loud—"

"Yeah, I can barely hear you," Anna said, even though she could hear her fine now.

"I'll call you later," Leslie shouted.

"Call me later," Anna shouted, and hung up.

She went to the bathroom, plugged in the flat iron, and turned it to high. Then she got out a tube of SPF 15 Sweet Tea tinted moisturizer and began to put on her face. Today she would call Brandon, Anna decided. She had assumed she would open the AVCCAM box together with Brie after she got back from kickball practice last night, bust out a box of microwave popcorn, and make it a roommate thing. But Brie never showed, so the box remained where it was, by the front door. She'd even sent Brie a text, *Yoo-hoo?* around 10:30, but never heard back. So now she would have to call Brandon. *It's probably for the best*, she thought. *Brandon's better at that sort of thing.*

Then again, maybe it would be better to get out of the house first, run a few errands? She hadn't left the apartment at all yesterday, not even to go downstairs for the mail.

She was halfway down the block when the phone rang again.

"Anna? Taj," came an unfamiliar man's voice. "You answered my ad yesterday."

"Hi," Anna said, feeling her pulse quicken.

"That was pretty funny."

"Funny?"

"Mr. 135 blah blah?"

"Oh yeah," Anna said, nervous. "Ha ha."

"Is now a good time to talk? I'm scheduling interviews this week, but first I just need to ask you a few questions."

"OK," Anna said. She walked by a sports bar with a huge banner outside reading CATCH ALL THE WORLD CUP ACTION HERE! Then she passed another small bar on the corner, with a handwritten sign taped up that said, ABSOLUTELY *NO* WORLD CUP COVERAGE EVER HERE (PHEW!). When she tuned back in, Taj was saying, "Sofia or Francis?"

"Um, Sofia?" Anna said.

"Dogme 95 or French New Wave?"

"Both?" Anna said, not knowing much about either.

"Black and white or color?"

"That depends—"

"Dolly or handheld?"

"Handheld."

"Pinhole or digital?"

"Are you being serious?"

"Semiserious."

She actually knew what a pinhole was because Brie had brought home one of those Build-Your-Own-Pinhole-Camera kits from Urban Outfitters one day.

"I guess, pinhole?" *This is supposed to be art*, she thought. *In which case, the weirder the better, right?*

"Bolex or Pixelvision?"

"What?"

"Bolex camera or Pixelvision?"

"Um . . ."

"That's OK," said Taj. "I was thinking of changing that one anyway. Bolex or Flip?"

"Flip." At least she knew what a Flip was. There was a longish pause. "Hello?" Anna said, pressing the phone closer to her ear.

"I've heard nothing but wrong answers," said Taj.

Well, that's that, Anna thought, automatically binding the familiar wound with a tourniquet of indifference. She was standing right outside the pharmacy now. She had something to do. After getting off the phone, she would fill her prescription. And then? Then she would go to Earthy Basket and get one of those fancy, superhealthy deli salads and have lunch, maybe grab a few things to go, for later. When she got home, she would call Brandon and they'd make a date to open the AVCCAM box. In the meantime, she could get back on craigslist, send some follow-up messages. Keep busy. Why hadn't she heard from anyone else yet?

"So, BING! You win," Taj continued. There was a smile in his voice. "I'm intrigued. Where do you want to meet?"

She felt her heart contract.

"Have you ever been to Café Gowanus?" There was another long pause and Anna thought maybe the line had gone dead, just now, at the crucial moment. "Hello?"

"They may as well call that place Café Schadenfreude," Taj said. "Let's keep it real. We'll meet at Halal Wireless Café on

Thirty-Third and Fourth in Brooklyn. Can you do tomorrow at three-thirty?"

"Yes," Anna said.

"I'll text you the address so you'll have it."

"OK."

"Bring a sweater. It gets cold in there with the air-conditioning," Taj said, and he hung up.

Anna walked into Health Aid, a little dazed. She needed time to think, so she walked around the aisles, looking at different things. Vitamins making sketchy claims. Shark cartilage pills. She would wear her blue dress tomorrow. The soy-based cotton one that she'd gotten on Etsy last spring. And instead of calling Brandon to open the box, she would watch a bunch of movies on Hulu tonight to prepare. Anna inspected the toothpastes, forgetting whether they were running low. It was only eleven o'clock. What should she do? Go to Earthy Basket for lunch and then home to watch movies? Or she could check the listings for Film Forum and IFC, see what was playing. She hadn't gone out to see a movie in forever. She pulled out her cell—an iPhone rip-off that came free with her shitty Verizon plan—to see whether there was anything good at Film Forum tonight. Before she knew it, a half hour had passed, she was still standing in the aisle, and the clerk was coughing softly into her fist.

Anna went up to the counter and handed over her thyroid prescription. Then, feeling in a celebratory mood, threw down a box of the shark cartilage tablets as well. That's what she'd do, go to the movies. Maybe Brie would want to come. Or Brandon. She would skip the popcorn this time, hide some wheat thins in her purse instead. It felt like a plan.

7

It was a neighborhood of fix-a-flats and squat storefronts begging to install neon lights underneath your truck or wrap your large vehicle in four-color advertising. Everything else—the kebab shops, the mosques, the all-girls Muslim school—came off as mere footnotes in the larger story of down-market goods and depressed real estate. Anna barely noticed them. She had taken a southbound R train to Thirty-Sixth Street, emerged onto Fourth Avenue, then walked three blocks, breathing in the halitosis of open-air garages and the burning sugar tar of the candy-nut vendors. Halal Wireless Café was an unassuming cinder-block square painted queasy yellow. It sat between a shuttered Off-Track Betting place and a bakery whose window was a tableau vivant of artificial food coloring. If she hadn't been looking for it, she would have walked right by.

Inside, the ceiling fan moved the air in slack circles and a television blared from a wall mount. Of the four people in the room, three sat together, crowded around a laptop. The man who was sitting at a table by himself near the window was brown-skinned. He was some indeterminate age between thirty and forty and wore dark slacks, a beige-collared shirt, and chunky black eyeglasses. There was a Moleskine open on the table next to a plate of half-eaten food, a basket of pita, and a coffee mug. With one hand, he waved Anna over. With the other, he pressed a cell phone to his ear.

"You graduated oh-eight?" Anna heard him say into the phone. He paused to write something down. "Tisch? Is there any chance you knew Chi-Wei? Production and Critical Studies? Ha! So Crick is still teaching that . . . ?"

Isn't it kind of rude, Anna thought, *to conduct another interview, knowing I'd arrive any minute?* She set her bag down on the chair opposite Taj and went over to the counter, where pretzel dogs were rotating sadly under a heat lamp. The menu was a bizarre mash-up of Middle Eastern and American food, casting doubt on the authenticity of either. Anna ordered a poached egg and coffee from a lady in a hairnet, then lingered by the toilet door, pretending to watch Wolf Blitzer on CNN until Taj was off the phone.

"Hey, Anna," Taj said, reading her name from a list in his Moleskine. "Did you find this place OK?" His face, Anna noticed, was lopsided, but in kind of a sexy way. His eyes were a dark liquid brown that reminded her of West Elm furniture. "I know it's kind of out of the way."

Anna nodded and took a sip of her coffee, which tasted like someone had done their laundry in it. She actually looked down into the cup to see if there might be a cigarette butt floating there, if some sort of mistake had been made.

"All right. So where were we?" Taj flipped open the Moleskine on the table. "I have in my notes that you're a big Lars von Trier fan."

Having never heard this name, Anna could only assume he'd confused her with somebody else.

"Actually, lately I've been getting really into Romanian New Wave," Anna chirped. "Lately" being since last night, when she had gone up to Lincoln Center to see a Cristian Mungiu double feature with Brandon.

"Oh, come on . . . ," Taj said, a half-bemused smile playing on his lips.

"What?"

"What *what*? Is that what you think I want to hear?"

"No!"

"You didn't think the first half hour of *12:08 East of Bucharest* could have been about half an hour shorter?"

"It maybe could've used some editing—" Anna began.

"And *The Death of Mr. Lazarescu*, how long was that movie? Maybe five hours? Weren't you like, 'Please die already, Lazarescu, I could use a fucking bathroom break'?"

Anna wasn't sure where to go with this whole line of inquiry, but felt like now she had to follow through. Go on the defensive.

"It won Cannes," she said with less certainty.

"Yeah, where they have a special jury prize for slowest film." He stirred his coffee boldly with one finger. "Seriously, don't you feel a little like the whole Romanian thing, it's almost like rewarding low expectations?"

"You're being reductive," Anna said and immediately regretted it. This happened sometimes; a bit of logorrhea left over from grad school would shoot out of her mouth before she could stop it. But Taj only smiled.

"Those movies, it's like they're almost *designed* to win Cannes," he said. "I think they have a secret Cannes-winning lab in Romania."

Anna giggled despite herself. "That lab should be in Transylvania."

"Doesn't it feel almost opportunistic?" He said this in a conspiratorial whisper, leaning in toward her.

"Like an infection?" She giggled again.

"Like an infection."

Taj held up a finger and wrote something down in his Moleskine. While he wrote, Anna studied his face: a very good nose, and his skin was more olive than brown up close. One eye, she noticed, was a little higher up than the other. Maybe that's where the sexiness came from? It made sense. She'd always had a weird thing for guys with amblyopia.

Realizing that Taj actually *enjoyed* sparring with her, Anna let herself relax a little. She stabbed her egg, letting the yolk spill across the plate. Taj generously pushed his pita basket toward her. She couldn't believe how well things were going.

"I was afraid you'd be like the other guy who was just here," Taj said. "He brought me his semiotics thesis. Check this out." Taj picked up the first page from the stack of paper on the table. "'Process Identification and *The Shawshank Redemption*—A Microanalysis,'" he read. "Who even knows what that means? I'm like, don't give me the *words* man, give me the *feelings*, you know?"

"I know what you mean." Anna smiled. "I'm all about the feelings." In fact, maybe now was as good a time as any to come clean. "Actually, that's sort of the reason I answered your ad. Have you heard of Paul Gilman?"

"Gilman?" Taj repeated.

"He did *Rurik, Rurik, Traffic Cop* and *87 Love Street* with—"

"Is this some lame attempt at irony?" Taj interrupted.

"N-no—"

"I know Paul," Taj said.

"Oh! So you know—"

"What I don't know, exactly, is how the *fuck* you people keep finding me." His voice was soft now, almost feral. "I never name-check Paul or even Simone, but Jesus, every time it's the same thing with you people. It's *incredible*, you know?" He leaned in closer. "Just explain to me how it works, OK? Do you really, really have nothing better to do than hang out all day on the Internet? It's like this piece of fucking shit I can't get off my shoe."

Anna felt her face get hot, stunned at the violence of this turnaround. "I swear, I really don't know what you're talking about." She was still chewing on Taj's pita, for God's sake. Hardly the body of Christ, but they'd shared a moment of communion, hadn't they? She wondered how soon she could leave, because now things were definitely superawkward, especially with the counterwoman in the hairnet wiping the table next to them. She would wait it out for five more minutes, she thought, trying to be like China.

"Yes, you do," said Taj.

"No," she said. "I don't. I watched *Age of Consent* the other night and it made me, I don't know, think of things a whole other way. That's when I found your ad. After that, I mean."

"I bet you watched it and thought, I can do that!" he said with a smirk.

Anna said nothing though it was true that those exact words had occurred to her.

"You really don't know who I am?"

"You're a guy who put an ad on craigslist?" Anna said, not knowing what else to say.

He searched her face for a long moment, then finally seemed to uncoil a bit.

"OK, you want to know about Paul?" He opened a creamer even though his coffee was gone.

"No, that's really OK—"

"Of course you do," Taj said, matter-of-factly. "So, first of all, Paul comes from money. And I know those movies 'didn't cost anything.' But movies that don't 'cost anything'? They all cost, *minimum*, twenty grand. So forget about the brutal honesty of 'exurban realism' or whatever it is he calls it. It was all family money."

Anna didn't really see what that had to do with anything, but she let Taj talk.

"And with Paul, the thing is . . . it's an aesthetic, OK, and I'll admit he's made it work, for himself at least, but where do you go from there? He's got his little game, 'Is it documentary or fiction, is it real or fake?' How interesting is that? This stupid manufactured intrigue. With me, I like to think it's really clear-cut. It's either totally, obviously real, or really, obviously fake, you get what I mean?"

Anna nodded, understanding nothing. She had googled Taj, but oddly her search hadn't yielded any results.

"*Age of Consent*, OK? It's a trick. Paul uses all his gimmicks, his faux realism, keeping everything so very, you know, *grim*? And what you think you're getting is honesty. But you know what you're really getting? Think for a minute about what you're getting. Do you know what it is?"

Anna shook her head mutely, feeling the way she had back at Columbia when trying to master impossible inflections, the complex morphology of Slavic declensions.

"You're getting sex," said Taj. "You're getting sex packaged as art, so you can go to a theater and sit there nicely with your friends feeling smart, and afterward you can go somewhere and talk about fucking without feeling like you're exploiting anyone, because it's *art*. But guess what? All those movies, *Calista* and the rest of them, they're nothing but porn. It's all one kind of porn or another. And don't even get me started on Simone," Taj said, though getting starting on Simone was something he clearly relished. "If there's one thing her story proves, it's there's no faster way to fame in today's attention economy than to show someone your pink parts."

"So what if it's titillating?" Anna said, surprised to find herself arguing. "At least it makes you feel something. If that guy in *Age of Consent* was obsessed with, I don't know, plumbing, and was reading from a bunch of plumbing magazines about pipes and things with a bag on his head, it wouldn't be the same. People wouldn't care. It's because he's sharing something *private*—"

"You're right," Taj said.

"I mean, maybe it's less arty, or more shallow or whatever," Anna went on, emboldened, "but I wouldn't want to watch it either if it was about plumbing. I guess I don't mind that Gilman uses sex to draw you in."

"No one's denying you your right to titillation, OK? I get it. Titillation is important, necessary even. But it can't be everything. You have to have titillation *plus* something else. If you're going to show me your nut sack, make it the Michelangelo of nut sacks. Blow me away with your craft, your insight, your *something*— shit—" Taj grabbed his pen and scrawled something down. "That's kind of a great idea: *Titillation Plus.* What if we call it that?"

"Call what what?" Anna said.

"A new framework for art criticism," Taj said, still writing. "Something's either just titillating or *titillating plus.*"

"Or it's just not titillating," Anna added.

"T, NT, or TP, then?"

"I guess."

Taj paused to spoon some ful mudammas into his mouth with a pita triangle.

"I'll tell you a story about Paul," Taj said, "but it's probably not the kind of thing he wants to get around."

"I promise," Anna said, trying to hide her excitement. It really only hit her now: she was sitting with a guy who *knows Gilman*! This put things on an entirely different level, didn't it? But then Anna realized something else. She wasn't just excited because Taj knew Gilman; she was excited because things were about to get fucked up. Already—and without getting drunk or high—they had stumbled into the zone of inappropriate intimacy. She could tell Taj things. And Taj could tell her things. Not everything, maybe, but a lot of things. Things they might not tell anyone else, because they either knew them too well or not well enough. Why was it that she never felt this way with other women? Brandon was the closest thing. But she and Brandon had something in common. They had been cubicle serfs at Pinter, Chinski and Harms together. A "loser bond" they called it. Because theirs weren't the kinds of jobs anyone aspired to but the kind you simply ended up at, sucked in by promises of health benefits and discounted Metrocards. You made excuses for being there until the excuses became the reasons themselves. So she and Brandon had Chinski and Harms, but what did she and Taj have?

"—had signed up for this special six-week seminar with Herzog out in LA," Taj was saying. "It was called Ephemeral Cinema or Cinema of the Ephemeral or something, and every week everyone in the class was supposed to make a three-minute movie and bring it in for crit. Paul was starting to get a name for himself in certain circles, but hadn't hit on the magic bullet yet. At the time he was in a Mario Giacomelli phase, shooting these supercontrasty, eight-millimeter films at night. Basically in the dark. Grain big as golf balls." Taj was tearing open a Sweet'n Low packet as he spoke, pouring its contents onto the table. "I think I still have some of those in a box somewhere."

Anna had no idea what Taj was talking about, but it was all interesting. She ate her egg.

"So Paul was showing his boring movies in crit every week and no one liked them. Then he comes home one day and his roommate is fucking some guy. He had found this cheap studio to sublet but it was a share, so he and this other guy basically lived in one big room together."

"I had a roommate like that once," Anna began. "In college we—"

"Yeah," Taj went on, ignoring her. "I forget all the details, but I think the guy was like, some kind of Puerto Rican queen. Or Vietnamese queen?"

"An ethnic queen?" Anna supplied helpfully.

"Something. And maybe he was fucking this other guy for money? I don't know. I remember Paul telling me there was something weird about it. Maybe they were dressed up like Pilgrims or, like, finger-painting with their balls—whatever it was, it wasn't exactly normal. Plus, of course, they're both totally jacked up on something. Paul had crit the next day and he hadn't made his movie yet, so he thinks, What the hell? And grabs his Nizo. He sets the camera down on something and hits RECORD. He shoots them for three minutes, all one take. They probably didn't even notice, or didn't care, if they did."

"That's so messed up—"

"Yeah, not exactly what you'd call a triumph of the human spirit." Taj paused to pour the contents of another Sweet'n Low on the table and began to draw a spiral in the sugar with his finger, a sort of *Spiral Jetty*. *Like land art*, Anna thought, *only table art*. After coming across Yagihashi's turd sculpture in City Park she'd done some Google searching on modern sculpture and now remembered that one of Smithson's other works was called *Broken Sugar*. Would it be funny, she wondered, if she subtly formed *Broken Sugar* out of sugar on the table, as a response to Taj's *Spiral Jetty*? Maybe not, she decided.

"Anyway," Taj went on, "the next day Paul had crit and of course his 'movie' makes a big impression. A lot of people hated it. Herzog was intrigued. But mostly—here's the thing—people *cared*. They argued. When he was showing his slow-as-shit 'abstractions' no one cared. Now that there was all this verbal fisting going on, everybody all excited, and Paul at the center of the whole thing, he was loving it. He told me that's when he had his epiphany."

"Whoa," Anna breathed, wondering how much of this was documented on the Internet, hoping none of it was.

"Whoa is right. In a way, Nowism was born right at that moment."

Anna was confused—hadn't Maoism been around for a long time?—but held her tongue.

"Even then, I remember thinking, you know, man, this is like a cliché that hasn't become a cliché yet. It's something you've just discovered that's actually been there forever. This all goes back to our theory. Where's the *plus*? Give me the *plus*, man. It just feels too fucking easy. And this is coming from *me*, who's all about hyperrealism, you know?" Taj pulled his chair in, closer to Anna. "Like, I was just thinking before you sat down—see those people?" Taj pointed to the threesome at the neighboring table, dropping his voice a register. "I'd love to film them."

There were two women and a man gathered around a laptop. The women both looked, as her mother would say, like they'd "lived a lot of life." The man had stringy hair and an uneven sunburn that reminded Anna of guys who hang around small-town bus stations asking for change for a twenty.

"They're looking at footage of mermaids on YouTube. They've been here all day," Taj whisper-hissed. The three heads leaned in toward the screen at the same time. "See? Imagine that shot from above. Their heads all coming together in this sort of white-trash pinwheel—"

She hadn't ever considered things that way, *shot from above*. But now Anna was thinking—and she was pretty sure this was racist of her—that these weren't the kind of people she expected to even have laptops. It was really something, though, the way even people in neighborhoods like this—places with too many notary publics and payday loan shops, where the bodegas all accept WIC—now had laptops and wireless cafés. And then Anna couldn't help but think, *What* is *a notary public, exactly?* And why did poor people need so many things notarized anyway? And why was it that she thought of them as poor and herself as not poor, anyway, when she still had nineteen thousand dollars' worth of student loans and no job? Where had *that* logic come from?

"This is it! This is it! It goes by really fast, see?" the fat lady said to the other two. "Shitsville. Tony, go back a sec. Uh-huh— there! That's not one of those fake suits. You can tell by the way it's flapping." Anna watched the woman tapping at the screen with her index finger, thinking, *You're not supposed to touch that.*

"My niece said there's a place in Florida where they do that. Girls in mermaid suits. They have a whole show underwater," said the man with the stringy hair. "She lives near there, in Tampa."

"Do you agree?" Taj was asking.

"Hm?"

"That anything could be a camera? You know, *this* could be a camera," he said, indicating his pen. "Or this," he said, tapping on his glasses. "You can tape whatever you want, but you have to shape it. Otherwise there's no movie. There's just footage."

"I see what you're saying," Anna said. It was true that Gilman's movies might be better if they were a little more shaped.

"So where'd you go to film school anyway? NYU? USC?"

"No—"

"Miami?"

"No, I mean, no film school," Anna said. From the look on Taj's face she feared this could be a deal-breaker. "I went to grad school for Slavic studies for a little while but—"

"You mean you've never even studied theory?" Taj enunciated each of these words slowly and clearly, as if Anna were a Japanese tourist asking for directions to Century 21.

"Well, not *art* theory, no." Anna said. Her eyes dropped to her mug as she waited for him to dismiss her. It looked thick enough to withstand a jihad.

"*Finally*," Taj said, almost to himself. "I could kiss you right now."

Anna looked up, wondering if she'd heard correctly, to find Taj staring at her with shining eyes.

"So here's the one thing I'm asking everyone. I don't need a person with skill, or experience, or even talent, though that would be nice," Taj added, chewing. "Not that you don't have any of these things, but I just need someone I can trust absolutely. One hundred percent. And someone who trusts me. This whole thing is stressful enough and I can't have people second-guessing me." Taj pushed his empty plate aside. He put his coffee cup on top of his plate, and on top of that, his napkin, fork, and knife. "Do you think you can give me that?" said Taj, still not looking at Anna, but rather at the ketchup bottle that he was moving to align with the condiments. "Your absolute, complete trust?"

Noticing these tics, Anna realized the ball was now in her court. "Of course." Her voice was clear and free of doubt. "Yes."

"OK?"

"OK."

"Cool," Taj said. "God, I'm sorry—I didn't even get a chance to ask you about your stuff."

Anna batted her hand dismissively, hoping this conveyed the notion her "stuff" was monumental enough to survive his disregard.

"Either way," Taj said, flicking an eye back down at his cell. "It's almost four. I better let you go."

Not wanting to be let go, she opened her mouth to suggest more coffee, but a pretty brunette had already appeared tableside.

"Sorry. Are you Taj?" She smiled down at him.

"And you must be . . . ," he said, consulting his list, "Béla Tarr?"

The girl swung her courier bag down on a chair. "That's me!"

"Well, thanks," Anna said, standing up and gathering her things. But Taj was smiling at Béla Tarr now. Her moment had clearly passed.

8

When Anna got home, she googled the shit out of Simone, whose real name, it turned out, was Gerda Bergner. Gerda's story was biblical in its dual simplicity and complexity. As a nineteen-year-old German exchange student, she had sent a video fan letter to a filmmaker she admired, a much older man, offering to fly to the city where he lived and have sex with him. In the video (which had been removed from YouTube, much to *Gawker*'s consternation), Gerda was reportedly wearing nothing but kneesocks as she cavorted around a dorm room reciting the *Duino Elegies*. The filmmaker pretended to say no before he said yes, and Gerda flew out to meet him. Over the next three days, she filmed their assignations in airport bathrooms, on motel bedspreads, and atop various wood laminate surfaces with her cell phone. The finished videos, which she first posted on her Tumblr alongside a series of brutally explicit diary entries, looked as though they'd been directed by American Apparel. The filmmaker consented to be taped for reasons unclear to anyone, including his longtime girlfriend, but perhaps once the nipple clamps were in place and the shaft of his penis slathered in Nutella, such concessions came easily. Nonetheless, Gerda gave the filmmaker the pseudonym James Franco and replaced his head with an ominous black dot. Neither of them could have anticipated the geyser of publicity that accompanied the publication of the videos on *Squeee!*, an obscure webzine whose audience, though small, consisted entirely of gladiatorial retweeters. One week and eight million views later, everyone was outraged and excited that Gerda had fucked this guy knowing he had a girlfriend, posted the videos online, called it art, and then had the gall to take as a pseudonym the name of the self-martyring Christian mystic Simone Weil. Everyone except Gerda, who accepted her notoriety with surprising sangfroid, as evidenced in an interview with *Gawker* that Anna dug up.

GAWKER: People hate you. Does that make you sad?

SIMONE: No.

GAWKER: Why not?

SIMONE: If people hate me, it means they hate women.

GAWKER: But a lot of women hate you.

(Simone shrugs.)

GAWKER: Wasn't Franco's girlfriend the real loser in all this?

SIMONE: If perception is reality, I could be any number of things. I don't believe I did anything wrong.

GAWKER: Your critics accuse you of seducing your way to artistic credibility.

SIMONE: Is that a question?

GAWKER: Are you just a slut with a cell phone?

SIMONE: I have a right to make art about my life with the face and body I was given, just as I have a right to shape my own narrative. If "James Franco" had seduced me, instead of I him, and I had filmed those encounters from the vantage point of victimhood, people would be much more accepting of that. They might praise me for "reversing the male gaze." But does "reversal of the male gaze" constitute a legitimate female gaze? I don't want my films to be viewed only as a counterfactual to a male point of view. The viewer feels threatened because I am a woman unafraid of expressing, exploring, and documenting my sexuality.

My advice to them? Get over it.

GAWKER: One last question: Who is "James Franco"?

SIMONE: "James Franco" is Paul Gilman.

By the time Brie came home two days later and asked about the box, Anna had practically forgotten it was still there, sitting by the door.

"It's good to see you getting into something," Brie said, and Anna could hear the unspoken "finally" at the end of that sentence. But mostly, Brie didn't want to talk about Anna, she wanted to talk about her situation at work, which had gotten fucked up lately. And her boss, Pom, so named by the other interns because she drank four Pom Wonderfuls at her desk each day—a $112-a-week juice habit, Brie pointed out.

"So Pom hands me her phone and tells me to dial star two and activate the international data plan from midnight on the tenth through the eighteenth, when she'll be in Iceland. So I'm like, OK, and I call the guy and give him the code or whatever and he puts it in the system." Anna was standing in the doorway of Brie's room, watching her sort through clothes she'd brought home from Rishi's, sniffing crotches, asses, armpits.

"Then, last night, I get this call from fucking Reykjavík. It's like, three in the morning, and of course it's her. She starts screaming that her phone doesn't work and her green light keeps blinking." Brie held a pair of jeggings up to the light. "God, I washed these like *once* and they're already totally faded."

"Sounds bad," Anna said.

"So she's like, 'Call Sprint customer service.' And I'm like, 'But *you're* the one with the phone. What if they want you to do something to it?' And she starts screaming, 'I don't give a shit, just call them! Tell them my green light is blinking!'"

Of course, here Anna thought about pointing out that it wasn't like this was the kind of job that, you know, *paid actual money*.

Surely Brie could just walk away, couldn't she? But that would only lead to some ardent speech about what a great networking opportunity this was, how all the interns who made it past April last year got sent to Bonnaroo, how much a recommendation from Pom would help with getting even-higher-level internships at places Anna had never heard of. It would only make her feel old, and besides, she didn't have time for all this right now. There was only one more night to finish Taj's assignment, and she hadn't even started.

He'd called her yesterday morning while she was still eating breakfast in front of the computer.

"Anna? Taj."

"I didn't think you'd call." She had begun to tell herself it was just one of those things.

"Sorry. Multiple situations," he was shouting, and Anna could hear loud noise in the background, some kind of jackhammering. "I'm on set and it's sort of crazy around here."

"If you're busy—"

"No. I've just been thinking, before we get started, it would be a good idea to sort of break you in."

"What does that mean?"

"Desensitize you a little. The way I work, it's pretty . . . well, I think I told you. It's going to require a different mode of thinking."

And then he'd explained the assignment: she was to go on Chat Roulette and record all of her video chats over the course of two unbroken hours. There was only one rule: she had to pose as anyone but herself.

"Don't worry, it's something I'm asking everyone to do," Taj had told her, which of course only made Anna worry more, knowing there was still an "everyone."

Chat Roulette. She vaguely remembered that fad. When had it been a thing? 2008? 2010? She was surprised to learn it still existed. What happened to sites like these after the Internet hordes had come and gone? It must be the digital equivalent of Area 51 by now.

"Isn't Chat Roulette all, you know, penises and stuff?" Anna said, stumbling over the word *penises*, getting over it.

"Then talk to them," Taj said. Anna could think of nothing she wanted to say to a penis, divorced from the head of someone she knew. "This is about losing your inhibitions," he added.

Her eyes skidded guiltily toward the door, and the Pandora's box filled with all the movies she would never make, movies as brave and raw as Gilman's. Taj's diagnosis was dead on—she *was* inhibited.

"Pretend like you're the star of a Gilman movie," Taj said, reading her thoughts. Anna turned the idea over in her mind, felt an unexpected thrill at the prospect of an adventure.

"What do I do with the footage?"

"You bring me a DVD," Taj said. "I'll e-mail you directions. We're shooting in Williamsburg."

By the time Anna felt motivated to go over to the dollar store to buy her disguise, the lights of the bodegas were smeared like cheap watercolors across the darkening sky above Fifth Avenue. She found two 99-cent stores right across the street from each other—a synthetic-housewares version of the classic Burger King/McDonalds face-off. She chose Lucky Gift 99¢ over 99¢ Plus and Gifts, where, either way, everything actually cost $1.08 with tax. Inside, it smelled like naphthalene and Febreze and there was barely any room to move. Everything gave off that sad feeling of cheap things about to be broken. Once in the party aisle, Anna found that her options were quite limited. Halloween was long gone. The only mask left on the shelf, amid the paddleball games and super cap guns, was a pair of oversize cat's-eye glasses covered in green sequins that came with a matching wand. It would have to do. Out on the street, Anna threw away the wand and slipped the glasses on, just to get into the mood. By the time she reached home, she regretted it; the plastic earpieces digging hard into her temples had given her a headache. Upstairs, she passed by Brie's closed bedroom door, through which she could clearly hear her retelling the story of Pom's Blackberry to someone on the phone.

Brandon had helped her set up the screencasting program without even asking why she needed it. Now she typed in the URL and the green light next to her webcam instantly flicked on. A lo-res version of herself, a person she didn't recognize at first, filled the square viewer on the bottom of the screen. She spent a moment adjusting, finding the just-below-the-chin angle of the webcam dispiriting, then decamped for the bed, where she lay down, balancing the computer on top of her knees. This would make it nearly impossible to type but at least it helped slim her face down a bit. She glanced at the clock on her screen—10:07 p.m.—and clicked NEW GAME.

Looking for a partner, please wait.

A youngish man with a goatee popped into the partner screen. "Connected," the screen said, "feel free to talk now." Anna tried to feel free. The man waved at Anna and Anna waved back, her hand sloughing off blurry pixels like some kind of cyberleper. The man bent his head, typing a message.

STRANGER: slm
YOU: slm?
STRANGER: hi
YOU: oh hi.
STRANGER: nerden from
YOU: nerden from?
STRANGER: turkiye
YOU: oh! America.
STRANGER: were are you

YOU: Texas
STRANGER: 78stanbul
YOU: Nice!

It was the lying that worried Anna the most. She hoped that the mask would help her fulfill some measure of the lying requirement, but had also decided that she would pretend to be from Texas or California or Minnesota, states she'd at least visited with her family when she was young. These weren't such great lies, but what if she claimed to be from Vancouver and the other person was from Vancouver, too? Next they'd want to know about her neighborhood or grammar school and Anna would be caught lying. But it made no sense. Why should it even matter if she was caught lying when she was *supposed* to be lying, was probably being judged on the quality of her lies, their audacity, the confidence with which she told them? Besides, these people weren't even real people, but a bunch of Rorschach tests composed of sad, anonymous pixels.

The Turkish man typed: "name?"

"Clarissa," Anna replied. Everyone else's lies would be better than hers, she thought, suddenly panicking and hitting NEXT GAME. The Turkish man vanished.

A black man with a ukulele and a pair of tweenage girls flashed by. She waved at both of them; both disconnected. Then three men playing cards around a table who never once looked up at the screen. Here was something: a faceless man masturbating with a cabbage leaf. He held each end of the cabbage leaf delicately between thumb and forefinger, running it up and down his considerable package. Anna couldn't help but notice the similarities between the ridges on the cabbage leaf's pale rubbery skin and the guy's scaly, weathervaning cock—all that Georgia O'Keeffe anthropomorphized flora shit made literal. *Kudos to you*, Anna thought. *It's not easy to eroticize a cabbage leaf.*

"Hello," Anna typed. And to her great surprise, the cabbage leaf actually stopped moving. Slowly, one hand drifted over toward the screen, bobbing over the keyboard.

STRANGER: you have a pretty smile
YOU: Thanks

The hand went back to the cabbage leaf and resumed its business. Anna waited some more, but that appeared to be all. Reluctantly, she hit NEXT.

She needn't have worried about the lies. There turned out to be very little lying required. The chats were short and circular. There were men with broken English, and headless men jerking off. The women always NEXTed her. She regretted not setting up some food next to the computer, some celery hearts and a thing of cream cheese. Her stomach was growling.

"Hi," a torso typed.

"Yes," Anna typed back.

STRANGER: I'M here to play fun and safe
YOU: You are upside down
STRANGER: would like to have fun too?
YOU: That depends
STRANGER: wanna see a big black cock?
YOU: you don't look very black, no offense
STRANGER: is that enogh proof?
YOU: It's pretty amazing that you can type and do that at the same time
STRANGER: can I cummm for ou?????

Connected, feel free to talk now
STRANGER: Hey
YOU: Hi
STRANGER: How old are u?

YOU: 108
STRANGER: hahah naah :;d

Anna was getting tired. She badly wanted to open a new tab and check *HuffPo*. She badly wanted to open up many new tabs, actually, and check Gmail, and Facebook, and her twitfeed, too. She wanted to get up, stretch, go take a piss, then do something physical and mindless for a good fifteen minutes, like pick the clothes up off the floor or scrub the ring of dead skin around the bathtub or lint-roll the bedspread. She wanted to bury her head in the refrigerator and eat and eat and eat. She even wanted to call back Leslie, who'd left a sad-sounding message about her failed IVF round that Anna had listened to for only three seconds before deleting it.

Every few minutes that she sat there, waiting to connect, she kept getting this little psychic hitch. Like, *What am I doing again? Why am I doing this?* It was the opposite of déjà vu, a kind of jamais-vu disbelief that she had even engaged in this stupid exercise to begin with, let alone that she was really still there, still herself. She was wasting her time for Taj. Because Taj had told her so. But who was Taj? She didn't know exactly. She didn't even know why she wanted to know, but it was true that she did. Then again—could this really be it?—maybe she just wanted to wake up tomorrow and have something to do, someplace to go. *I have a shoot tomorrow*, she'd said to Brie, careful to keep her tone light but secretly thrilled by the velocity of this strange new word leaving her mouth. Was it that simple? Well, if she wanted to go on the shoot, she would have to do her best on the assignment so as not to lose out, as she so often did, to the invisible "everyone." She thought of "Béla Tarr" and wondered if it wasn't time to take things up a notch. Time, as Brandon might put it, for some *serious, next level shit.*

Connected, feel free to talk now

STRANGER: hihi

YOU: hello

STRANGER: your missing the world cup

YOU: I can say the same about you

STRANGER: and you chose chatxroulette instead

STRANGER: perfect choice

STRANGER: world cup or sexy chat . . . ?

YOU: How about nonsexy, normal chat?

STRANGER: then why have chatxroulette?

YOU: Haha

STRANGER: are we not adults here?

YOU: Ok, tell me all about your exciting sex life. I'm ALL
ears.

STRANGER: yeah?

STRANGER: ok

STRANGER: im single now

YOU: Uh huh

STRANGER: for about a year or so

STRANGER: no girlfriend

YOU: sad

STRANGER: a few girls ive gone out with

YOU: yes?

STRANGER: but nothing worth keeping in touch

STRANGER: they were fun

STRANGER: but no serious keepers

YOU: I see

STRANGER: and yours now

YOU: Well, it's good to see you've got such high standards

STRANGER: I do

STRANGER: need a fun smart sexy independent woman

YOU: Maybe you need a personal ad

STRANGER: I do!

STRANGER: ive never tried online dating before

YOU: May I suggest OkCupid?

STRANGER: is that your pick?

YOU: I swear I don't work for them

STRANGER: im sure

STRANGER: you just get on here and sell memberships all day

STRANGER: its all a scam!

YOU: Haha. Right. When I'm not watching the World Cup

STRANGER: I think that top wants to come off

YOU: Subtle

He isn't bad-looking, Anna thought, *despite the bald spot.* And he was at least a little bit funny, sort of normal, even, wasn't he? But it was the way he said it—that top *wants* to come off—as if her "top" had desires separate from her own. And she couldn't help but think about her tits, and what they wanted. She leaned into the screen a little to feel the heavy push of them against her forearms, wondering how it would feel to lift her shirt up and feel the cool air there. Wasn't this what Taj was asking for? This *letting go*? She could already feel the cycle of fucked-upness accelerating, anticipating what Taj would think when he saw what she had done, what he would think when he knew what she was willing to do. But was she really even pretending to be someone else anymore? What difference did it make, Anna thought, as long as Taj thought she was. She checked the clock: seven minutes to go. It was enough time.

A grim new determination settled over the face of the man in the viewer.

STRANGER: Show me your boobs

And so she did.

9

She had expected skinny guys in faded band T-shirts and sloppy/
sexy Greta Gerwig types spilling out of an art-dorm warehouse.
But the address Taj texted her was nowhere near Bedford Avenue.
Instead, she found herself deep in south Williamsburg, lost in a
nondescript neighborhood of cheap taquerias and soapstone-
fronted apartments. Finally, she stopped a man pushing a snow-
cone cart down the street and showed him the address.

"That's Morris Martin Houses, down on Krueger. You passed
it. Go back and take a left." The man inspected her dubiously.
"You know someone there?"

Anna thanked him and turned back toward Krueger, slightly
alarmed. Five minutes later she arrived at a red brick tower set far
back from the street with a NYCHA symbol hovering over the
door. She was just about to text Taj to reconfirm the address when
she spotted a man on the lawn holding a light meter up to the
building. He was wearing a beige cargo vest, the kind with a million pockets. She walked over to him and he carefully pretended
not to notice her.

"Excuse me," she said, "do you know where Taj is?"

The man turned to look at her and Anna saw that he was
older, maybe forty, which instantly made Anna feel less loserish.

"You are new PA?" The man spoke with a thick Russian
accent.

"I don't know," Anna said. "I think so."

"You're late," the man nodded at the entrance. "Second floor."

Anna made her way back to the concrete path with the faux-antique lampposts. The doors were heavy and institutional and blammed shut too loudly behind her. Inside, she confronted a metal panel with a Braille-like forest of call buttons. Through the glass pane, Anna could see an old woman scrubbing the floor of the lobby with a wet tennis ball stuck on a metal pole. She waved. The woman saw her and didn't wave back. Anna tried the handle, just in case, but the door was locked.

Back outside, she approached the Russian man with the light meter again.

"Excuse me," Anna said, in Russian this time.

"What?" the man snapped back in English, clearly annoyed.

"Is there a code?" Anna said, switching hastily back to English herself.

"I sent instructions to PAs yesterday." The man continued grimly adjusting his dials.

"Sorry," Anna said.

"Apartment seven-B. Sam Leung."

"Sam Leung," Anna repeated.

"Here," the man said, and from one of his many pockets he extracted a cell-phone-size two-way radio. "Take walkie."

Anna took it without saying anything, silently admonishing herself for greeting the man in Russian. Hadn't casual encounters like these contributed to her undoing in grad school? There was no point to studying Russian. She may as well have been studying how to be black. She may as well have taken ESL classes—Ebonics as a Second Language—and spent her year abroad in Harlem. The sheer ludicrousness of it. This time when she reached the door, it was mysteriously propped open. She was halfway to the elevator when the walkie-talkie beeped, interrupting this train of thought.

"Sasha, where are you?" came a voice. "We're totally having white-noise issues here."

"This is Anna."

"Anna? What are you doing on Channel One?"

"Taj?"

"Ugh. Never mind. Just get up here."

"Room seven-B?"

"Who told you that? Third floor. Fourteen-A."

"OK," Anna said to the already dead receiver.

The third floor looked exactly like the first floor, only with more doors. Same paint, same vinyl flooring, same blurry prints of seashells and white gazebos in scuffed-up frames. The smell of floor polish and Bengay. A folding table with some food was set up in the windowless dead end of the hall. Feeling disoriented, she headed toward the food, thinking some breakfast would help slow time. There were trays of sweaty cheese and sweaty turkey slices and pieces of bread that were already hard on top. She opened a packet of Yogi Berry DeTox tea and threw the bag into a foam cup. This was her new thing: calorieless drinks. It was an interesting theory that Brie had advanced, that by cutting out soda and juice and (here was the tough part) all that carby alcohol, Anna could shave off a good quarter of her caloric intake. She'd gone on CalorieCounter.com and composed the following chart based on her drink consumption that week:

Cranberry Juice, 100ml	120 calories (but a *real* glass of cranberry juice was more like 200ml, effectively making this more like 240 calories)
Fizzy Lizzy (Yakima Grape), 12 ounces	120 calories
Ginger Beer, 12 ounces	124 calories
Stella Artois Lager, 100ml	221 calories
Lemonade (sweetened), 16 ounces	328.3 calories
Margarita (frozen, fruity), 14 ounces	450(!)

The evidence was pretty convincing, Anna had to admit. Brie had also suggested she try Master Cleanse—apparently Beyoncé had lost twenty-two pounds in ten days—but Anna didn't feel like she was ready for Master Cleanse.

"Ay!"

Anna turned around to find a pear-shaped man in a green uniform peering at her.

"You with the crew? You need to get your food and get back in the room."

"Sorry," Anna said, grabbing a sugary scone despite her better impulses. She slid past him, making her way to room 14A, but the man kept calling after her.

"I don't get paid for this! I'm not even supposed to leave the boiler room!"

The door to room 14A was closed, but Anna could hear voices. She raised a hand to knock, then thought better of it. What if they were in the middle of a scene? She decided to wait and stood there in the hallway, blowing on her tea. Bored, she examined the aphorism printed on her Yogi tea bag: *Your life is based on the capacity of energy in you, not outside of you.* Whatever that meant.

There was arguing behind the door, what sounded like a Chinese woman barking orders at someone. *Why is it*, she thought, *that Chinese people always sound angry?* That was probably her own prejudice talking. Was there, for example, such a thing as a Chinese lullaby? It would be interesting to know. Now contrast the angry-sounding Chinese with the maximally soothing and self-effacing Japanese. Wait, but hadn't the Japanese defeated the Chinese in some war Anna couldn't remember? She tried to picture this: an army of soft-spoken, oppressively polite people subjugating the angry Chinese, but came up short. When she got home, she would google "Chinese lullaby."

"Ow!"

A willowy woman with a clipboard had thrown the door open

and run straight into her, spilling tea down the front of Anna's shirt.

"Holy hell!" the woman said, slapping at her wet arm.

"Crap." Anna set her cup down on the floor. "Are you OK?" she said, but couldn't help thinking, wasn't *she* the one with the scalded breasts here? Then Anna realized the woman looked familiar. Maybe one of Brie's friends from the kickball team, the one who'd brought the marshmallow-topped chicken casserole for last month's Midwest-themed potluck dinner?

"Anna!" Taj emerged from behind the girl, a giant pair of headphones around his neck. *He looks different without the chunky glasses*, Anna thought. *Better.*

"I have my DVD for you," Anna said.

"Give it to Lauren. Lauren, put Anna in my phone." Taj handed Lauren his iPhone. "I'll be right back."

Anna held her DVD out to Lauren. "I'm sorry," she repeated lamely.

The woman thumb-typed something into the iPhone without responding.

"You're thirty-seven," she said.

"What?" How did Lauren know her age?

Lauren held the screen up to Anna's face and she could see that she was, indeed, number 37—the last entry on speed dial. Lauren took the DVD, unclipped a Sharpie from the clipboard, scrawled the number 37 on its face, and circled it. Then she strode off toward the elevator without another word.

Now Anna noticed an elderly Chinese woman was centered in the doorway. Had she been there this whole time? She was very short—shorter than Anna—and her face had the pocked texture of an almond shell. She wore a cotton robe over drawstring pants and paper-thin slippers. Flashes of white scalp shone through a bad bottle-dye job. The woman pointed to the dark stain spreading down Anna's shirt. Anna looked down, brushed the wet spot helplessly with the sleeve of her jacket.

"Get you clean up," she said, grabbing Anna's arm. Anna bent down to pick up her cup and allowed herself to be pulled through the door.

She had imagined a scaffolding of lights, a sea of cables strewn across the floor. But inside there was no sign of a film shoot anywhere, no additional crew. Instead, there was just a middle-aged Chinese man sitting at the kitchen table working his way through a pile of scratch tickets. He looked up at Anna, then said something to the woman in Chinese, who immediately barked something back. *They sound angry*, Anna couldn't help but think.

"Sit!" the old woman said to Anna. "Sit! Sit!" She pushed Anna toward the couch, which was upholstered in a cheap and scratchy but immaculately clean floral print, and disappeared into the bedroom. From her place on the couch, Anna could see a little Buddha in the corner where a shrine had been set up. Some wan slices of orange, two apples, a dying bouquet of carnations, Chex Mix in a shiny bowl. *That's what being an all-knowing deity gets you*, Anna thought. The apartment smelled like boiled chicken; Anna decided to breathe through her mouth.

The woman emerged from the bathroom waving a billowing red pajama top.

"Oh. That's really sweet of you," Anna demurred, trying not to sound nasal. "That's OK."

"Nokay!" the woman barked. "It fit you." She unfurled the top like a parachute.

"I can just wear this jacket. See?"

"You stain!" The woman dropped the shirt in her lap, jabbing Anna's chest with one finger. "Dirty." And at this, the man looked up and let loose a long stream of accusatory Chinese at the woman, who retreated to the bedroom again.

"Sorry about Mama," the man said in perfect English. "She's been very excited with the crew here all day."

"That's OK," said Anna.

"She stayed up late cooking and now everyone's a vegetarian." He shook his head. "Chinese hospitality."

Before Anna could respond, the door opened again.

"Sam, sorry, man, all they had at the bodega was Sweet Million, Take Five, and Quick Draw," Taj said. He walked into the kitchen, followed by Lauren.

"No good."

"Sorry. It's all they had."

"I told you Mega Millions. The only other one I play is New York Power Ball. Except Sundays. Sunday is Power Play." Sam took a stack of lotto cards from Taj and inspected them, dubious. "I don't even know how these work."

"I think you scratch them," Taj deadpanned.

"Scratch them however you want," Lauren added. "Pretend like they're Mega Millions."

"We'll get you some Millions tomorrow," Taj said. "Where's Mrs. Leung? Mrs. Leung!" Taj walked back to the door and poked his head into the hallway. "Sasha?"

Mrs. Leung announced herself with the sad scuffing of slippers. "We take again?" she said. She scuffed over to the counter without waiting for an answer. "Take, take," Mrs. Leung muttered to herself. She pulled a potato from the colander in the sink and started peeling.

"Sasha!" Taj yelled again as Lauren grabbed a boom mic from behind the coatrack. Taj handed her his heavy-looking headphones and she plugged them into the recorder unit clipped to her belt.

Happy for some excuse to occupy herself, Anna slipped away to the bathroom to change shirts. When she returned, Sasha was standing in the doorway holding a paper plate of minimuffins.

"Is raining outside," Sasha intoned.

"You've got the camera?" said Taj.

"Yep." Sasha took his place by the table next to Sam, pulling a camera from the depths of his cargo vest. It was tiny, a tourist cam that easily fit in one palm—a Kodak Zi8, Anna realized.

"Anna, keep your eye on Sasha if you want to learn some moves. He's the man," said Taj. Then, turning to Sasha, "Ready?" Sasha nodded. "Sam? Mrs. Leung?"

"Take, take," Mrs. Leung muttered to the potatoes.

"Good. OK, everyone. Scene one, A, take three." Taj clapped his hands twice. "Action!"

"You like pigeon with that lotto," said Mrs. Leung, placing a peeled potato in a bowl of water next to the colander. "Chk, chk, chk! Always scratch."

"What's your birthday, Ma?" said Sam, penny poised over a Mega Millions.

"Always scratch, always po'."

"I know your birthday," Sam said. He bent his head and began to scratch.

"I too old fo' birthday." Mrs. Leung shook some scabs of potato from her peeler.

"Four and twelve and nineteen and twenty-four. I'm feeling lucky, Ma."

"You feel stupid, like pigeon."

"I need one more number. How many potatoes you have there?" But Mrs. Leung didn't respond, so Sam went over to the bowl and counted for himself.

"Always borrow money," Mrs. Leung muttered.

Sam sat back down and began to scratch.

"I have two out of five, Ma." Sam held the ticket up to Mrs. Leung's back, but she didn't turn around.

"Ma?"

"Your brother, he stay in China, he make big money. Big money *in China*. And you here! You in America, an' still po'."

"I think we won something—we already won something with four—four numbers, Ma!"

Lauren and Sasha tightened their circle around Sam and Mrs. Leung, as Taj silently conducted them from the back wall. Anna, acutely aware of her tent-size shirt and her own inactivity, felt suddenly self-conscious.

"I think I won, Ma," Sam said, his voice skidding higher. "Four. Twelve. Nineteen. Twenty-four. Eight." Sam's penny bobbed over the ticket as he counted, his voice thick with disbelief. A small pile of silver shavings had accumulated on the table.

Lauren stepped right in front of her to bring the boom closer to Sam, and in that moment, seeing her in profile, Anna felt a jolt of recognition—it was the Celtx girl, from Café Gowanus!

"You go to Key Food later, you get me shrim' an' also green banana," Mrs. Leung said, throwing another peeled potato into the bowl.

"Ma," said Sam. "I won! I won, Ma!" He stood up, waving the ticket. Its foil squares glinted weakly in the light. He looked directly into the camera. "We're rich!"

Mrs. Leung said nothing. She turned on the tap and scraped the dirt from a potato with her fingernails.

"I don't know," Mrs. Leung said.

"Cut! That's a wrap," yelled Taj. "Fantastic."

Lauren lowered the boom and pulled off her headphones. "Really great, you guys."

"I actually won three dollars." Sam grinned, showing his ticket to Sasha.

Sam got up and walked over to the Buddha shrine, where he tucked the used ticket in between a pair of apples.

"Did you get that?" Taj called out to Sasha. Sasha nodded.

"You want me to do it again?" Sam asked. "I was going to light a stick of incense, too."

"Sam, you go to Key Food," Mrs. Leung said, but no one was listening.

"No, skip it," said Taj. He took Lauren's boom pole and began unscrewing the mic head.

Anna continued to sit on the couch, feeling both exhilarated and confused. Should she offer to help? Should she ask a question? She regretted not buying a Moleskine yesterday.

"How do you feel?" Taj said, unexpectedly plopping down on the couch next to her.

"Well—" Anna began.

"Totally clueless? Don't worry." Taj smiled. "We'll grab a drink later and I'll explain."

"OK," Anna said, some of the awkwardness she felt lifting. "How do *you* feel?" But it was Lauren who answered for him.

"Like someone going for the Gugg?" Lauren said, smiling down at Taj. She put a hand on his shoulder, but something in his face made her drop it again.

"Thirty-seven?" It took Anna a moment to realize Lauren was talking to her. She nodded toward the door. "We need you to break down the buffet table."

Anna wandered back to the table of cold food and began to stack the coffee cups. Through the window, she could see the identical red towers of Morris Martin Houses tessellating across identical patches of yellowed lawn. She found a box of ziplock bags under the table and bagged the scones and the minimuffins, put the tea bags back into their box. Though dogged by a feeling of age-inappropriateness, Anna did her best to keep her mind on the small picture, to not telescope out and see herself as a thirty-seven-year-old woman with a master's degree, ziplocking minimuffins in the cul-de-sac of a Brooklyn housing project. *There is no I in* crew, she reminded herself. Things might not have been ideal, but it still felt good to again be the recipient of marching orders. At the very least, the inflationary spiral that had rendered the hours of her formless days all but worthless had slowed. Sure, she still felt the gentle tug of online flash sales and trending memes lapping at the edges of her consciousness, but she hadn't checked her phone once during the shoot. Wasn't that reason enough to celebrate? These thoughts were interrupted by the sound of footsteps rapidly approaching. She felt an uncharacteristic burst of goodwill. She was *full of patience and open to everything*. If it was Taj, she would give him a big hug. If it was Lauren, she would forgive her for being beautiful. If it was Sasha, she would compliment his moves and his camera, even though it was just a crappy Zi8. Anna turned around, already beaming. But it was only Mrs. Leung. And she wanted her shirt back.

10

How was it that she'd never even thought of coming to a place like this? That it never occurred to her all these five-hundred-dollar-a-night hotels, glowing cubes wedged into the shadows between exhaust-darkened buildings, had bars and restaurants open to anyone? Now here they were, tucked into a leather booth with tranquilizing music throbbing overhead. Illuminated rows of Stoli, Maker's Mark, and curaçao glowing behind the bar like the Manhattan skyline rendered in liquor.

They were dreams. That's what she'd learned over the first drink. Or maybe the second, while Sasha was still with them. Taj found them by putting up flyers at supermarkets and Laundromats in unlikely neighborhoods. People would call and he'd interview them about their dreams. He took the best ones and made them into films. Or was it the worst ones that became films? Anna remained confused on that point.

Sam Leung had seen Taj's flyer at the Key Food in Greenpoint and called right away. His dream was to win the lottery and buy his mother—who had grown up with nothing but sticks and dirt for toys—a cream-colored Aston Martin with a leather interior of breath-mint blue. And since a portion of each ticket sale went to the government, he convinced himself that playing Mega Millions was patriotic, or charitable, the same as dropping money into the March of Dimes cup next to the register. It was this combination of greed, patriotism, and filial devotion that got Sam

$83,000 into debt. When he lost his house, his wife also left, together with their daughter. But he didn't move into Morris Martin Houses with his mother until years later, by which time he'd slid quite a few more rungs down the ladder.

"I have this book, well, actually, like three books, Moleskines, where I transcribe all the dreams," Taj said. "And I was thinking, when it's time for the screening I'll exhibit them under glass, you know, like art objects."

"I think that's really beautiful." Anna knew she had to stop saying "beautiful"—she had already used the word twice when Taj explained he was giving people the chance to star in their own dreams—as well as *generous*. Thank God she had enough sense to stop at *noble*. She was a little drunk.

"The fucked-up thing is some people's dreams are so—I mean, you really can't make this stuff up. The reality of it is so much better than fiction."

Anna nodded, picked up her cocktail, drank deeply. Instantly, she regretted the calories. She had started out with a relatively dietetic vodka tonic, but then decided to reward herself for not having any of those minimuffins from the buffet earlier by ordering a sangria. Doing some quick math, she realized she'd already lost whatever gains she'd made earlier in the day, and at this thought her eyes slipped over Taj's shoulder to the mirrored wall where certain cold facts confronted her. It was true—she was fat. But her blue eyes were still very striking, and tonight she'd done a good job outlining them in black. Moreover, the dual benefits of bigness were also on display in the plunging décolleté of the tank top she'd worn beneath her tea-stained blouse. It was with no small satisfaction that she'd noticed Taj's eyes dip a few times over the course of the evening. First when she opened her purse to fetch a mint, and again when she'd pretended to scan the dessert menu. Seeing herself in the mirror now, she hoped what she always hoped, that men saw her as Rubenesque. Women, she already knew, saw her only in the hypothetical sense, as pretty-if-she-lost-weight.

They weren't quite playing the "vulnerability game," as Brandon would put it, but she had still learned a great deal between drinks one and three. Taj had told her about being born in India, which he couldn't remember at all, and growing up in Kansas City with his two sisters. Neither his hobbies (squash, Final Fantasy) nor his college major (economics) or family background (both parents were doctors of the gut region), explained how he'd ended up an experimental filmmaker. In truth, he was not so different from the bright Indian guys she'd known in high school, who'd all gone on to med school or law school and, come to think of it, seemed almost supernaturally predetermined to succeed. But there was an obvious gap in Taj's narrative, the period after college and before now when everything had changed and he'd come into his own. He wasn't particularly forthcoming about this period, however, so Anna told him about her mother and growing up in suburban Connecticut where the streets all circled one another like bored house pets until they just collapsed into culs-de-sac. She also discovered the entirety of her time at Pinter, Chinski and Harms could be condensed into the space of one depressing tweet.

"So how did you meet Gilman?" she finally asked. It was the arrival of drink four that gave her courage.

"Jailbreaking his iPhone," said Taj.

"Random," Anna said. Her Google searches were still turning up nothing. According to Google, there was no Gilman and Taj. No Taj and Simone. No Taj at all, actually. How could that be? It hardly seemed possible that a person who didn't exist on the Internet could exist at all. Even *Anna* existed on the Internet, albeit only on Facebook, uninteresting mentions in the PCH newsletter, and, worst of all, the Association for the Advancement of East European, Slavic, and Eurasian Languages and Literature website, which listed her as a Ph.D. even though she'd only managed to slink out of Columbia with a master's. She poked at her ice cubes with a stirrer straw, trying to deduce how Gilman and

Taj's relationship had progressed from this quotidian hipster interaction to, well, whatever it had become.

"Was it a setup for another one of his movies?" she joked.

"*1-800-Jailbreak*. Ha-ha. No, that would be too boring even for Gilman." For a moment his face clouded over. "Humiliating people is the only thing that gets Paul's rocks off." And as Taj's eyes flitted over the drink-bearing torsos passing by their booth, she realized the feeling between them was slipping away. She regretted bringing the conversation around to Gilman. "But enough about me," he said, throwing back the rest of his drink.

"No!" Anna piped, knowing she was scraping conversational resin from the bowl but unable to help herself. "It's not."

It was too late, though. Taj had clearly already hit some internal reset button.

"You know what I love about this place?" he said. Knowing she had only the flimsiest reason to hope the answer might be *her*, *them*, Anna leaned forward anyway. "The bathrooms," Taj continued, raising a finger for the waitress. "The walls are all one-way mirrors. It's totally fucked. You should check it out."

The next morning, in their bathroom, Anna asked Brie why they had never bothered to move the mirror down. They were both standing at the sink, brushing their teeth and staring at their eyebrows in the mirror. The mirror had always been too high. When they put on lipstick, they had to jump for just a brief glimpse of their mouths.

"I thought it was bolted to the wall, but I think those are just big nails," Anna said, pointing her toothbrush at the waterlogged wallpaper near the ceiling, the twin disks of rust holding up the mirror.

"Pain in the ass," Brie spat, wiping her mouth on Anna's bath towel. "What kind of crazy shit were you listening to last night?"

"I can't pronounce the name," Anna said. "It was a Chinese

lullaby." She had googled "Chinese lullaby" when she got home and learned the Chinese do not, in fact, yell at their babies. The songs were dulcet, almost cloying. These moments of enlightenment, Anna hoped, would help dispel her latent racism. It certainly strengthened her resolve to pursue the Middle Way. The Chinese were nothing if not enigmatic in their balancing embrace of disparate extremes.

"Huh. I was just thinking it reminded me of this new band we're working. They sound totally Chinese even though they grew up in Florida."

"What are they called?"

"Cheap Sex," said Brie. "It's brilliant. Electro-dance party with Cheap Sex. Get it?"

"Oh," said Anna, pausing to spit. "Ha-ha."

"If you want to be my plus one, they're playing Santos House on Friday."

"I can't," Anna said, "I have a thing." When they parted ways last night, Taj told her to meet him in Bushwick on Friday and to keep her day clear.

"OK," Brie said. "Next time."

But on her way back to her room, Anna wondered when the next time would be. The last time Brie had invited her to go anywhere had been ages ago. In the beginning—the honeymoon phase of their roomiedom—Brie had dragged her everywhere. Art-show openings, readings, Roller Derby matches, indie-rock shows. But Anna had sulked, hadn't she? There was no better word for it. She had no one to talk to at the after parties, and ended up drifting around with her sad plate of cheese and crackers, unsuccessfully trying to attach herself to various groups. A moon without a planet. She had found the readings tedious. (Was she missing something or was this about watching a person sit on a folding chair and read from a book for an hour?) And what about poetry? God, *poetry*! She wanted to like it—could even remember reading some good stuff in college—but to her it sounded like these people were just pulling random words from a bingo tumbler. No matter how dismal the attendance, a dude with a safari-grade lens on his camera would always be on hand, circling whatever scruffy trust-fund kid happened to be on stage, intent on documenting every itch-inducing minute of this nonevent.

She didn't care who won the Roller Derby matches, and sensed the audience was there more out of bloodlust anyway. Indie-rock shows she couldn't get into unless she already knew the songs, which she never did. Otherwise, it was just like being forced to listen to the entirety of someone else's favorite album in a high school basement. She always ended up staring at the bobbing backs of other people's heads, letting the fizz go out of her beer. If there was a surgical enhancement that would affix a look of permanent attentiveness to her face, Anna would seriously consider it.

Brie, on the other hand, never seemed to have a problem enjoying anything. Her appraisal of any social occasion was inevitably expressed entirely in caps. Parties were unfailingly GREAT! Shows were always SOOOO FUN! The thing was—and Anna hated herself for feeling this way—fun things *weren't* fun. Sooner or later, the necessary inconveniences always began to grate: the delays on the F train, the overpriced drinks, the wait at the door and then the beer line and then the line for the ladies' room, the way you had to sit for the entirety of the show, or stand for the entirety of the show, and the obligation to keep passing the same careworn questions back and forth with the uninteresting person to your left or to your right, asking them where they were from and telling them where you were from, when hadn't both of you ditched those godforsaken holes as soon as possible to move here? Inquiring as to what they "did" and explaining whatever it was you didn't do. She was constantly being forced to agree something was awesome when that thing was at best mediocresome. In fact, she was convinced there was actually some kind of vast left-wing conspiracy afoot to recast mediocresome things as awesome. And that somehow Brie was part of this movement to enshrine mediocrity, a movement powered by ecstatic *Flavorpill* bulletins and overcaffeinated, PR-driven previews in some online hipster broadsheet. It was always someone else's marketing that landed her in this club/café/shop/rink/piercing salon. Somewhere, some-one's neck was on the line. Someone was being paid to make sure asses filled seats. These people were hyping the shit out of every-thing out of pure self-interest, and the truth was that it was im-possible to fill the quota of fun they promised, not without a flour sack of cocaine. Why is it that her favorite activities were never trumpeted? She had half a mind to go put up her own stupid flyers: *Stay home and have a long circular conversation with a friend! Why not take a bath? Just sleep in! Sleeping is awesome!* The hard sell was just meant to pry her away from what she really wanted to do, which was stay home and work on her laptop tan. And when did it become shameful? Why couldn't she brag about the hours logged surfing the same way Brie bragged about the number of mai tais downed? Why was the breathy admission "I got soooooooooo wasted last night" a marker of stamina or derring-do at least wor-thy of a giggle, whereas the equivalent "I surfed until my eyes felt dry" earned her only a sad look, an awkward pause, or an invita-tion to someplace she didn't want to go?

The morning after these events, Brie would always get up early to google herself and read about the time she'd just had. There would be a guilty encounter at the kitchen table, where Anna would make excuses for having slipped away early. "I came back from the bathroom and couldn't find you!" But it didn't matter to Brie that Anna left early, what mattered was that Anna was a buzzkill for the brief time she was there. No, more like a buzz *slaughter*. So it had been months since Brie had asked her any-where. Sometimes Anna wondered whether her antifun stance was really just the cold hand of agoraphobia on the back of her neck. Even worse, because of all her buzz slaughter, Anna feared that a subtle chill had descended over her relationship with Brie.

When Anna first began her life-coaching sessions with Leslie,

Anna had announced she wanted to be more like her roommate. Leslie had, of course, pointed out the obvious: that Brie was ten years younger, a serial intern with no direction in life and named after a cheese. Leslie also couldn't help but add that Anna had only found Brie on the Internet a year ago. It's not like they'd grown up together, like she and Leslie had.

"Yeah, but I like the way she can do things unironically, just because she feels like doing them. Just because she *enjoys* them," Anna had said.

It was true. Brie once wore Lee Press-On Nails for a month, unironically. Not in a showy, making-fun-of-the-proletariat-while-pretending-to-be-them kind of way, just in a wouldn't-it-be-fun-if-my-nails-looked-like-giant-Tic-Tacs? kind of way. She had a lightness to her, Brie did. She never seemed to overthink things. And her pixieish attitude served to insulate her, keep her strangely unreachable. Everyone always shaped themselves around Brie, her random whims and verdicts, not vice versa. Everyone including Anna, even though she hated herself for it. Even now, Anna fought the urge to take back what she'd just said and agree to go see the horrible-sounding indie-rock band—to burst out and apologize to Brie for all her prior social failures as well. Realistically, though, she knew that she would never do any such thing, because she and Brie didn't talk, not really. Brie made sure their conversations only skimmed the surface of things, like the animated ball bouncing over the lyrics on a karaoke screen.

There was a sudden muffled thud from the living room.

"Fuck," Brie yelled. "Anna, when are you going to move this crap away from the door?"

"Sorry!"

The door slammed shut. She kept forgetting about the AVCCAM box, but it would have to wait another day—now she needed to figure out what to wear for lunch with her mother.

Once a month, her mother came down to the city from Connecticut to shop at Century 21 and have lunch with Anna. She always stayed uptown with her friend Margaret, a woman who shared her interest in energy drinks and hangar-size department stores. Today her mother had suggested they meet at a French restaurant in midtown, even though she knew Anna was a vegetarian. This, Anna assumed, was her mother's subtle way of inducing her to eat salad. Still, the right choice of outfit could help Anna negotiate even these treacherous channels. Her mother had always been the kind of woman who looks at a person's shoes before their face. More than once, the scrutiny of a choice scarf snagged at Barney's once-a-year warehouse sale had saved her from closer inspection of the bulk that lay just below.

The A train was delayed, of course, so Anna had to hump across the avenues, estimating the ratio of blocks to minutes as she ran—that depressing New York calculus of lateness. Billboards of angular women dangling from uncomfortable furniture or angular women sucking inexplicably on jewelry or men with scalloped cheeks laughing explosively into their TAG Heuer watches flashed by. She looked up at the skyscrapers, thought of tycoons vomiting billions into one another's mouths overhead. When she finally arrived at La Petite Folie, she found her mother already seated.

"Anna," her mother said, smiling as much as her taut forehead would allow. Anna kissed her cheek. "How are you?"

"Fine," Anna said.

"It's OK if you don't want to tell me."

"I'm fine."

"Well, you weren't fine last time."

"That's because I *wasn't* fine last time."

"So you found a new job?"

"No."

"How is that fine?"

"Would you like it better if I said I *wasn't* fine?"

"Of course not!"

"Then I'm fine." Anna was almost out of patience and she hadn't yet sat down. "Did you already order something?" she asked.

"Just a water," her mother said, relenting.

Things, Anna thought as she inserted herself between chair and tablecloth, *were already off to a brilliant start*. She opened up the menu and found a parenthetical calorie count inserted next to every appetizer and entrée. Flipping it over, she noticed another section subtitled in red: "Meals Under Six Hundred."

"I'll have the Niçoise," Anna said to the waitress who materialized, sensei-like, as soon as the menu hit the table.

"Two," her mother said.

"So . . . ," Anna said, bracing herself for the sinking prospects for their conversation.

"You don't have to say anything; your face is very expressive." Her mother pulled a pack of Capri cigarettes out of her purse and laid them on the table. "But I'll be gone tomorrow. And would it kill you to wear some makeup?"

"How was Century 21?" Anna had long ago adopted the anti-conversational strategy of ignoring most of what her mother said.

"I haven't gone yet."

For the past eighteen years, Anna's mother had worked as an admissions officer at a community college outside the small town in Connecticut where Anna had grown up. Now that she was retired, she sold clothes on eBay.

"Mostly I came to see you."

"Oh?"

"Well, I'm concerned."

"Oh."

If there was one thing Anna hated, it was her mother's concern. That free-floating cloud of anxiety waiting to be ionized by the misery of others. If not Anna's misery, then the misery of people she barely knew. Better still, the misery of unknown, unseen relatives of barely known people. Denis Dystck's son went back into rehab for the third time, Anna's mother would announce with relish. Eva Rohneson's baby was diagnosed with nonketotic hyperglycinemia and will spend the rest of his life in a diaper. Valerie Omarshadian found her husband making out with their babysitter at a stoplight outside Starbucks. Mr. Kim's anal tumor? Malignant. *So terrible. Can you believe it?* This is how their lunches usually went, with her mother recounting a litany of horrors, eyes glistening with synthetic sympathy.

But just at that moment, and to Anna's great relief, their salads arrived and her mother was distracted by the lack of Dijon mustard, which she had ordered on the side. The ensuing argument with the waitress gave Anna a rare chance to examine her mother's face unobserved. She tallied up the latest damage. Her mother had had her first face-lift back in the eighties—the horse-and-buggy era of plastic surgery—and the scars from those two incisions still stood out clearly just below her earlobes. Back then Anna had remembered dismissing it as a symptom of being bored and living in Connecticut. The "vacations" to Antigua started only after Anna finished college. After that, her features kept moving steadily north as though someone had selected them in Photoshop and repositioned them with a mouse. First, her eyes were pinned higher on her forehead. Then her cheekbones seemed to grow closer to the tops of her ears. Her nose tilted skyward. Was this the hidden key to beauty? Eyes, nose, cheeks, all racing toward the hairline? Anna felt sure she'd had other work done, too—*down there*—but she never asked her mother that for the simple reason that she and her mother had never discussed any of her surgeries. Not once. Not even the Botox treatments that were sometimes so fresh her face looked like it had been raped by bees. Of course, why should Anna bring it up when it served her better to say nothing? The undiscussed surgeries lay like a weapon on the table before them. Her mother knew, despite the jabs about Anna's weight and the pointed comments about her unemployment, that as someone who wandered the plasticized wilderness somewhere between Joan Rivers and Michael Jackson, she should go only so far.

"What?" her mother said, and Anna realized she'd caught her staring.

"Nothing." Then quickly, "No, something." Because suddenly, she didn't want it to be this way. What was it Leslie had said? *Act the way you want to be.*

"Mom, what was your dream?"

"Last night? I don't usually dream, Anna." Her mother raised her twin black arches, charcoal gravestones marking where her eyebrows had been. "Only if I eat chocolate at night, which you know I never do."

Anna pushed aside thoughts about the respective speeds at which they were eating their Niçoise. "No, when you were young. Your *dream*."

"Why would you ask me that?"

"Because I want to know."

For a moment, Anna felt sure her mother would wave her away with one of her passive-aggressive bons mot: *Save your breath and chew more slowly—you'll feel fuller afterward.* But that's not what her mother said.

"I wanted to run a funeral home," she said. And then she laughed, surprised by her own words. "Sounds funny, doesn't it?"

"Why?" It was the least likely thing she'd heard her mother say today. Possibly ever.

"There was a funeral home and it was on my way home from school, and every day these expensive cars would pull up. Mercedes, limos, Cadillacs. Always black. There were hearses, too, but to me they were just fancy cars. The women would stand outside, smoking cigarettes on the sidewalk in long dresses, hats. To me it looked glamorous, like a dinner party. But we didn't have a lot of money back then, and I was just a stupid kid," her mother said. She chewed her salad, then added, "Well, you asked."

"Weren't they crying?"

"From a distance, crying looks like laughing."

Anna could see that.

"Then I grew up and figured out what the place was. Can you imagine?" Her mother gave a bark-like laugh. "I bet the fumes would take the paint right off your nails."

"Well, what was your dream after that?"

"After that? I don't know. To work in college admissions, I guess. To marry your father." She poked her olives. "Of course, that's before I knew what was what. I might have been better off with the funeral home. Have you heard from him, by the way?"

"Dad?"

"Since last time?"

"Not since last time." Anna's father had last called her a year ago from Thailand. Her phone rang at 3:30 in the morning and they talked for fifteen minutes on a crackling line, mostly about her father's business investments. Something about exporting souvenirs made from coconut shells and the exchange value of the baht—she hadn't understood a thing. How was it that even such a hallmark domestic tragedy, her father leaving her mother, had insinuated itself into their lives so uneventfully? His business trips had grown ever longer and more frequent until one day he'd simply eroded into nonexistence. No papers filed, no divorce. It sounded bizarre when Anna explained her father's absence to others, but back home it was treated as just another stale fact, like the square footage of the garage.

"Anyway," Anna's mother said, exhaling heavily. "I sent you an e-mail a while back and you didn't write back."

"What e-mail?" Anna said, knowing exactly what e-mail that must be.

Without a word, her mother took a brochure out of her purse and slid it across the table toward Anna. It was a brochure for the Aveda Hair Institute.

"Mom—"

"I'll pay for it. Tuition. Books. Hair-cutting utensils or whatever. Twenty thousand dollars, Anna."

"It's—"

"Eight months. Then you take your test, get certified. Voilà!"

"But I don't *want* to cut hair."

"Maybe it isn't what you planned to do in life. I know we all have these pictures of ourselves, these 'dreams,' but Anna, it's time to grow up. Take a look around." Her mother took a dramatic look around. "Everybody has hair. Everybody needs a hairdresser."

"Everybody needs an undertaker, too," Anna said.

"You see an undertaker once, when you're dead, but hair keeps growing. Even after you're dead." Her mother moved the egg from the top of her salad to the side of her plate as if it were a cancerous cyst. "This Brie person still doesn't have a job yet either, does she?"

The chance for communion, Anna realized, was slipping away. Without thinking, she suddenly blurted, "I met someone."

Her mother's hand froze on its way to pick the remaining potato wedges from her salad. "Another one from the Internet." It wasn't a question.

"No," Anna said. It was technically true, depending on your definition of *met*. Hadn't they first met in fleshy person, at Halal Wireless Café?

"Oh, Anna. I don't know . . ."

"What don't you know? I haven't told you anything!"

"But I know *you*."

"So?"

"So I worry."

"Stop worrying. Please. Just stop."

"Instead of looking for a job, you're looking for men on the Internet."

"He's *not* from the Internet."

"What about that one from Delaware?"

"That was five years ago. Why do you have to keep bringing it up?"

"Because he had two kids."

"I know that."

"He's a total stranger, Anna. You don't know him."

"Everyone's a stranger until you know them!" Anna practically yelled.

And even her mother couldn't think of anything to say to that, so she changed the subject.

"How much of Clara's money have you got left?"

"A lot."

"How much?"

"Mom—"

Her mother gave a loud exhale. "I worked in admissions for eighteen years, Anna, and believe it or not, I know a thing or two about things. You have a gap in your résumé right now and you're not filling it with anything. At least not anything you could explain to a potential employer. Your gap is growing. I want you to think about that. And think about this," she added, tapping the brochure significantly. As her mother stared at her, tapping, Anna couldn't help but wonder about the relative rates at which her gap and her hair were growing.

Suddenly it was clear this little speech had used up what little self-control her mother had left. A "fuck it" look crossed her face as she grabbed a cigarette from the pack on the table and lit it. The waitress was upon them in an instant.

"I'm sorry ma'am—" she began, sounding not sorry at all. But it didn't matter; lunch was already over.

12

"Hope used to live in bookstores, in record stores," Taj was saying. "Now people think hope lives in a fucking URL."

Anna simply nodded, following him up the subway steps.

"But that's not true," he continued, waving a hand. "This is where hope lives. It lives right here."

She found that a little hard to believe. They had just surfaced at the Halsey Street station in Bushwick and were now making their way past a series of ambitiously named but depressingly shabby buildings. Roman Court. Wyckoff Manor. Without bothering to turn around, a man peed in a doorway.

"Careful!" Anna said, pointing to a dog turd on the sidewalk. Taj barely managed to skip over it.

"I saved you." Anna smiled.

"You are my turd GPS," Taj said, squeezing her shoulder. Serving as her guide to all things Bushwickian had apparently put him in a good mood today. The sun hit the cheap clapboard siding of the row houses a little harder and she felt a shiver of pleasure. They stopped at a deli where Anna got a coffee with skim milk, Sweet'N Low, and a banana—what she liked to call her "poor man's banana split." Friday had rolled around slowly, with many uneventful days in between. Her mother had lingered for an extra day, demanding to be taken to tedious museums, which had prevented Anna from getting back to J&R to return the AVCCAM and the sound equipment. Brie had also vanished again, responding neither to texts nor calls. Despite herself, Anna couldn't help but wonder if this had anything to do with the growing stack of unopened utility bills on the table. Their A/C bill, in particular, had been recklessly high all summer, owing much to the fact that neither of them understood the symbols on the remote control.

"Sunflower isn't working," Brie would say, helplessly prodding the buttons. "Should I try tiny droplet?"

Frustrating though it was, Anna found herself missing even this stupid ritual. The apartment had been lonely and still all week, inducing mid-afternoon naps and late-night existential crises.

Two guys were carrying a sofa left outside for curbside pickup into a heavily graffitied doorway. They both nodded at Taj, letting him pass by first. He steered Anna inside with a light touch to the small of her back. She was eating her banana, which somehow made her feel like a child. A man was asleep in a La-Z-Boy in the hallway. It seemed like he had been there since the night before, as he was still wearing a coat and his face was mashed directly into the cushion. He didn't move, not even when the strap of Anna's backpack trailed across his bare arm.

"Who are these people?" Anna whispered.

"Members. It's a co-op."

Later Anna would realize that the Compound, whose basement served as Taj's studio, was basically a metaphor for the lives of its denizens: a former warehouse in an endless process of "conversion," lightless corridors leading to nothing, not zoned for residential living. A squat, in other words. But now she just nodded, feeling the simple thrill of the new.

Open doorways revealed microuniverses of hipster aspiration. One bathroom had been repurposed as a DIY brewery. Band gear, camera equipment, and unfinished canvases clogged the hallway like dust bunnies. The lone window was covered with so many stickers, it achieved a kind of stained-glass effect. Taj led her down a staircase lit by a series of caged lightbulbs. They emerged into a large windowless chamber where a stage had been set up against the back wall. In the middle of this subterranean piazza stood a giant plywood box. A room within a room. Its glass-cube windows glowed a warm yellow. The plywood door practically flew open at Taj's touch, and as Anna stepped inside, she couldn't help but feel like they were animating a giant dollhouse.

Inside, Lauren, Sasha, and two hoodied guys—one of whom Anna recognized as the guy from Café Gowanus—were sitting around a small table on chairs vomiting stuffing from assorted wounds. Everyone "Hey"ed one another, and Anna offered a small wave to the guys she didn't know.

"This is Fifteen and Sixteen," Taj said, indicating the guy from Café Gowanus and the other one. The two men nodded at her, their eyes glittering darkly from within their hoodies. *If the horsemen of the apocalypse were to ride today*, Anna thought, *this is what they would wear—matching black hoodies.*

"So, Anna," said Taj, "after reviewing your materials, we've all agreed. You're in." Anna felt a warm flush spread up her neck. "You'll be engaged in all stages of production, starting today."

Lauren, who had been chipping the blue nail polish from her thumbnail onto the table, flashed Anna a look. Sasha raised his eyebrows at her, not unkindly.

"Thank you," Anna said. A chorus of "Cool" sounded around the table.

"And just in time," he added, "because today is totally fucked."

"The band will be here at ten," Lauren said, consulting her iPhone.

"The stage should be ready by eight," one of the hoodied guys said. "That's when we're getting the PA from the sound-rental place."

"Sasha, Anna? We need that room completely covered in tinfoil by eight," Taj said, making a few furious notes in his Moleskine.

"Sorry, what is this for?" Anna said, feeling a bit bolder now that she was to be "involved in all stages of production."

"We're stage-setting the future. Tonight we're shooting a live show in here. But it has to look like the future."

"Tinfoil looks like the future?"

"On camera it will," said Taj.

"All that foil will never fit in my Civic, Taj," Lauren said.

"Yeah, we will need truck for Costco." This from Sasha, whose Russian accent made everything sound like a cattle call to the gulag. Like Stalin himself were calling to announce you'd just won an all-expense-paid trip to Dudinka.

"Is there a script for this movie that I can maybe look at?" Anna said.

"Anna," said Taj, "you need to find us a truck."

"I don't know anyone with a truck."

"Think like a poet," Taj said, rising to his feet, "thrive within the constraints."

"We're late," said Lauren.

"OK, gang, chop-chop!" Anna was the last to stand. Lauren, Taj, and the two hoodied men filed out, leaving her alone with Sasha.

"Do you know anyone with a truck?" she asked him.

"No," said Sasha.

"What's the budget for this stuff? Can we just rent one?"

"Zero budget," Sasha said.

"Shit." Why had she been stuck with Sasha when Sasha was clearly useless? Then she had a sudden epiphany. Anna took out her phone and dialed 411.

"New York," she said. "Brooklyn. Home Depot." A moment later, she was connected.

"Yes, hi, I'm calling from Habitat for Humanity and we were hoping you might have a rental truck available for donation this afternoon? We have a load of Sheetrock we have to get up to Sunset Park for a house we're working on . . . uh-huh . . . Krestler. Anna." Anna hung up.

"Wow," Sasha said. It sounded like "Vow."

"I used to volunteer for Habitat in college. If no one was using the rental truck at Home Depot they'd let us have it for free."

"You are very wily," he said. His smile revealed some seriously sketchy bridgework and a gold incisor.

"Thanks," Anna said, not at all sure this was a compliment.

On the way to Home Depot, Anna asked Sasha how he and Taj had first met, expecting him to name a URL. But Sasha told her they'd met two years ago, at an amateur film-screening night Taj used to host at Quantum, a now-defunct venue in Williamsburg. Anna tried to realign this new information with her image of Taj. Because wasn't hosting an open-mic night for amateur filmmakers kind of loserish? Less loserish than actually participating, but still. She pictured the clientele with their sad, outsize dreams, tossing back beers laced with the backwash of failure. But maybe she was being overly harsh. Anna remembered the box by the door and considered what it would be like to make a movie as raw and unadorned as Gilman's, to sit unseen among a crowd of strangers as they devoured it in the dark. A little shiver raced down her back.

"It sucked, this thing," Sasha said. "It sucked very much. The movies people brought were terrible. They had a lottery system. You arrive and they give you a number. Sometimes you wait only half an hour to screen your movie. Sometimes four hours. I would have many different feelings about myself at this time, sitting and waiting."

"Why did you do it, then?" Anna asked.

"In Russian we have an expression—to soak in one's own juices. And I did not want to sit home with my movies, soaking. I had ambitions but nowhere to go. When all doors are closed to you, when you have no connections, what can you do? Quantum took everyone, so I went to Quantum." In this, Anna had to admit they had something in common. "He gave me award one night. A coffee mug," Sasha continued, "for best movie. That night we talk, very late, at the bar. The next week we talk again. Soon, he hired me."

"He pays you?"

Sasha shot Anna a look from the corner of his eye. "A little." And then the question Anna had been dying to ask finally slipped out.

"So, then, what does Taj do, you know, for money?" She suspected family money, of course, figured that shame of his own privileged cushion was what fed his bitterness toward Gilman. It was only human nature.

"He has a poetry scheme," Sasha said. Then, seeing Anna's uncomprehending look, "SAP. The Society for the Advancement of Poetry."

"Taj runs a poetry society?"

"Once a month, the society holds a competition and the best poem gets an award."

"Whoa," Anna said. This was truly unexpected. Though, if she stopped to consider it, the distance between the experimental film and poetry worlds was probably small, and both involved the same sorts of very intelligent people working hard to ostracize a vanishingly small audience.

"So what else does the society do?"

"Nothing."

"Nothing? It's just a contest?"

"Taj started it. He judges competition for fee."

"How much is the fee?"

"Thirty-five dollars."

"Well, what's the award?"

"You get tweeted."

"And?"

"Taj has very good business sense. He studied economics."

"Wait, your poem gets tweeted and that's it?" Anna said, unable to keep the incredulity from her voice.

Sasha shot her another look. "The SAP has more than seven

thousand followers, you know." *Thirty-five bucks for a chance to get tweeted?* Didn't contests usually involve more tangible prizes: money, a trip somewhere, a crappy Lucite plaque? "Is only one winner per month," Sasha continued. Then, perhaps concluding that math was not her forte, added, "Twelve winners per year."

Anna mulled this over. Taj's exhortation to "think like a poet" now took on a new significance. So he earned his money exploiting some sort of loser economy, generating and profiting from an artificial scarcity of poetry prestige? Then again, it wasn't as though Taj were like Brie, trapped in some interminable intern feedback loop with no clear endgame. He was a real artist with clear-cut goals, just prebloom. Once he became successful like Gilman, the money would cease to appear ill-gained. It would become a necessary investment. Just another of those endearingly quirky schemes artists resort to in order to fund their dreams. Thus Anna reasoned all the way to Costco, where they filled five shopping carts with three hundred rolls of tinfoil.

At the checkout counter, Anna was relieved when Sasha pulled out a platinum AmEx. She watched him sign for the tinfoil, wondering why, if there was some kind of budget, they couldn't have just rented a truck to begin with. Was she still being tested, pitted against the invisible "everyone"? And if that was the case, then Sasha must be a coconspirator only *pretending* to be useless, which brought him up a notch in Anna's regard. Either way she supposed it was fair enough, manufacturing a minor crisis to see whether Anna mustered a response or folded under pressure. And she *had* managed, hadn't she? The knowledge that she had somehow "passed" gave her a boost, and when they arrived back at the Compound, Anna strode back and forth through the scabbed hallways carrying armloads of tinfoil with a new measure of confidence.

Now, Anna thought, she was finally living in Brooklyn. Not just residing here—taking the subway to work and back, traversing the four short blocks that reliably delivered her to pharmacy, supermarket, and coffee shop—but really *living*. She remembered a recent night when Brie had come home breathless from a party she'd attended at someone's penthouse loft. There had been a miniature carousel on the roof and a fountain filled with absinthe. Famous artists were there. OK, not famous famous, but New York famous, like the artist whose resin-cast penis had been included in the New Museum's "Younger Than Jesus" show. And as Brie recounted her evening—the starfucking, the dancing, the making and unmaking of ephemeral friends—and shared her Instagrams, Anna couldn't help thinking, *This city is wasted on me.* Right then she swore to herself that she would turn this period of forced inactivity into an opportunity to explore. The next day, when Brandon called to see if she wanted to go gallery-hopping in Chelsea that weekend, she'd eagerly agreed. But come Saturday, she found herself calling Brandon to cancel. It was too hot out. Chelsea was an hour away. There were no good, cheap places to eat in that neighborhood. Et cetera. What was wrong with her if it wasn't depression? Agoraphobia? Claustrophobia? Lifeophobia? Whatever it was, it seemed to have lifted since she'd met Taj. She felt an almost helpless gratitude toward him.

"Crinkled or flat?" Sasha asked Lauren as he unspooled the first roll of tinfoil at the base of the stage.

"As flat as possible," Lauren replied, not looking up from her phone.

And for the next five hours, Anna and Sasha tinfoiled first the stage, then the rest of the room. They wore canvas gloves, which helped with the sharp edges and securing each sheet in place with silver pushpins. Someone put LCD Soundsystem on full blast. Someone else ordered Thai food delivered. Anna ate *pad kee mao* with crispy tofu from a paper plate and joked with the hoodied guys while Taj spray-painted the ceiling silver. Taj *was* going for the Gugg; this she learned from Fifteen. The Guggenheim Fellowship. And they were steering him capably toward this goal, one purring engine of productivity. Sixteen even started a singalong: "He's going for the Gugg, he's going for the Gugg. Hi-ho, the derry-o, he's going for the Gugg." For the first time in a very long time, Anna felt happy.

When the room was done and the band gear deposited on-stage, the crew slumped down on a decomposing sofa for a PBR break. Confident that she had already burned a Pilates session's worth of calories hanging tinfoil, Anna didn't even bother to check the nutrition information on the bottle before knocking one back.

"This is totally craptastic," Anna said, looking around the room in awe.

"It's like a million disco balls exploded," one of the hoodied guys seconded.

"Or a Lady Gaga video," said Sasha.

"The band will be here soon." Lauren, who, Anna had noticed, had scarcely touched her Thai food, was still in business mode. "Guys, sorry, but we need those lights set up."

There was a reluctant shuffling as the men rose and stretched, revealing the hair on their lower abdomens and the worn elastic of their boxer shorts. Then it was just Anna and Lauren.

"Anna, we need you for something," said Lauren. For once she wasn't looking into her phone; she was looking straight at Anna. And she hadn't called her Thirty-seven, which Anna took as a good sign.

"Sure. What?"

"We need you in the test shoot—we're blocking the scene."

"OK," Anna said, whatever that meant, though she had half-hoped to loiter behind the camera with Taj.

"Great. You'll be wearing this." Lauren bent down and retrieved a plastic bag from under the sofa that said "Have a Happy Day." She handed it to Anna. Inside was a red, tubular, glossy one-piece suit, made from some kind of rubbery material. It was exactly the kind of clothing that would delineate every roll of Anna's back fat, mercilessly cast her arm flab into high relief, and generally reveal her lightbulb shaped figure in the least-possible flattering light.

"Um . . ."

"Have another drink," said Lauren, producing a potent stout from the bottom of the cooler. "Don't worry about it. You'll look great."

And because she both badly wanted Lauren to like her and didn't want to ruin such a good day, Anna found herself taking the bag and heading back toward the office to change. While Anna was coaxing her abundant flesh into the red unisuit, the band arrived. Three men, all dressed in black. They had already taken their positions onstage by the time Anna emerged from the office, their fauxhawks slicked up and pointing in different directions, like cartoon road signs at an ominous crossroads.

"What do I do?" she shouted out to Taj, who was staring into the viewfinder of a camera set up by the stage. The room was so huge it seemed to swallow her words as soon as they left her mouth.

"You look great," he yelled back. "Get up there. Take the mic."

Anna made her way across the room, highly conscious of the fart-like squeak emanating from the nether regions of her unisuit whenever her thighs brushed together. There were no stairs, so she was forced to clamber awkwardly up onto the wooden platform. Once she was onstage, the band suddenly began to play a dissonant and highly aggressive sort of postpunk samba. They moved jerkily as one in some kind of choreographed dance.

"Loosen up," Lauren yelled up at her. "Improvise!"

"I don't know how," Anna yelled back. But reluctantly, she began to sway from side to side—the standard lame, white-girl dance.

"Where am I supposed to look?" she called out into the darkness. The lights flashing off the tinfoil had blinded her completely. She could no longer see Taj, Lauren, or the camera.

In response she heard a distant laugh, then Taj's voice.

"Look forward," he called out, "into the future!"

13

Step one to getting her shit together, Anna decided, was to take Brie's advice and order those prescription diet pills online. Brie had mentioned the site back when she first moved in. How else did she manage to get Ambien without paying a shrink two hundred bucks per session? Besides, the whole thing was a racket, Brie said. Anyone who got to the point of making an appointment with a shrink had already done the necessary Google searching and knew what they needed. Brie believed in cutting out the middleman.

It's not that Anna had hang-ups about being full-figured, per se, but being on camera last night, even for a moment, even just for the sake of "blocking the scene," had opened up new pastures of insecurity. And being around Lauren all day, whose clothes sloughed so elegantly from her coat-hanger frame, didn't help. They didn't even *make* clothes like that in Anna's size. The experience had planted notions in Anna's head, a new hope for thinness. Why shouldn't that be part of her transformation, shedding the physical as well as the metaphorical weight?

Anna had the site bookmarked. But when she clicked over to CanadianPharmaPharm.com it rerouted her to another site, dominated by a glossy, half-naked woman, that called itself Masculus. At first glance, the site seemed to offer only Viagra Pro, Max Viagra, Cialis Pro, and, for the fence-sitters, a multipack of all three. Only when she scrolled to the bottom of the page did she notice the tiny link for "other medications." Just as Brie said, she was easily able to order a one-month supply of phentermine.

That done, Anna could move on to the main business of the day. Taj had given her a list of filmmakers who had influenced him and she had dutifully Netflixed all of them. *Everyone is so weird*, Anna thought, as she watched a video starring a talking pony head on a stick by the filmmaker Ben Coonley. Where did they get these ideas? Taj, Gilman, everyone made it look so easy to just ignite with some random-passion, and yet Anna still had no clue what it was she wanted to make movies about. Sometimes she wished she could just go to Earthy Basket and pick up a microwavable pouch of artistic inspiration, a six-pack of ideas. A few short weeks ago, considering Yagihashi's shit sculpture, she couldn't help suspect that inspiration wasn't actually an innate mystery of human nature, that the whole thing was a lot more calculated than that. Seen with a cynical eye, it was easy to imagine Yagihashi simply exploiting a gap in the art world by carving out an esoteric, scatological niche for himself. The idea that maybe art was just a lifestyle choice flashed through her mind; Yagihashi didn't give a shit about shit, but did enjoy swanning around art galleries, dating girls like Lauren, and having the heads of various pompous institutions kiss his sweet Japanese ass.

But now that this strange fever had taken hold of Anna as well, she finally understood. She understood Gilman's bizarre predilections and Yagihashi's and her own. Why Gilman filmed men finger-painting with their balls was the same reason Anna spent seven hours wallpapering a basement with tinfoil and squeaking around in a tight red suit: because losing yourself in an idea—any idea—made life worth living. And didn't fetish websites prove that it was possible to turn *anything* into an object worthy of love, obsession, scholarship? An amputee? A pointy shoe? Macaque dung? And here a new thought struck her; sitting here all night with her Netflix and her e-books, wasn't that an awfully *consumer* approach to art-making? There was something to be said for book learning, but she had the sense that the Duplass brothers, Andrew Bujalski, Lynn Shelton, Ramin Bahrani, this guy Coonley, and, of course, Gilman, had learned their craft on the job. The kind of emotion-drenched, impulsive, jagged-edged filmmaking Taj exalted required the thrill of discovery. Didn't it?

Anna closed her laptop with a satisfying click. She went out into the hall and tapped on Brie's door. Brie had finally come home last night, but had been locked inside all morning.

"What?" came Brie's muffled voice.

"Hey. Do you want to come open this box with me?"

"Can't. Don't feel well."

"Oh no. Can I get you anything?"

"No."

"OK, feel better," Anna said, with a false sympathy she hoped masked the suspicion Brie was simply blowing her off. There was no way that she could get Brandon over here in the middle of the afternoon—he was still clinging to his job at Pinter, Chinski and Harms. It was just her and the AVCCAM box.

She opened everything at once, ripping into the boxes like she was satisfying a long-suppressed cardboard fetish. The date for returning the AVCCAM had passed and shredding the packaging to the point of no return felt like a christening of sorts. To her great surprise, the camera turned out to be easy to assemble. There were only three parts and they easily snapped together. It was shocking how remarkably clear and bright everything was when viewed from the other side of the lens. The AVCCAM seemed to have magical, gloom-lifting properties. Even the gross, fuzzy crack between the radiator and the wall transformed into a mystical, Mordor-like landscape when viewed at full zoom. Anna wandered over to the refrigerator, camera glued to one eye. Inspired by some moldering fruit, she arranged three half-melted bananas in a bowl around a dead tomato. It was so incredibly beautiful. More beautiful than any still life by Morandi, or Zurbarán, or Steenwijck.

When the phone rang, Anna answered it automatically, somehow sure that it was Taj calling, so she could tell him about the AVCCAM and the beautifully rotting fruit. But it was only Leslie.

"Just calling to say I'll be ten minutes late. The N's stuck on the bridge again."

Shit, Anna thought. She'd forgotten Leslie had changed their session to Saturday this week. Now she would have to take a cab.

"Ditto," Anna said. "Take your time."

She hung up and with great reluctance laid the camera back in its foam cradle like a reliquary.

The seating situation at Gorilla Coffee was even worse than at Café Gowanus. Laptop people crowded every seat of the four long tables jutting from the back wall. They contemplated leaving, but where to go? The pita place? The juice bar? Ambience was important, and the pita place had been occupied, Palestine-like, by an aggressive cult of lactivists who aimed their loaded breasts at childless passersby. The juice bar was irradiated with guilt. Anna always felt like she should order something with wheatgrass, but ended up asking for a coconut mango shake with crushed almonds instead. Besides, it was hard to linger over a glass of juice. So Anna filled Leslie in about her apprenticeship with Taj as they loitered by the milk station at Gorilla until two seats opened up.

"OK, so it sounds like you know what you want to do, you just have to find a way to make money doing it," Leslie said, settling down.

"Exactly," Anna replied, even though she hadn't given the question of money a second thought.

"I mean, is there a job down the line here?"

"I think some of his crew gets paid . . ."

"What are we talking?" Leslie said, no-nonsense. "Beer money? Rent money? Health benefits? 401(k)?"

"No. I don't know. Probably not that much," Anna admitted.

"Well, this sounds like a great résumé builder, but we have to consider the exit strategy."

"Les, I just officially joined the crew."

"I'm just encouraging you to think long-term. Making a career for yourself in the arts—any art—is a major campaign. We can always map it out both ways: filmmaking as career and filmmaking as hobby." Leslie was already pulling out a pen, searching around for a napkin.

"No way it's a hobby," Anna said, annoyed at Leslie for not just letting her talk.

"OK, OK. Last week it was criminology, remember?" Leslie said, putting up her hands in mock surrender. "I'm only trying to keep up with you."

As Leslie eyed the line for the bathroom, Anna gave herself free rein to think treasonous thoughts. After all, what the fuck did Leslie know? Hadn't Leslie simply followed the predictable route from college to B-school to McKinsey? Leslie, easily six dress sizes smaller than Anna, would never squeeze herself into a red rubber unisuit to gyrate on a tinfoil stage for the sake of an unpaid art project. No, it no longer made sense to seek out Leslie's advice. She lacked an artist's perspective. And suddenly it hit her: There *was* no map. There *could be* no map. Everything she wanted to accomplish, everything worth accomplishing, was off the grid, in the weeds, underwater. The kinds of places Leslie didn't want her to end up. The place she was trying to drag Anna out of right now.

Before it was time to wheelbarrow Dora to some activity or another, Leslie handed Anna a book called *The Fatal Flaw*, written by some guy in a lab coat. Anna made another visit to the counter to procure a testicular twist of dough and a fresh latte, then settled back to peruse. The lab-coat guy's thesis, her skim revealed, was that everyone had a fatal personality flaw but that no one would tell you what it was, most especially not the shrink collecting your hush money. Lab Coat favored a rigorous, scientific approach. He posited that only an anonymous and representative survey of friends, family, lovers, coworkers, and scant acquaintances could reveal the exact nature of one's douche-baggery. Anna flipped to the back—there was an ad for Lab Coat's consultancy. His was a crack team, filled with the kinds of truffle hunters who keep college alumni databases updated, and for a mint, they would pan the river of your regrets, sifting the piecemeal disappointments from the chronic stuff.

She found herself thinking of various people she knew. Leslie, Brie, Taj, Brandon—what were their fatal flaws? *More interestingly*, she thought, taking a sip of her latte, *if each of them were a coffee, what kind of coffee would they be?* Leslie would undoubtedly be something expensive, one of those fancy pour-overs the new place up the street was charging six bucks for. Brie? Something sweet with foam. A Cinnamon Dolce Crème Frappuccino with a shot of hazelnut. Brandon, who always liked to get things done quickly, would no doubt be instant. Taj . . . now, Taj was complicated. Perhaps he would be one of those exotic free-trade coffees the barista was always expounding on, holding up the line. Grown in some Himalayan village where each bean is wrapped in muslin, carried down the mountain by virgins, and bathed in unicorn tears before being left to dry in the sun. But what kind of coffee was Anna? Something not too bitter and a little diluted. An Americano, maybe. *Or a latte*, she thought, contemplating her latte.

The lights were off in the apartment when Anna arrived, so she was surprised to hear Brie's voice sounding in the dark.

"Hey."

"Hey!" Anna said. She flipped on the light and there was Brie, sitting on the couch, wearing a slept-in pair of sweatpants and a T-shirt emblazoned with a dancing piece of tofu. Her finger was stuck, mid-rewind, in the sprocket of a plastic cassette tape whose magnetic intestines were unspooled across the floor. The whole table was, in fact, covered with tapes. Tapes and their dusty cases, many cracked, all of them looking as though they'd been scrubbed with steel wool. Brie sat there as though she'd always been there and always would be, like a figure from a Greek myth—Cassettrodite.

"Are you OK?"

Brie shook her head no.

"What's wrong? Is it work?"

Brie shook her head again.

"Rishi?"

"No."

"Kickball?"

Brie began to cry. "F-fuck kickball," she said.

Coming from Brie—a person who stopped reading a book if she thought that "things were maybe about to get sad"—tears were shocking.

"Do you want me to make you a peppermint tea?" Brie didn't say anything and Anna decided to take this as a yes. She went over to the electric teapot, glad to escape the toxic orb of misery surrounding Brie and busy herself with something. She returned a moment later with a steaming mug.

"Too hot," Brie sniffed.

"I know. We'll wait."

They waited.

"I'll blow on it."

"Good," said Anna. Then, after an awkward span of silence, "I ordered some diet pills from that website you told me about."

Brie nodded, blowing on her tea.

"They said they'd send them in a couple weeks."

Silence.

"You were right, it was totally easy."

Brie could only close her eyes as the tears streamed harder, gathering under her chin.

"Brie, what's wrong?"

"I-I can't say it."

"OK."

There was just the sound of Brie blowing and sniffing.

"I'll write it down," she said, finally.

"OK," Anna said. She dug a pen out of her bag and handed Brie a bodega receipt.

Brie scribbled something down on the receipt with one hand and slid the note across the coffee table to Anna. She let the cassette clatter to the floor—she never did explain what the cassettes were for—and left Anna to read the note. Anna read it and then read it again, even though it contained only two words: *I'm pregnant.*

14

Looking back, Anna wondered whether her relationship with Taj would ever have advanced to the next level if Brie hadn't become pregnant. Would she have invited Taj over that night if Brie hadn't gone to stay with her parents in Framingham and she hadn't had the apartment to herself? There was no denying that she had felt lonely ever since Brie left. Then again, it was almost worse with Brie there. After that one discussion on the couch, Brie hadn't brought up her pregnancy again, and this filled the apartment with a weird tension, the withheld revelations giving Anna a severe case of conversational blue balls. A week later, Anna had come home from a shoot at the Compound to find a handful of checks for Brie's share of the bills tucked under the pepper mill and Brie gone. The text from Framingham only arrived two days later.

When Taj called, Anna was editing her fruit footage. Brandon had given her a promotional copy of Final Cut Pro he had cadged from an old friend at film school. Threatening pop-up boxes appeared whenever Anna launched the application, but she just clicked OK and, to her relief, things seemed to indeed turn out that way. She didn't like the idea of stealing software, but a new copy of FCP cost a few hundred dollars and, since she had decided against returning the AVCCAM, money was getting tight. Besides, Brandon reassured her that no one who was serious about film actually paid for editing software and so, by paying for it, she would only be reinforcing her own poor perception of herself. It would practically be an act of self-sabotage.

"I'm upset," Taj had said as soon as she'd picked up the phone.

"Oh, no!" said Anna, happy to find herself a recipient of this, Taj's upsetness.

"I feel like you're the only one who can get me unupset."

"Why's that?"

"Because you're new," Taj said. That made sense to Anna.

"Do you want to come over? I'll make you soup." Or rather, Anna thought, she would heat him soup. She'd picked up a quart of corn chowder and a pint of split pea at Earthy Basket that afternoon.

"You would soup me?" Taj said. He promised to be there in an hour.

But although he had sounded raw and even a little tender on the phone, by the time he arrived something had changed and he just seemed angry.

"When did you get this AVCCAM?" he said, waving at the camera on the table with a vague air of hostility.

"A while back," Anna said, feeling oddly guilty. For some reason she hadn't found time to mention the AVCCAM to Taj, or the thing with Final Cut Pro.

"Fucking waste of money."

"Well, I needed something with two mic inputs—"

"You'd have been better off with a Kodak Zi8. It has a really good lens. You can always just record the sound separately on a Tascam DR-100."

She should introduce Taj to Brandon, Anna thought, so they could have conversations that consisted solely of passing strings of letters and numbers back and forth. Then something else jogged her memory. *Good lens*. Shit. Maybe that was what the salesman at J&R had been trying to say about the Zi8.

"Do you want some soup?" Anna said, as much for Taj as to

distract herself from calculating how much money she might have saved by buying the Zi8 instead.

"Scotch."

"I might have some Absolut in the freezer."

And she did, buried under two ancient bags of frozen edamame. Anna filled a shot glass for Taj, which he tossed back immediately.

"I got rejected," he said.

"Oh, no. Was it the Gugg?" Anna said, feeling caught off guard. "Because you shouldn't feel bad about that. No one ever gets those."

"God, no. Nowhere near as good as the Gugg. Some crappy festival."

"That's so fucked up."

"On many levels. But that's not even what bugs me. They rejected me but they didn't even *tell* me. I had to find out from Lauren, whose crappy short got accepted and who, by the way, has no idea I submitted, so we didn't have this conversation."

"Of course not," Anna said. She went to the cabinet and got out the good chocolate she'd been hiding from Brie. She put the chocolate on the table, but Taj didn't touch it. "What happened?"

"Lauren tells me she got in and I've heard nothing, so I call the festival people and they go, 'We have no record of your application on file.' And I'm like, 'Really? Because I noticed the check for my application fee was cashed two months ago.' And they're like, 'Oh? OK, we'll call you back,' in this annoyed voice like I'm this *drag* they have to deal with now. Like, 'Oh no, this stupid, annoying retard is hassling us'—"

"No!"

"Yeah. Then the next day I get a call from some fucking Tisch *intern* or something and the guy just goes, 'Is this Taj?' and I'm like, 'Yeah, this is Taj' and he goes, 'You didn't get in.' That's it. Hangs up. How *un-fucking-professional* is that? Who *does* that?"

Anna exhaled and shook her head. No one does that. No one should do that. It sounded awful. She had the urge to interrupt Taj to tell him about the day Professor Kagan had sat with her all through a congenial lunch, chatting away about the amazing colloquium series the faculty had set up for the fall semester—the semester Anna would not be invited back—before shooting her down in the graduate lounge in full earshot of two of her fellow classmates, both Slavs, of course. But Anna could sense that it wasn't her turn to talk. With Taj, she wasn't sure when, if ever, it would finally be her turn.

"Seriously, don't say anything to Lauren," he was saying.

"I won't," Anna said. "And you know, there are a lot of other festivals. You can always submit it somewhere else."

He poured himself another shot.

"There's South by Southwest, there's Sundance, Toronto," Anna listed. She began eating the chocolate herself.

"Fuck it," he said. "Fuck Tribeca and Slamdance and Toronto. At the end of the day you know what? It's between the creator and the public." Taj's eyes glistened the way they did whenever he slipped into speech mode. "The truth is that all the self-anointed gatekeepers—agents, managers, lawyers, producer reps, festival selectors, talent spotters—all the fucking cockroaches and jumped-up arrivistes, have no power to either stop or help you. They only exist if you believe in them. And I'm going to tell you something else," Taj said, "but you have to promise to keep it to yourself."

"I'll put it on the list," Anna said, thinking a little jokiness might help lift his spirits.

But Taj regarded her unsmiling. "I am not shitting you."

"I will," she said, then quickly, "*I know.*"

"Gilman was on the jury."

Anna sucked in her breath. "Oh."

"Yeah. Oh."

"Maybe he didn't know it was you?"

"He knew."

"But why would he do that? Does he have something against you?"

"I don't know. Apparently. Who knows?"

"Well, I'm sure it's not your fault."

He threw her a sharp glance. "Why?"

Anna did her best to recall something Leslie might have once said about the Power of Yes, or how optimism is like a muscle you have to work to develop, but suddenly decided to try a different tack.

"You know, I actually think what you are doing is way beyond Gilman. Conceptually, that is."

"Anna, you *love* Gilman. You want Gilman's cock in your mouth!"

"I maybe did at first, love him, I mean," Anna said, flustered, "but that was before I started working with you."

"So now you've seen the light," Taj said, his voice flat. "Hallelujah."

"It's like what you said, remember?" she continued. "About the difference between titillation and titillation plus. I really think you've got it. You've got the *plus*."

Taj considered this for a moment, lining up a few things on the table: a votive candle holder shaped like a tree trunk, a tiny notepad from Muji, a box of diuretic tea. Then he looked up. She looked back at him, not without hope.

"Come here," Taj said. She stood and went over to him. He drew her into a full embrace. "Thank you," he said, exhaling deep into her sweater.

It seemed as though they stayed that way for a long time.

Two drinks later, Anna and Taj were on the roof, which was strictly off-limits. The roof had no railing and was covered in peeling tar paper. Strange protuberances erupted from its lunar surface like calligraphic symbols from some unknown language. The downtown Brooklyn skyline squatted low on the horizon like it was bending down to wipe Manhattan's ass. Taj and Anna sat underneath a satellite dish, kissing. It was cold out, but the combination of vodka and Taj's warm mouth sent a liquid heat coursing through her.

"I don't know anything about you," Taj whispered. "I'm such a selfish pile of shit."

"You're not!"

"I am."

"I don't need to talk about me," Anna said, meaning it. "I already know about me."

"The clock tower looks really nice from up here."

"I know."

"Tell me something. Something you've never told anyone."

Taj's hands were moving all over her now, causing Anna to regret certain folds of fat. She tried to reposition herself to allow for better access as she considered Taj's question. She could tell him about Kyle, her boyfriend in freshman year of college, who she had dated for a year but never kissed. Or about the time she had sold some of her eggs to pay for her summer in Europe. She could relate the story of her embarrassing failed suicide attempt in high school, how she'd drunk half a bottle of her mother's hydrogen peroxide, then immediately dialed 911—but instead she found herself saying, "I'm addicted to the Internet."

Taj laughed, his hand fumbling around her back in search of bra hooks that were, unfortunately, located in the front.

"You and everyone else."

"No. I'm really, not-jokingly addicted. I-I can't get anything done. I think it's why I'm so . . . fucked up. Maybe why I got kicked out of grad school."

"Internet addiction is the meme of our generation."

"It's not just getting things done," Anna continued. "It's everything. Life, relationships. I have this fantasy. Want to hear my fantasy?" Taj said nothing so Anna decided to keep going. "It's that someday Google'll figure out a way to make real life like Gmail so then you can, you know, trash bad conversations, run people through filters, delete them—"

"Clean out your cache?" Taj added. "Junk your preferences?"

"Yeah." Anna laughed. Taj laughed, too. Suddenly it was funny, even though, really, it wasn't.

"I get up in the night and check my e-mail—"

"Shhh," Taj said. But this was annoying, because now Anna *wanted* to talk.

"—like some old guy with a bad prostate who needs to pee all the time. Two, three times a night sometimes."

The whine of an ambulance sounded in the distance and suddenly she felt ashamed of her ridiculously bourgeois complaints. "But I guess it's probably not a big deal, as addictions go, right?" she added.

"It's not like you're dying of cirrhosis," Taj said. "My dad sees a lot of those cases."

"No," she agreed. Still, she suspected it was exactly these sorts of embarrassingly petty revelations that would bring her and Taj closer together. Brandon would be proud of her; without even realizing it, she was playing the vulnerability game.

"Anyway, I bet Gilman got rejected a lot, too, you know. In the beginning."

"Yeah, well, Gilman found a work-around," Taj said in a cryptic voice.

"You should keep submitting. You're so good," Anna said, not caring about Gilman anymore. The tips of Taj's fingers were darting around her breasts like cold little fishes.

"I'm never submitting to anything again."

"Taj . . ."

"Fuck it. I'm done. Fucking gatekeepers."

"But the Gugg—"

"Fuck the Gugg."

"It's just one—*oh!*"

"Shhh . . ."

"But you—"

"That feels good?"

"Y-yes—"

"Right there?"

"Mmm . . . yes."

"Or maybe there?"

"Oh!" Anna breathed into Taj's neck, surprised. *Addiction*, she thought. *A. Dick. Shun.* She giggled. It had been a very long time.

"Yeah, yeah . . . right there . . ."

15

As Taj drove Anna sat silently in the back, staring out the window and cradling thoughts of the two of them together. She had spent the past two days since the roof episode having conversations with Taj in her head. She was careful not to call him, instead trying to enjoy the Tajy tint he'd lent to her life. Tajiness was hard to quantify or describe. She felt herself quicker to judge, if not to express that judgment. Sharper. A little meaner, maybe. Even wasting time on the Internet, she'd started clicking and mousing more deliberately. *Be careful*, Leslie had said after Anna filled her in on the latest developments with Taj. *Don't do what you always do*. And Anna had taken these words to heart, even though Leslie failed to elaborate on what she meant. Last night, though, she had started to get the jitters, fearing it would be weird seeing Taj in front of everyone the next morning without having debriefed their encounter. But a jokey e-mail from him yesterday had dispelled all doubts. It was a link to an Internet addiction rehab program. Subject line: Online, natch :)

Now the crew was on its way to Islington, New Jersey, to shoot a carnival on the edge of town. They were traveling down a ratty two-lane highway past tract houses decorated with American flags and ceramic fawns, trucks on concrete blocks, plastic polycarbonate jugs filled with colored water. *What an unspeakably real and poignant place*, Anna thought. She was in the kind of dangerous mood that made even the eighties pop music blaring from the stereo resonate with meaning. "Falling in love is so bittersweet," Whitney Houston sang. *So true*, Anna thought. *Both bitter and sweet, yes, only at the same time!*

She imagined herself and Taj inhabiting one of the dreary houses that lined the highway, wondered what their life together would be like. Of course, the thought of Taj—who was probably born with an iPad in his hand—living *here* of all places was hilarifying. It hardly mattered, though. Anna was so boozy with desire she could location-scout their future anywhere. McDonalds. Alcatraz. The Moon. Their movie would be shot with a blue filter. She could already picture herself at the kitchen sink, staring through the faded curtains, past the browning lawns and all the way back to her old life, which had been entirely devoid of real things like love and lawns and deflated kiddie pools. In the seat in front of hers, Fifteen and Sixteen were palming twin Zi8s and filming the same scenery. She pretended not to notice when they panned the camera her way, and was careful to keep the melancholy look on her face.

The highway ended in a delta of chain restaurants and cheap motels. Another mile down the road and the tremulous outline of a Ferris wheel hove into view, its lights Crayola bright.

"Welcome to our John Waters movie," Lauren murmured as Taj ratcheted back the parking brake.

Was it just Anna, or had some distance opened between Taj and Lauren? When it came time to unload, instead of forming their usual intimidating little clique, they circled each other like opposing magnets. In addition to Sasha and the hoodied crew members, they had brought along the star of the production: Lamba, a forty-seven-year-old Sikh man whose dream was to fall in love at a carnival. Privately, Taj acknowledged Lamba was a hard sell given the rot that was spreading across his front teeth. Still, here they were in central New Jersey, where anything was possible.

Thinking that Lauren looked—could it be?—a bit lonely, set-ting up a tripod at the edge of the parking lot for an establishing shot, Anna decided to approach her. But once she was standing beside Lauren, she could think of nothing to say, found herself yearning for a Google search prompt. Like how when you start typing *crotch* into Google, it might suggest "crotch rocket," "crotch rot," or "crotchety" to speed you on your way. And this reminded her how during a break last week at the Compound she'd wandered over to Taj's Mac Air and typed Gilman's name into Google, revealing Taj's search history for the same name: "Paul Gilman narcissist" and "Paul Gilman backlash."

"Your hair looks really nice today," Anna ventured at last, thinking maybe this was something Brie would say.

Lauren breathed a heavy sigh. "If you have mid-length hair and you want to look like a natural blonde in New York City, it will cost you about three hundred dollars." She looked directly at Anna. "Such a rip."

Though well versed in the brutal economics of highlights and lowlights that made wage slaves of so many women, Anna still found herself with absolutely nothing to say on that score. She tried again.

"So what do you think of this place?"

"I don't know." Lauren shrugged. "Same old, I guess."

Then the conversation dried up like it always did with Lau-ren, who probably hated her. Who probably thought Anna was an unbearable neophyte, a clingy wannabe and pathetically lack-ing in dietary self-restraint. *That's it*, Anna thought, and vowed to stop trying. But as it turned out, she didn't need to worry about Lauren being left alone. Somehow it fell to her to accompany Lamba through the souk-like cluster of game booths crowding the midway, scoping out lonely women in search of a savior with a pocketful of quarters. The hoodied crewmen followed them with their Zi8s while Sasha monitored the sound on their wireless mics from a distance. This left Anna and Taj free to retreat to the shadows of the Tilt-A-Whirl to make out.

"Shouldn't you be out there filming?" Anna whispered.

"Five more minutes," said Taj, snaking a hand warm and dry as a fresh Xerox under her shirt, up her bare back. She straightened up and sucked her stomach in imperceptibly. The Tilt-A-Whirl was making a huge, ground-thumping sound that echoed in Anna's rib cage as it swung on its axis. "Your thing is beeping," Taj breathed into her neck.

It was true, Anna realized. Her cell phone was pinging away.

"I don't care," Anna breathed back. But despite the circumstances, it wasn't true. She found herself badly wanting to check her caller ID. Why was it that whenever she missed a call, she automatically assumed it was Yahweh calling to inform her that her whole life was fixed now?

"We should go," he said at last. They were already testing the boundaries of propriety; it turned out small children exclusively were the ones interested in patrolling the undersides of the carnival rides. When they emerged into the klieg lights and the thick smell of burning sugar and dough, Anna slipped her hand into Taj's. Just as quickly, he removed it.

"We should probably keep things on the down low," he said. "I wouldn't want to confuse the guys." At this Anna could only nod, confused.

It was halfway down the midway that the incident with the woman took place. Rather, the girl—she couldn't have been older than eighteen. Taj stopped so suddenly that Anna was already well past the Bottle Ring Toss when she realized he was no longer beside her. The girl was sitting on a bench chewing on an enormous thing of blue cotton candy, an orb so garish that for a second Anna thought she might be eating a clown's wig. She was wearing cutoff jean shorts that showed off her long, tan legs and a buttondown shirt knotted above her midriff, like Britney Spears in that video.

"Wow," Taj whispered. "Look at that. Isn't she hot?"

She was, Anna had to admit. Heart-shaped face, eyes blue as sea-whipped glass, dark wind-blown hair, a nose that belied Nordic heritage. It was rare that all the elements aligned so perfectly. When Anna ran the girl's face through the TSA scanner in her head and matched it against the universal profile—the cutter from which supermodel cookies emerged—a bell clanged somewhere in her head, activating her fight-or-flight impulses.

"Mmm," Anna managed.

"Those eyes! Killer."

The girl's lips, blue from the cotton candy, now matched her eyes as well. She blinked and ate and stared off at nothing in particular, not noticing either Taj or Anna. Eventually they started moving again.

"I swear, you only see girls like that in places like this," Taj said. "Totally unspoiled."

What is this? Anna wondered. Hadn't Taj just been kissing her? Weren't they—even in some marginal, non-hand-holding way—together? Did he even consider she might feel hurt or insecure by his gawping openly at a beautiful young woman? And wasn't it borderline autistic of him to ask Anna to join him in extolling this girl's hotness when he'd never so much as complimented her choice of earrings, let alone the entirety of her person? They walked the rest of the midway in silence until they finally spotted the crew huddled around the Crossbow Shoot, where Lamba was taking aim at a clothesline of moving paper bull's-eyes.

"How's it going?" Taj asked Lauren.

"He doesn't want to talk to any women. He just wants to play the games," Lauren said. She pointed to a row of plush Disney characters dangling from nooses under the awning. "He's obsessed with that Tweety."

They watched as Lamba shot another round. The cap gun popped loudly several times and a little plume of smoke emerged from its barrel. He brought the barrel up to his nose, inhaling deeply.

"Smells good!" Lamba said, to no one in particular.

"Maybe if he wins a prize," Taj said, "we can just walk around with him afterward and find a girl he can give it to?"

"Then we're going to need a lot more tickets," Lauren said. They all watched grimly as Lamba fired at the target rapidly, intently, and with what appeared to be a total lack of accuracy.

Taj turned to Anna. "Hey, can you get us some tickets?"

"How many?" Anna said.

"Fifty bucks' worth." Taj touched her shoulder then lowered his voice a notch, adding, "I'll get you later."

Anna walked away, irked. The hand-holding incident, the girl, the fifty dollars—in the space of five minutes, all of this bad juju had suddenly accrued, threatening to spoil her mood for the rest of the night. She did her best to channel Leslie's thinking. Repositioning one's disposition, as she'd told Anna, required taking responsibility for her own role in the way people treated her. Perhaps Anna had subconsciously invited these slights. Or somehow failed to subconsciously invite the requisite compliments. Regardless, Anna reminded herself, nothing had actually changed. Taj—an actual guy, and not some elusive on-screen avatar—liked her, wanted to work with her, better still, wanted to kiss her, even if that latter activity was relegated to obscure and uncomfortable locales. Wasn't she still a creative partner whom he could both trust and build a lasting professional relationship with? And right then, Anna made a new resolution: to be *easy*. She would not ask for the fifty dollars at the end of the night when Taj dropped her off. In fact, she would not mention it at all, unless he brought it up first. Hadn't he asked her for his trust in the very beginning? Thus resolved, she bought herself a funnel cake, both as a reward for being sensible and with the justification that traveling to Islington, New Jersey, was akin to visiting an exotic country where funnel cake was the indigenous specialty. She was, in a sense, a locavore.

Anna bought fifty dollars' worth of tickets and headed back to the midway. But when she rejoined the crew—now cheering Lamba on at Plinko—she found there was nothing for her to do. Taj and Lauren had gravitated back into their usual whispered consultations; the rest of the crew was busy filming.

Anna tapped Taj on the back and he turned around quickly.

"What?" he said, not altogether happily.

"Do you mind if I walk around and film for a while?"

"All the cameras are tied up."

"No, I mean, I brought my AVCCAM. It's in the van."

Taj considered this for a moment.

"We don't really need another cameraperson on him now, but if you want to get some B-roll . . ."

"I was thinking I'd shoot a little of my own stuff," Anna said. Then, suddenly afraid that if she seemed too excited he might shoot her down, added quickly, "Only if that's OK with you."

"We'll probably need you in a bit. Twenty minutes, max," he said, handing her the keys to the van and turning back to Lauren.

The chaos of the fairgrounds soon crowded out her worries. With her AVCCAM cutting off circulation to her shoulder, Anna stumped past the ticket booth and along the broad dirt path that wove through the rides. The greasy smoke and winking popcorn lights, the epileptic fits of the Sky Swat, the Condor, and the Disk-O, combined with theme music from twelve different rides, assaulted her from all sides, congealing into a kind of unholy audiovisual soup. Anna stopped, uncertain of where to go. That's when she spotted the fortune-teller.

She didn't appear to be an official part of the carnival. Otherwise wouldn't she have a booth on the midway? All the fortune-teller had was a blanket, two low stools, and a hand-lettered sign that looked like a toddler's art project. REAL ESOTERIC

TEACHER, it read. She had set up on a sad and weedy little patch of grass just past where the rides ended.

The fortune-teller was eating a German sausage from a foam container on her lap. She looked to be in her late fifties, with hair bleached to the color and consistency of a Dorito. Her dress was black and very tight and, not to be ageist, but Anna found the plunging décolleté more than a little off-putting. Once Anna arrived at the edge of her blanket, she noticed another sign, Sharpie on cardboard, leaning against an empty beer stein on the ground. DONATION, it said. Anna took five dollars out of her wallet and placed it in the beer stein. The fortune-teller immediately removed the bill, regarding it disdainfully.

"For twenty dollars," she rasped, "I could give you a real fortune. What do you want me to do with *this*?"

"Um," Anna began. She wouldn't have expected such hostility from an unauthorized psychic working for tips on the outskirts of a carnival in Islington, New Jersey.

"How about I just tell you five things?" the fortune-teller said, tucking the bill into her cleavage.

"Five things would be fine," Anna said. "Would it be OK if I filmed you?"

"Can I finish my sausage?" she countered.

Anna busied herself with setting up the AVCCAM on a monopod while the fortune-teller chewed her sausage. Once she had finished eating, she picked up a pack of fatigued-looking tarot cards lying at her feet. She shuffled the deck and set it down in front of Anna with a bored *plop*.

"Cut it," she said.

Anna did as she was told and the fortune-teller began flipping the cards back in solitaire-like rows before Anna: the Wheel of Fortune, the Sun, the Hierophant.

"You are very visually attuned," she said, flipping back more cards. "Both visually and aurally attuned."

Well, duh, thought Anna. This statement seemed to apply to anyone whose head came with the standard-issue orifices.

The fortune-teller riffled through the deck faster, throwing cards down on the blanket in a dizzying array at Anna's feet. Sixes. High Priestess. Stars. World. Twos. Fool.

"You have a lust for life and this leads you to take risks. Unhealthy risks. You must take precautions. I see some kind of abyss in your future."

At this, Anna perked up a little. It was true that she had a lust for life. Or at least a lust. And hadn't she taken a number of risks lately? The purchase of the camera? Joining the crew? Taj? During her weaker moments, Anna herself marveled at the speed of her metamorphosis, even wondered whether her behavior was entirely "healthy." But what about her old life? The tedium of long days at Pinter, Chinski and Harms enlivened only by the occasional smoothie run to Jamba Juice or bitter lunches with Brandon? Collecting spam, was *that* healthy? Was *stagnation* healthy, even if it was the de facto mode of almost everyone she knew? Everyone, that is, except Taj.

More cards. The Hermit. Nines. Temperance.

"Vacation plans?" the fortune-teller now asked, picking a loose bit of sausage from her teeth.

Anna shook her head.

"Someone is going to ask you to go somewhere," she said with a significant look. "It's very important you take this journey. Consider it a quest."

"Quest?" Anna repeated dumbly. She did not associate sci-fi vocab with this woman's gauge of hoop earrings.

"Like a vision quest."

"Oh!" Anna said, getting it. File under crystals, druids, Arizona sweat lodges intended exclusively for white people.

The fortune-teller passed a hand over the cards, muddying them into a pile. She shuffled the deck again and laid down the top card. The Magician. Draped in a red robe, the Magician held what looked like a double-ended dildo aloft in one hand. The fortune-teller shook her head.

"Not good, kiddo."

"No?"

"You are a good person, but that doesn't mean that people always treat you the way they should." Now the fortune-teller was looking directly at Anna, who couldn't help but notice her lipstick bore only the vaguest relationship to the actual borders of her mouth. "You give too much, and people take advantage of that. Am I right?"

Anna nodded.

"There is a man," the fortune-teller continued. She glanced back down at the cards. "Married?"

Anna shook her head.

"Boyfriend?"

Anna shrugged, thinking, shouldn't *she* be the one asking the fortune-teller things, not the other way around? Then again, what did she expect for five dollars?

"But there is a man?"

Anna nodded.

"Well, watch out, honey," she said, tapping the Magician's dildo.

"Is it bad?" Anna felt her throat tighten. She reminded herself again that a make-out session on a rooftop and a grope under the Tilt-A-Whirl did not necessarily constitute the underpinnings of a permanent union.

"I don't mean to be Debbie Downer, but yeah, probably bad. I've been doing this a long time. Get yourself a cat, that's my advice. Unless he's taking care of you." The fortune-teller swept up the cards, giving them a desultory shuffle. She eyed Anna shrewdly. "Is he taking care of you?"

"Is who taking care of you?"

Anna looked up, surprised to see Taj staring down at her, a Zi8 in one hand, corn-on-a-stick in the other.

"Well, there you go," the fortune-teller said. "You sure you don't want a real session for another fifteen? I do palmistry, tea leaves, crystal ball, numerology—"

"But that was only four things!" Anna said.

"You really owe yourself a deep reading, hon," the fortune-teller went on, as though she hadn't heard. "It usually costs forty-five, but I can tell you're a good person, and it's not a good time for you. I'll do it for thirty, OK? It's a lot cheaper than a therapist."

"We have to get back," Taj said to Anna. The fortune-teller's face fell back into its default sulk and Anna guiltily stuck two more dollars into her beer stein.

As they made their way back down the midway, Anna wondered exactly how long she'd been gone. There was no sign of the crew at the Bottle Ring Toss or the Puck Shuffle or Down-A-Clown and most of the concession stands had already shuttered. Empty carousel cars swung in the night sky. If earlier the crowd had struck her as gaudy, the few passersby that remained looked as forlorn as figures in an Edward Hopper painting, casting long shadows under the sulfur lights.

"How are you?" said Taj, suddenly taking her hand.

"Sad," Anna said, feeling happy her hand had been taken.

He squeezed her hand.

"Me, too," he said. "Want to make a suicide pact?"

"Ha."

A lone drunk guy being whipped to a puree in the Orbitor howled somewhere above them. Anna wondered whether he would bring up the fifty bucks. Why was being easy so hard?

"Why are you sad?" Anna said.

"Something's not clicking with the dreams," Taj said. "Conceptually. Gilman was onto something when he rejected me. He could smell it."

"I love the dreams."

Taj shook his head. "It's stock."

"No! I had this great idea once, too." She made a spontaneous decision, plunging into the cloudy waters of unsolicited revelation. "I wanted to write a book about late bloomers. Kind of a compilation of inspiring success stories, you know? But someone else beat me to it. Your dream thing, it's a great idea *and* no one else is doing it."

Taj took this in as he gnawed the last kernels off his corn-on-a-stick.

"What's funny about that is nobody actually feels inspired reading those stories."

"Of course they do," Anna said. "I do."

"No, you don't. Just think about it. How does reading those long, glowing profiles in *The New Yorker* make you feel?" He didn't wait for her answer. "Bad, right? Jealous. Scared. Insecure."

Anna wasn't sure, but nodded anyway. Taj's voice, his knowing tone, felt like a hand at the back of her head, forcing her to nod.

"Know what people really find comforting?" Taj continued, "Failure. Humiliation. Defeat. *That's* what makes people feel better."

"You think so?" she said.

"Think about it. Nothing brings people together like a good scandal. Nothing makes them happier than to see someone fall from a great height. Hell, even a footstool!"

"Well, I guess everyone's had a bad experience at some point in their lives . . ."

"Anna, it's genius." Taj stopped suddenly, his eyes ablaze with a strange new light. "A humanist angle on humiliation. That's the missing piece! *We* are the ninety-nine percent!" He grabbed her and kissed her so hard on the mouth, she didn't even have time to breathe or to properly parry with her tongue, could only stand there like a wind sock with her arms thrown stupidly behind her back. When she finally opened her eyes, one of the hoodies was there.

"Sixteen!" she said, so surprised she momentarily forgot the unspoken rule that only Lauren and Taj were allowed to call people by their speed-dial number. How long had he been trailing them?

"Hey," said Sixteen, pretending not to notice the moist ring around their mouths, "We need the keys, dude. We're locked out."

Shit, Anna had forgotten she was the only one with keys! They hurried back to the parking lot, where the rest of the crew sat slumped against the van. Seeing her, Lauren said nothing, simply held out her hand with barely suppressed annoyance. She unlocked the back hatch, and Sixteen and Fifteen started loading the camera bags and tripods right away. Anna remembered her phone and pulled it out to check her message. It was a text from Brandon asking about lunch on Friday. She tapped back an assertively lowercase, unpunctuated reply to signal her newfound busyness. When she finished her text, she wandered over to Sasha, who she noticed was emanating a somewhat friendlier vibe.

"*Privet!*" she called in cheerful Russian. Sasha said nothing, but waved his glowing cigarette in response.

"So did that guy ever fall in love?"

"Sort of," he said.

He made a motion for her to follow him. Together they walked to the other side of the van. And there was Lamba, asleep on the ground, his face resting between the legs of an enormous Tweety bird.

16

When Anna looked at herself in the mirror the next morning, or more accurately, when she examined just the top of her head, she found herself experiencing a panic that could be described as life-choices dysmorphia. Even though she'd unquestionably moved from "inaction" to "action," and from "boredom" to "excitement," hadn't she also moved from "security" to "insecurity"? Her bank account was dwindling while her gap was growing. When gripped by doubt, she'd taken to rereading a particular e-mail from Mr. Brohaurt, just to remind herself of what things had been like pre-Taj, under the regime of Pinter, Chinski and Harms. She padded out to the kitchen, took a seat in front of the laptop, and moused over to a Gmail folder labeled "Thing." There was only one thing in the "Thing" folder, a message from Chad Brohaurt. Subject line: Detailed Instructions.

> *Anna,*
>
> *Here are your instructions: Start with any of the 4 source files. As I showed you on screen, do the following: Look in the 3rd, 4th, & 5th major column headings: For each "Multi Unit" in column 3, look under "Tenancy." If there is a number in the last sub-column, headed "MU," COPY & PASTE that entry into the first table of the target file headed "Theme: Individually Parceled Properties." Copy & paste it into the middle column labeled*

"Housing Tenure" IN THE APPROPRIATE PERSPEC-TIVE based on what is indicated in the 5th column of the source file. Keep working down in each perspective, starting under the last entry. Add more rows for each entry as you need to. Then, copy & paste the "Indicator" from column 1 of the source file into the 3rd column for ". . . Indicators Addressed." In the source file, if an entry has a number under "Owner Occupancy" in the subcolumn headed "H," COPY & PASTE that entry into the SECOND (last) table of target file headed "Theme: Co-op and Condo." When you've finished one source file, move on to the next until you've done them all.

I hope this clears things up.

Cheers,
Chad

She read the message three times, pressing on past the point where it froze her brain, smote her individuality, bored her to the brink of suicide. When even that process failed to Reposition her Disposition, she called Leslie.

"He made me stop and look at this woman with him," Anna said, dismally aware of exactly how whiny this sounded. "He wanted me to agree she was hot."

"Did you consider that as a filmmaker, that might just be how he processes experience?" Leslie was deploying her maddeningly calm "mom" voice. "Through an aesthetic lens?"

"But *I* want to be the pretty one."

"Maybe you are."

"He never told me I was."

"It's a lot easier to say something like that in abstract about a stranger, behind their back, than to someone you care about, to their face."

"He *doesn't* care about me."

"Why do you always think that?"

"And I'm not pretty. I'm fat."

"Don't you think this is more about your own insecurities? If you actually thought you were pretty, you wouldn't care about that girl."

"No, I would," she said. "I would totally care!"

This is how Anna ended up accompanying Leslie to her hot yoga class. Leslie thought it would be good for her to "engage in a physical discourse with her self-image." Anna, having nothing better to do that night, agreed. She took the Q express train to Herald Square and met Leslie outside the Chakra Shack in midtown. The powerful smell of foot hit her halfway up the stairs. It was so humid you could have grown mushrooms on the landing. Leslie met up with her on line at the front desk.

"So what did you bring to wear?" she asked, giving Anna a quick scan.

"This," Anna said, indicating her sweats, T-shirt. "Nothing."

Leslie looked at her, alarmed. "You're going to die. It's a hundred and five degrees in there."

There was no way Anna was going to wear one of those kiwi-size stretch bikinis.

"I'll be fine." She smiled at Leslie. "I like it hot." At this Leslie raised both eyebrows but said nothing. The guy in line ahead of them was taking forever.

"Do you want to work for money or for yoga?" she could hear the receptionist asking.

"Uh, I want to work for yoga, for money."

"I mean, do you want to trade hours for free yoga?"

"What if I just trade hours for money, and then money for yoga?"

This exchange went on for five more minutes, and when at last they reached the desk, Anna bought a coconut water and a tube of electrolytes to go along with her mat and towel rental. Her introductory class was free, so why not splurge? They made their way to the changing room, which was tastefully decorated in bamboo and stone tile. Leslie peeled off her clothes with a professional ease, revealing a body unmarred save for a few stretch marks and a cesarean scar. Of the two of them, Leslie had always been the prettier one. But recently Anna had noticed time was carving a pair of parentheses on either side of her nose, as though her face were whispering, *Psst! By the way, I also have a mouth.* Looking at Leslie now, Anna felt she had a chance of catching up.

She waited on the bench, observing the bitter trade-off between boobs and body fat enacted in live flesh all around her. Sure, their bellies and thighs were flat as Pyrex pans, their faces chiseled into bas relief, their bodies offering no resistance to the superior tailoring demands of spandex, but undressed didn't they look a bit, well, mannish? Last she checked, men still enjoyed a nice rack and a serious backside, Anna thought with no small satisfaction. Leslie was right to bring her here—yoga was already doing wonders for her self-esteem.

"—because when I have sex, there tends to be a lot of, you know, *clenching*," one of the women was saying.

"—the second time we'd had to call the super in one week—"

"—but if you ever check the box, soy is actually—"

"—the injections aren't so bad. I used to be the biggest baby about needles and now it's just part of the morning routine. You know, brush your teeth, breakfast, shot."

Anna suddenly tuned in—this was Leslie speaking to an older woman with impeccable abs.

"—no guarantees, though," said Abs. "Took *five* tries for my sister-in-law."

"Well, I had two friends over forty get pregnant just using clomiphene—" said Leslie.

"No, you were right to skip to the IVF."

"The doctor says statistically—"

"I told you, *five* tries. It's just a question of how much can you afford. You know it's free in Israel? That's why my brother ended up making aliyah. They live in Tel Aviv now."

"Yeah, well at least it worked."

"And at least you have the one kid," Abs said, snapping the waistband of her yoga panties decisively.

"Yeah," Leslie said. She sounded sad and distant.

Thinking back to their earlier conversation, about the hot girl with the blue cotton candy, Anna felt a sudden stab of shame. She had spent the past few weeks so self-absorbed in her manufactured crises that she hadn't even bothered asking Leslie about her own life. Who knew how badly Leslie wanted this second baby? What psychological toll infertility was taking on her marriage as each month that pastel negative sign swam to the surface? How Leslie felt when she picked Dora up from day care and watched siblings chase one another around their father's legs? Maybe Dora had asked for a little sister for Christmas? At this thought, tears actually filled Anna's eyes. She would have to be a better friend. Next time they saw one another, for sure, Anna would start right off by asking Leslie, *How are you?* She would have to be tenacious, otherwise sweet, modest Leslie would selflessly redirect the *How are you?* right back at her. She would write it on the palm of her hand to make sure she remembered, give it an acronym so Leslie wouldn't notice. HAY.

Leslie was done changing. She was wearing practically nothing and had swept every bit of hair off her neck in a tight bun. Anna followed her into the yoga studio, where the foot smell increased by several degrees of magnitude and temporarily threatened to overwhelm her. Leslie unrolled her mat and placed a white towel over it. Anna watched her and did the same. They both lay down. The room was incredibly hot, but also dry. Lying still, Anna closed her eyes. She felt pleasantly baked. It was like being at the beach, if that beach were located inside an armpit. Before long she was completely relaxed. Why had she been so resistant to accompanying Leslie to yoga for so long? Now Anna pictured herself walking purposefully down the street with her yoga mat tucked under her arm. On the way out, she would ask about that discounted one-month pass for new students.

She must have dozed off, because suddenly everyone was on their feet and the instructor, a middle-aged woman reassuringly lumpy around the middle, had taken her place on the dais at the front of the room.

"Please bring your feet together and place your hands below your chin for pranayama: deep breathing in standing pose," she said.

Anna put her feet together and placed her hands below her chin. Leslie had assured her that Chakra Shack's was a no-nonsense approach. One of the things Anna had always feared about yoga was being asked to chant something in Sanskrit, only to discover later she'd just spent twenty minutes worshipping Ukkar the Suction God. Of course, simply standing around and breathing struck Anna as almost disappointingly easy. Still, it was a step up from lying down.

Anna breathed, unfolding her elbows until they hovered just above her ears, then pulling them back down beneath her chin. For the first thirty seconds she felt pretty confident—she was no Cirque du Soleil contortionist, but she could bring her elbows up higher than at least one woman in the front row. Quickly, however, she noticed an alarming ache setting in. Holding her elbows up around her eyes wasn't quite so easy. Her elbows were heavy, apparently. Who knew? They moved on to the next series of exercises, which Anna found presented a new series of challenges to her unequipped muscles. Soon she had to stop to roll up her pants above her knees. Parts of her she hadn't known could sweat were sweating. Her earlobe. The bottom of her foot. The instructor told them to focus on their own eyes in the mirror, but Anna only had eyes for Abs, who was standing directly in front of her, and whose bones had apparently all been replaced with pipe cleaners.

"I want you to lift your foot and forgive your foot," the instructor called out, her face nestled snuggly against her ankle bone. "Forgive it for causing you pain. It's the concept of karma. Whatever bad feeling you put out there will circulate through you, infect your chi. Even bad feelings toward your foot. And remember to breathe. Let it all go."

Anna pretended to lift her foot, forgave Taj for the blue-eyed girl.

The instructor detached her foot from her face and Anna considered the possibility that all her limbs were actually removable and infinitely reconfigurable, that she was in fact a human Mrs. Potato Head.

"Now tuck your right elbow behind your left ear," she said, doing something impossible with her arms. "Forgive your elbow."

The air was undeniably hot when she had first lain down, but now Anna felt as though she were deep-tonguing a blowtorch every time she inhaled. She was starting to feel woozy and sank down to her mat, tried to fold herself into an appropriately lotus-like position, but ended up sprawled there like an aborted origami crane. To Anna's shock, the dizziness and nausea were even worse now that she was sitting down.

"You'll feel better if you don't leave the room," the instructor called out to Anna as she began to pick her way across the moist carpet. Anna shook her head to indicate *Please stop humiliating me*, but it was a signal the instructor apparently failed to pick up.

"Once you acclimate you'll see what an incredible instrument your body is and how much you are truly capable of," the yoga Nazi continued, casually switching legs. "But if you leave now, you'll never know. Leaving the room won't make you feel better, it'll only make you feel worse—"

Her perp walk finally complete, Anna pushed open the glass doors to the lobby and instantly felt better. She slid onto a bamboo bench, put her head in her hands. A moment later she felt a slap of hot air against her legs as the studio door opened once more.

"Are you OK?" came Leslie's voice. Anna looked down at Leslie's tan, dry lap and felt the overwhelming urge to lay her sweaty head there, curl into a ball, and let the horrible Celtic pan flute music saturating the lobby lull her to sleep.

"I should have guessed it would be too much." Leslie sighed, pressing a tube of Electrolyte Stamina tablets into Anna's hand. "It's the computer. You lose so much mobility hunched over like that all day. I'm such a jerk. I should have started you with Anusara, where they use supports and things. Will you be OK?"

Anna felt Leslie's hand on her shoulder and inadvertently stiffened. Leslie knew she wasn't spending all day in front of the computer anymore, not since becoming a "creative." So why was she going out of her way to remind Anna who was the "bottom" in this relationship?

"Will *you* be OK?" Anna said, an almost-credible hitch in her voice. "I heard you talking to that woman earlier, you know, about how things are going."

"Oh." Leslie stiffened, plucked at the fat she didn't have. "Yeah, it's not looking good for the IVF and Josh isn't sure how he feels about adopting."

This triggered an automatic association. "I read this weird thing on *Squeee!*—did you hear about this?" Anna began "—that couples are purposely adopting black babies so they have a better chance of getting their kids into private school and Harvard and stuff. Isn't that fucked up?" Even before Leslie gave her that look, she wished she could take it back, scroll up through the history of their conversation to the part where Leslie was still lecturing her and making her eat electrolytes.

"I can't believe you read that shit," Leslie shuddered. "That site's a cesspit."

"Oh no, yeah, I know," Anna said quickly. "Ridiculous."

Through the door, she could still hear the instructor encouraging everyone to flex some inflexible part of themselves, then forgive themselves for it. Leslie began talking again, in great gushes, about adoption and Josh and the problems they'd been having, but now Anna was distracted by what was going on in the yoga room and the memory of that terrible smell. This somehow got her thinking how the only perfume she'd ever loved had been the first she'd ever bought, Colors de Benetton. She wondered if it still existed—were there vintage perfumes the same way there were vintage wines?—and suddenly, more than anything, all she wanted to do was search eBay for an original, unopened, 1987 bottle of Colors de Benetton.

"So Josh goes, 'I believe in genes,' and I was like, 'Well, what if *I* believe in destiny?'" Leslie was saying.

Anna tried forcing herself to listen, but all these concepts—genes, destiny, Leslie's hypothetical second baby—were wisps of dandelion fluff compared with the totally concrete image she had of the 3.3-ounce bottle of Colors de Benetton perfume that had stood on her bedroom dresser all through high school. Her thoughts skidded toward the locker room, where her phone waited inside her jacket pocket. Even though she always made fun of those cyborg people who walked around with those horrible "augmented reality" glasses, she saw the sense of it now, almost wished she had a pair.

". . . unfair, right?" Leslie said, and Anna realized she was supposed to say something.

"Totally," Anna nodded, guessing. "Especially because you guys have everything. Money. The apartment. Dora. I mean, I know people having babies who totally don't have their shit together. Who don't even have *jobs*—"

"What?" Leslie cut in, eyes narrowing. "Who do you know?"

Anna looked at her and, before she answered, felt a sudden surge of . . . what? Triumph? Meanness? Adrenaline?

"Didn't I tell you?" she said. "Brie's pregnant."

17

"I'll have the veggie burger, but can I have no bun, no onion, and no sprouts with that?"

The waiter nodded.

"And the avocado on the side?"

"No problem."

"Instead of brown rice and beans, I'll have the steamed vegetables."

Now the waiter looked at Brandon with open hostility, furiously scribbling. "Will there be anything else?" he said in a voice tipped with acid. But if Brandon noticed, he didn't let on. He simply handed over his menu and turned his attention back to Anna.

"Did I tell you about the cat?" he said.

Anna shook her head. "What cat?"

"Manx. We just adopted him. Philippe's idea."

Anna had googled "black baby adoption" after coming home from yoga with Leslie and learned that people were adopting African babies not to take advantage of affirmative action, but because restrictions on international adoption were tightening. China and Russia had passed laws. While this made her feel worse about her comment to Leslie, it had one unexpected benefit. Ever since the "black baby adoption" search, Google had been sending her new personalized ads. She'd been alarmed at the first suggestion that she consider freezing her eggs, but after a few days, began to appreciate the new maternal role Google was playing in her life.

Maybe freezing her eggs wasn't such a bad idea? And thinking back, maybe it was Google that had first planted the idea she take a class after losing her job. Maybe instead of listening to Leslie or her mother, she should just listen to Google, let Google be her life coach . . .

"—they don't have tails. More like a dog-cat," Brandon was saying.

"That sounds cool," Anna said.

"Philippe wants to train it to pee in the toilet."

"You can do that?"

"Sam from Torts did it with his cat. Haven't you seen his Facebook page? Personally, I think it's disgusting."

"It's a little weird—"

"Selby already fell in once. That's the cat."

"Ew."

"Don't act like it's *my* idea. Philippe loves that thing like a baby. He sifts through the litter box to examine its poo. Says he wants to make sure he's regular. A week ago he found pink streaks in his stool and totally freaked out."

"God."

"The vet bill—get this—four hundred dollars."

"Four hundred? Wow," Anna said, gumming her straw thoughtfully. "Hey . . . do you think maybe *I* should get a cat . . . ?"

"A cat? God, no. What makes you think that?" Brandon waved a hand as though to ward the specters of unwanted cats away from their bread basket. "So anyway, you're a filmmaker now?"

Anna blushed. "I didn't say that." And yet she had to admit, the footage she'd shot of the fortune-teller at the carnival felt more precious to her than all her material possessions—save for the AVCCAM itself. She had already watched it countless times, memorizing every fold in the old woman's neck, the rhinestone rings clogging her knuckles like tumors, the lurid whine of her Jersey accent. Anna replayed the footage in her head, cutting and recutting it in the shower or while lying awake at night. She wasn't ready to edit it yet. For now, she greedily wanted to keep every little piece of it intact. Every stomach-tossing lurch of the camera. In fact, the unfocused bits, which reduced the carnival background to a hazy, Froot Loop soup, were some of Anna's favorite parts.

"Is the Shoe Lady still there?" Anna asked. The Shoe Lady was a secretary whose synthetic Payless pumps let out an odor so dire that when she took them off under her desk, it sent the suits at Pinter, Chinski and Harms scattering through the lobby like so many silver mercury balls.

"Can we not talk about work? I really want to hear about your movie."

"It's not a movie, Bran. It's just footage—"

"You were so right to leave, Anna. Best fucking decision you ever made."

Anna decided not to remind him it *wasn't* a decision she made.

"PCH is such a wasteland. I hate it. I really hate it." Brandon asked, his eyebrows shooting up, "You know what my first thought is in the morning, when the alarm goes off?"

"What?"

"'Fuck.'"

"That is a little sad . . ."

"Sad? It's fucking Shakespeare-level tragic."

"Maybe you should just quit?"

"Yeah," Brandon said, looking as though she'd just suggested he lather himself with olive oil and scale the high-rise across the street. "Right."

The thing with Brandon—and this Anna had noticed in the early days of their friendship—was that he seemed to have a fixed quota of disappointment demanding to be filled regardless of how well his life was going. Conservation of angst: Brandon's own empirical law of physics. If he got a raise and a promotion at Pinter, suddenly his relationship with his boyfriend, Philippe, was falling apart. If Philippe surprised him with a Groupon for a weekend balloon ride over the Hamptons, work became intolerable. And if he couldn't manage to engineer any kind of crisis at home or at work, he would find something else to freak out about: the intolerable living conditions at his $4,000-a-month Brooklyn Heights condo, a perceived pain in his spleen, the perilous rise in the global incidence of melanoma.

The waiter arrived with Brandon's "burger," a solar system of sides and condiments arranged around a bare vegetable patty on his half-empty plate. Anna had ordered a salad, but before the waiter had even set it down, badly regretted not ordering the fettuccine Alfredo. Brandon drizzled some balsamic vinegar on a lonely tomato. *No wonder he's so fucking skinny*, Anna thought, watching him chew. Then Brandon stopped chewing and looked at her, his eyes suddenly bright.

"Anna Banana?"

Anna stopped picking at the salad she didn't want anyway and waited for him to tell her she smelled like 1987. She'd found a bottle of original Colors de Benetton on eBay for only thirty-nine dollars with free shipping. It had arrived yesterday.

"I think I have an idea," Brandon continued, in the same slow, awed voice. "We should do something. Together. You already have all the gear. The AVCCAM, the mics—"

"You mean, a movie?"

"—and I have the skills."

"But I thought you hated movie people and you hated USC?"

"I never said I *hated* it."

"You said—"

"I just hated Los Angeles. Los Angeles is a pile of lies shaped like a city. But film . . . I've totally been thinking of getting back into film for a while now."

Then how come, Anna wondered, Brandon had never mentioned these thoughts to her? Not during their umpteen apocalyptic lunches at Pinter, or when she asked for his advice about the

AVCCAM, or when he dropped off that pirated copy of Final Cut Pro last week? Was it just her, or did *everyone* suddenly want to be a filmmaker?

"There's this idea I've had since back in college." Brandon exhaled excitedly, pushing a pickle around his plate.

"Uh-huh."

"You'll love this. Ready?"

"OK."

"It's a freestyle adaptation of Joseph Conrad's *Under Western Eyes*."

Anna stared at him with blank eyes.

"You haven't read it?"

"No," Anna admitted.

"It doesn't matter. I'm thinking this would be an updated version, happening in the present day on some East Coast campus. It would be told through the eyes of an associate professor giving testimony, with, of course, brief flashbacks to the backstory. You know, sort of the way *Heart of Darkness* was adapted into *Apocalypse Now* by Coppola or *Secret Agent* by Hitchcock . . . ?"

Anna had no idea what Brandon was talking about, but nodded anyway.

"Jesus." Brandon exhaled excitedly. "I can see directing the fuck out of this. We're talking massive Dostoyevsky-grade material. Actors will love it! It'll be so much fun to write. And it's all in the public domain, so—"

Anna did her best to project enthusiasm through a forkful of arugula, but in truth, all she felt was the dull throb of annoyance. Brandon, clearly, was trying to save himself from utter soul annihilation at Pinter, Chinski and Harms by clinging to the life raft of her newfound purpose. Not to mention her AVCCAM, her lavalier, and her Sennheiser mic! Anna suddenly felt oddly territorial. Didn't she have her own footage and her own plans? And what about her work with Taj? With a happy little shock, Anna realized she was *busy*. She didn't really have time for Brandon and his crazy schemes.

"Wouldn't it be amazing to work together again?" Brandon was saying. Anna noticed his plate was looking more and more like a painter's palette as dollops of aioli and organic mustard merged with islands of homemade ketchup.

"It would," Anna said, choosing her words carefully, "but you're light-years ahead of me. You studied film in college. I can barely turn on a camera. I don't know what half the buttons mean—"

"It doesn't matter. It's all about your *sensibility*."

"You'd get frustrated working with me. I'm slow."

"Remember how fast you learned how to draft statutory liens at Pinter when you first started?"

"That's different—" Anna began, and just at that moment she felt the miraculous vibration of her cell phone against her ass. With a glance at the screen, she murmured her insincere apologies and stepped outside to take the call.

"Anna, Anna, Anna, Anna," said Taj.

"Taj!" Anna said. "Taj!"

"I have a brilliant idea for you—"

"Oh."

"What?"

"What?"

"Why do you sound so defensive?"

"S-sorry. I didn't mean to. What's your idea?"

"I'm going to make your dream come true."

"*My* dream?" Anna didn't know she had a dream. If she did, it probably involved Taj in a way that wasn't shareable.

"We're going to Silver Lake."

Quickly, Anna ran through the possibilities in her head. Was Silver Lake a bar? A lake? A jewelry store? A band? A website?

"Where?"

"Silver Lake, California. It's a neighborhood. In LA."

That was the one Silver Lake Anna hadn't even considered.

"LA?"

"To break your addiction."

For another disquieting moment, Anna had no idea what Taj was talking about. Then she remembered: their conversation on the roof. In truth, her condition had metastasized into "addiction" only that night, when she found herself forming the word in response to Taj's question.

"But they have Internet there—"

"Roight," Taj said, affecting a cockney accent for no reason. "Well, you won't be using it. No smartphones. No computers. Cold turkey."

"Wouldn't it be better to go to some desert or a mountain or something?"

"Except for that it would be superboring? Yeah. But in Silver Lake you'll actually be testing your resistance. A mountaintop is too easy."

"I can't just go to LA just because you say so."

"Why not?"

Anna had to admit there was no particular reason.

"How long would we be gone?"

"Five days."

"When would we leave?"

"Tomorrow."

"You're crazy!"

"Maybe." A smile had crept into his voice.

Anna turned back to the window, where she could see Brandon cutting his veggie-burger patty into what were probably equilateral pieces. Is that the kind of person she wanted to be? Someone who minced and quibbled all the joy out of life?

"Yes!" Anna said. "I mean, I'll go, but I have to go. I'm having lunch with someone."

"Call me after."

"OK." Taj hung up and Anna turned back to join Brandon, feeling her pulse quicken. She took her seat and happily stabbed at her salad while Brandon prattled on and on about his god-awful

Conrad adaptation, leaving Anna free to contemplate Taj, their trip together, what it all meant. When the dessert menu came, Anna snatched it up.

"Jesus, I'm so excited," Brandon said, sucking the noncaloric soda that had appeared by his elbow. "But wasn't I just about to say something? What was I going to say?"

"You were about to tell me about LA," Anna said. Her inclination toward the white chocolate mousse was tempered by her strongly held belief that white chocolate was never chocolatey enough. "Hey, did you ever hang out much in Silver Lake?"

18

She didn't tweet right away. She waited until after she'd talked to Taj again after lunch and he'd reaffirmed his plan to take her to LA. Anna wasn't much of a tweeter. As in life, she was more a follower. But such was her feeling of uplift at the thought of leaving Sunset Park that she decided to go for it, demonstrating an admirable economy of characters: *Off to LA with Taj!*

Her followers were a questionable lot of authors promoting their self-help books, the largest U-Haul dealer in Canada, a German woman whose name was also Anna Krestler, and seven people she didn't know who described themselves, variously, as "an airborne pathogen," "a purveyor of hipster bullshit," and "a breeder of cartoon dogs." But among all these fake followers was one real one, which is why her phone rang immediately post-tweet.

"Why would some man you just met on the Internet want to take you to LA?" her mother demanded, sans hello.

"It's not like he's paying for my ticket," Anna said, but it was too late: her mother was already googling "craigslist murders."

"Donna Jou disappeared in 2007 with a guy pretending he needed math tutoring. That same year, Katherine Olson—didn't you go to sleepaway camp with an Olson?—was murdered after answering an ad for a nanny. A *nanny*, for God's sake—"

"Mom, I'm hanging up now."

"Then in 2009 a guy was trying to buy a car and—"

"Mom—"

"—not even a good car, Anna. A Chevy! And the guy selling it shot him. Are you listening to this?"

Of course she was listening, she could never hang up on her mother. She put the phone on mute, popped some frozen Morningstar veggie patties in the oven, and waited. In the end, her mother's grisly list did nothing to dissuade her from going to LA with Taj, but it did make her think twice about contacting Perry in Manhattan about the Fiesta ware mug in Shamrock (a much-coveted color, retired after 2003) she'd been ogling on craigslist.

If her mother was someone she could be honest with, Anna would have admitted that she herself had wondered about Taj's motives, and it had been something of a relief to pry the confession from him—after he'd gone on for a bit about the dangers of her "Netaddiction" and quoted the part about "being open to anything," from his ad—that he had other business to take care of in LA. She'd felt uncomfortable with the idea that this trip was all about her, but now that it was clear Taj had his own reasons to go to LA, Anna could relax. She was incidental to the trip and being incidental had the paradoxical effect of making her feel more secure. So secure, she didn't even bother to press him about the nature of this "business" he was being purposely slippery about.

Of course, there had never been a real possibility of saying no. What would she do home alone all week without Taj? It was a little disturbing to think how thoroughly he'd supplanted her entire routine, or lack of one. How it was only the promise of the next shoot or lunch or phone call that sculpted the hours in between into some semblance of a life. But it wasn't just being left alone that scared her, was it? It was being left alone with her *footage*, which had remained firmly glued to something called "Timeline: Sequence 1 in Untitled Project 1" in one long unadulterated strip within Final Cut Pro. All the "viewers" and "browsers" and "canvases" had proved too confusing; she'd confessed to Brandon that she needed something easier. Final Cut Amateur. Of course,

Brandon had bristled, told her to "show some sac" and stick with it, which had the exact opposite effect.

She busied herself with the logistics. Anna had exactly $4,409 left in her bank account. Her share of the rent was $950. Taj still owed her fifty dollars, but that was beside the point. Living frugally, her savings might last another three months in Brooklyn. With the trip, she'd be out of cash by the end of next month, if not sooner. She spent the rest of the afternoon lost in the Bermuda Triangle of Orbitz, Travelocity, and Expedia. The irony of it all was that she had barely spent any time online since unpacking the AVCCAM, but now that she'd been tasked with airfare comparison for their trip, had slumped right back into the virtual miasma. After the fare comparison would come the hotel research and the itinerary planning, not to mention the required background reading on underground lucha libre venues, the latest trends in molecular gastronomy, and any number of other tangential topics that would keep her tethered to this chair, this table, this apartment until it was time to board the A train to JFK. Moreover, because the fare comparisons always took at least thirty seconds to load, staying on task proved impossible. A tub of avocado dip and a bag of vegetable chips soon materialized at her elbow as she found herself opening a new tab and typing "Nicole Kidman plastic surgery" into Google Images. But why, *why*? she wondered, compulsively clicking through JPEG after JPEG of Nicole's endless butte of a forehead. For no apparent reason! Perhaps she was suffering from some kind of Internet Tourette's syndrome that caused her to vomit noxious search terms into the ether with complete lack of impulse control? "Obama love child!" "Bedbug movie theater seats!" "Phentemine sex drive side effects!" As if to shake off this compulsion, she did three quick Gmail/Facebook/Twitter laps, hardly breaking a sweat. Maybe this was a better way to look at it—she was an Internet athlete, a Gmail jockey, a NASCAR driver hugging the bends of the information highway.

"Hi."

Anna jumped. There was Brie, and she looked different. Not pregnant—just drawn and worn out. She reflexively hid her browser, momentarily forgetting she had nothing to hide.

"Brie!"

"I'm going to put this stuff away," she said, dragging her duffel bag down the hall into her room.

Brie shut the door and Anna thought, *That's it?* With full and total respect for whatever Brie was going through, Anna felt that as the roommate of a pregnant person, she deserved some answers. This wasn't just another Friday night after kickball practice when Brie could breeze by, jab her finger into Anna's crab dip on the way to the shower, and dismiss her with a flip remark. She'd announced she was pregnant, then gone and disappeared for three weeks with barely a text or tweet. Now Anna wanted to know: Was Brie still pregnant? If so, would she remain pregnant? Was she moving out? If so, when? And what about the Con Ed and Time Warner accounts that were in Brie's name? Had she quit her internships? Was it Rishi's child? Did Rishi even know? In sum: What the flying fuck was going on? Partially just relieved to have some reason to step away from the computer, Anna rose and followed Brie down the hall. She knocked tentatively on the door.

"Come in."

Brie was sitting on her bed, contemplating her foot, one shoe on, the other off. Anna noticed that Brie's room was almost eerily clean. For once the shoe was the only thing on the floor.

"So . . . ," Anna began, settling awkwardly into Brie's faux-fur butterfly chair, "what's up?"

"I'm pregnant."

"Is that," Anna began, searching for the right words, "how it's going to be?"

"I think so."

"You don't look pregnant at all."

"It's early."

"So you're . . . staying?"

"What do you mean?" Brie asked, suddenly suspicious.

"I just thought maybe you'd want to move in, you know, with Rishi. Or something."

"It's not Rishi's."

"Oh. Sorry."

"It's OK. He wasn't anything."

Well, whose is it, then? Anna wanted to ask. Then again, even if Brie gave her a name, described some guy from the kick-ball team, would it mean anything to Anna? Probably not.

"Want to Netflix tonight?" Anna said. "My instant queue is pretty awesome."

To Anna's surprise, Brie nodded yes.

"I just need a nap first," she murmured, slipping off her other shoe. "So tired . . ."

On the way to the bodega to pick up a box of microwave pop-corn, Anna called Leslie.

"She's back," Anna said as soon as Leslie picked up the phone.

"Did she say anything?" Leslie's habitually reserved tone van-ished as she snapped into gossip mode.

"She's still pregnant."

"Well, I just hope this Rishi has a good job."

"It's not Rishi's," Anna said, suddenly distracted by a flyer taped to the bodega window. "LEARN HOW TO BLOG!" Next to the flyer, another sign read: "We now sell Boeef Soup <u>and</u> Ice Cream."

"So now you're going to, like, help her raise this baby?"

"What?" Anna said, tuning back in. "No!"

"You can't live with a baby, Anna. It's impossible. You don't know what a baby is."

"I do need to find a new job," Anna conceded.

"We should have another session. Next week."

"I can't, I'm going to LA." The Korean man behind the counter knew her. He winked as she set her popcorn down by the register.

"What? With what money?"

"I have some money," Anna said, defensive.

"Why now? Why LA?" Anna mashed the phone between ear and shoulder, scavenging for change in her wallet. "Where are you?" Leslie continued. "What's that stupid music in the background?"

A wiry Hispanic guy holding a Stouffer's frozen dinner exhaled loudly behind her.

"I'm going with Taj," Anna said, sliding her change across the counter.

"Hello? You're breaking up."

"I'm going with Taj!" Anna yelled.

"You're totally fucking him, aren't you?" Leslie yelled back so loudly that Anna was sure both the Korean man and Mr. Stouffer's had heard. She looked around, embarrassed.

"No bag," she said to the Korean man, grabbing her popcorn.

"What?" Leslie yelled.

"I said no." Anna pushed the door open with her shoulder. "I'm not."

"Well, Jesus, you should be," Leslie said, with a sharp laugh, "if you're going to LA together."

And this, Anna had to admit, was probably true.

It was three-quarters of the way into Ramin Bahrani's moving, yet stultifyingly slow and ultimately sort of boring, immigrant swan song *Man Push Cart*, that Brie told Anna she was going to have the baby. This was after Anna burned the second bag of popcorn and the fire alarm went off. Brie had opened all the windows then plopped down next to Anna, who was sorting the still-edible kernels into a plastic bowl at the kitchen table.

"Are you sure?" Anna asked, totally bewildered as to why any woman would choose to have a baby before the mandatory threshold of thirty-five, let alone an intern without any visible means of support and/or interest in children.

"Yeah," Brie said. "I think it will help. I was just starting to feel really . . . blurry."

This new Brie seemed so quiet and serious that Anna had no idea how to reply. She wasn't used to Serious Brie. When someone suddenly replaces your roommate with Diane Sawyer, it takes some getting used to. She had even filled the refrigerator with serious foods; there was a brick of tempeh in the refrigerator that looked like it could power her laptop.

"What are you going to do?" Anna said.

"I don't know. My parents are cutting me off. I guess I could go live with my sister, but I really don't want to."

Anna tensed, sensing that she ought to say something to Brie about not worrying about the rent. But that would mean giving up her trip to LA, wouldn't it?

"It's good to have options, though," Anna offered.

"It's all trees and meth addicts out there. I'd go nuts. I'll figure something out," Brie said, pulling herself to her feet. "Sorry to bail, I'm really tired. Tell me what happens in the morning."

"It's OK. I think that guy's just going to push his cart some more," Anna said, to which Brie responded with a wan smile.

But after Brie padded off to her room, Anna didn't go back to the movie. Instead she flipped up her laptop to check her e-mail. A Groupon. A Twitter notification. An online bill from Verizon. A message from Leslie. Wait: three messages from Leslie. She felt highly unmotivated to open Leslie's e-mails, certain they'd contain something healthful and guilt inducing—New Study Reveals No One Should Ever Eat Cheese, or Laptop Screens Linked to Eye Cancer—but clicked on the first one anyway. Subject line: FYIski.

There was just a single line, written in a faux-casual style that did nothing to hide the desperation underlying it:

btw, wud Brie consider adoption?

The second message cascaded directly from the first: Re: FYIski.

I mean, how is she going to support this child? It's ridiculous.

The last message had the subject line: Contact?

Can you forward me her number? Maybe I should just talk to her directly?

Anna didn't know whether Brie had considered adoption, but she resented Leslie putting her in this position. Brie's baby? This went well beyond the bailiwick of craigslist. A baby wasn't a Pokémon beanie or even Fiesta ware of some breathtakingly rare shade and vintage, and she felt uncomfortable serving even as the most tangential broker in this exchange. Not knowing what else to do, she starred Leslie's e-mails and shifted them to the folder labeled "Important." Then she reloaded her e-mail seven times in the space of thirty seconds, only to get dick-smacked each time by the brutal reality that no entity, either corporate or human, was striving to contact her at that particular point in time. Suddenly, on the eighth reload, a new message *did* appear in her box. From Brandon.

Anna!
I sensed that I might have scared you off the other night with my Conrad adaptation. Although I'm glad you like the idea, it seems the best course for me right now is to work that one out on my own, at least through

initial drafts. However, I actually had another idea for an original feature that I think would be more suitable to our dual strengths. Here's my pitch: A young woman, ambitious but financially strapped (aspiring actress? Or scientist/social worker to work humanist/Sundance angle?), receives a mysterious package one day containing a $20,000 couture dress. She puts it on (of course it fits her perfectly) then wanders into the night without a plan. Suddenly our heroine finds all the doors to the city's ne-plus-ultra nightspots open to her. She is ushered into a hotel lobby where a Hugh Hefner type, mistaking her for his paid escort, whisks her into a high-stakes dinner. At which point a bunch of other shit happens, et cetera.

The dress makes a perfect MacGuffin because of its costume-as-mask metaphor. A designer dress reifies you, puts a price tag on you, gives you access like a shibboleth, makes your body a commodity. Directorially, I much prefer masks as a time-honored theatrical tradition (from early rituals to Japanese theater to commedia dell'arte) to the cheap-ass obscene sub-Method histrionics often on display in mumblecore and indie drama in general (no offense). Moreover, what intrigues me about masks and costumes is the paradox described by Slavoj Zizek: a mask doesn't hide, instead it reveals the true essence, because we are what we pretend to be. Knowing you, I'm sure you agree.

Of course the ultimate archetype here is Cinderella. Can we use it and subvert it? What genre could we bounce off of? A satire? A dark fantasy/allegory? Can it be Dick-ensian in the way Slumdog *was? Or Gogolesque instead (*The Overcoat*)? Or is it* The Prince and the Pauper *with the old switcheroo?*

I know, I know. This helps not at all. But it's my way of showing that I'm excited. Maybe our next step should be to set up a meeting with your friend Taj? Does he have industry contacts? My college roommate used to work at UTA and I could def check in to see whether he might still be able to set us up. If at all possible, it would be great to sell this off a pitch rather than go through all the rigmarole of actually writing and selling a spec (esp in this market!) so maybe we should prioritize getting a rep first? Just a thought . . .

Anyway, lots to discuss once you get back, obvs. Safe travels and thanks for getting me all revved up about getting back into film. Almost makes going into work everyday semi-bearable ☺

Smooches,
Bran Flakes

Anna had no idea what a shibboleth was. Or what had gotten into Brandon. He sounded just like one of those intolerable industry douche bags on *Deadline Hollywood*—one who happened to have swallowed both a *Roget's Thesaurus* and Jacques Lacan's *Écrits* for breakfast.

Totes! Anna wrote back to Brandon. *You know me, I'm up for anything. See you when I get back :) hugs, Annagram.* She hit send, sincerely hoping that by the time she returned, Brandon's pipe dreams would have dissipated, leaving nothing more in their wake than the toxic resin of disappointment that had drawn her to him in the first place.

19

Anna found Taj at the Continental ticket counter at JFK. Since she had done such a good job economizing on plane tickets, Taj insisted on a nice hotel. Despite the pinch to her wallet, Anna understood the reasoning. She was the same way. Nonfat yogurt with grape nuts for breakfast meant a club sandwich with everything for lunch. A Cobb salad for lunch earned her a liberal mound of creamy risotto for dinner. Et cetera. But secretly she hoped that the upgrade was some kind of metaphoric investment in their relationship. Even though, of course, they were splitting the cost of the room. At least, Anna assumed they were.

When she spotted Taj by the bank of automated check-in machines, he looked both relaxed and mysteriously unencumbered. Anna, on the other hand, had already come completely undone. Her journey from the AirTrain terminal to the ticket counter had involved trying to pull an oversize suitcase behind her while fighting a losing battle with a shoulder bag that kept slipping down the length of her arm to become, in sad fact, an elbow bag. She had also made the unfortunate choice to wear a long-sleeved maroon shift that usually ingeniously cocooned her flab within an immobile and (hopefully) eloquent column, but now merely provided a vivid road map to her sweat stains. Yet, if Taj took notice of any of this, he didn't let on. He greeted her by planting a cool kiss on her cheek. Without meaning to, Anna inhaled as Taj exhaled, as though a maître d' had just uncorked a bottle of fine wine for her approval. His breath was a potent mix of coffee and Altoids.

"Did you bring your laptop?" he asked.

"No."

"iPod?"

"No."

"Good girl. Tablet?"

"I don't have a tablet."

"OK, give me your phone."

Anna handed it over and instantly regretted it, wishing she'd taken one last look at her messages. She hadn't checked since she'd left home, had she? Which made it almost an hour and a half. Potentially some kind of record. The lengthening gaps between e-mails checked and tweets tweeted: were these not the milestones by which Internet addiction was cured? What was the equivalent of hitting dirt bottom for an Internet junkie, she now wondered. It must be dying online. Literally dying—not just murderizing one's Gmail account. Dying in an imitation Aeron chair mid-tweet, mid-Amazon-order, mid-porn-browse, the way an alcoholic drowns in his own vomit on a flophouse floor.

"Here's your phone for the week," Taj said, handing her something heavy and shaped like a deodorant stick. For a moment she just stared at the electronic relic, this destroyer of ass silhouettes. Then she opened it. There was just a number pad, a sliver of screen. "My number's preprogrammed," Taj continued, then, noticing her bags, "Jesus, what'd you bring? It's only five days."

"I brought the AVCCAM," Anna said. The camera was her only defense against the Internet, its thrall.

"Oh, come on," Taj said. Her heart sank as his mouth pulled up in a half sneer. But just as suddenly, he reversed course. "Great idea, you'll need something to keep you busy while I take care of work stuff."

"What is this work stuff again?"

"I know," he said, ignoring her question. "You'll do a video diary. About your recovery!"

"Totally," Anna echoed, unsure about this idea, its rumored greatness. "So where's *your* stuff?"

"Laptop. Couple clean shirts. Five-pack of boxers." Taj patted his bag. "I'm good."

When they arrived at the gate, the departure monitor delivered the unsurprising news that their flight was delayed. Armed with bottled water and dehydrating snacks, they settled in for the wait at the terminal lounge.

"Finally, a vacation, huh?" Taj murmured, sliding his butt down to the edge of the pleather seat, stretching out his long, skinny-jeaned legs.

"So nice," Anna agreed, though in truth, taking a vacation when she'd already been out of work for months actually required quite a bit of mental reconfiguring.

"I have a little surprise for us," Taj said.

"What?"

"Not here." Taj opened his copy of *New York* magazine. "On the plane." He laid the magazine across his face and closed his eyes, leaving Anna alone with her thoughts.

Tiresome as the day had already been, Anna was still excited, girlishly grateful for this time alone with Taj, away from Lauren, the crew, and the stillborn dreams of random losers. In truth, they still barely knew each other. A part of her feared that with her antediluvian notions of what was and wasn't fun, she might not be able to handle five days alone with Taj. Nonetheless, seeing how unperturbed Taj was, watching his chest rise and fall, Anna felt reassured. Leslie would be proud of her: at long last, she was making good on her intention statement to Live in the Now.

Once they had stowed their bags into the overhead compartments, settled into their seats, ignored the seat-belt and oxygen-mask demonstration, and half-dozed through something called "cross-check," Taj gave Anna a nudge. He raised the armrest between them, removed a wad of cocktail napkins from his pocket, and pressed it into her hand. She glanced down into the nest of tissues and there, to her surprise and horror, lay a handful of shrooms. Anna turned to Taj, eyes bright with disbelief.

"No!"

"Oh, but yes." Taj smiled.

"Security—"

"One of the easiest things to get through."

"You're nuts."

"Hey, if you don't want any—"

"Of course I want!" Anna's own indignation came as a surprise, given she had never actually tried shrooms before.

"Then shut up and thank me," said Taj. He shook a single shroom into her hand and palmed the rest. It felt eerily light and dry, like a long-forgotten cat turd. Anna thought about the last time she had done drugs. It had been in Amsterdam, the trip she'd sold her eggs for back in college. The "grand tour." Some globe-trotting young Aussies at the hostel had offered her a giant pot cookie, which she'd taken back to her room and downed with a hot cocoa from the vending machine in the corridor. Scarcely had a smooth and miraculous mellowing taken hold, before she'd even had a chance to reach for her Pocket Rocket, did her heart start racing. The panic attack lasted a full day, during which her cracked psyche did nothing but circle the drain of a single terrifying thought: everyone she knew was going to die. She would die. Her mother and father would die. Leslie, her college friends, all the nice polylingual young people running the hostel, all the nice polylingual people living in Amsterdam, all of Europe . . . A holocaust of death, inevitable and horrible, loomed over the entire population of the planet and for some reason this was calmly accepted as a fact of life by everyone. Everyone except Anna. Should she run screaming through the well-lit, crimeless streets to warn everyone of the horror to come? In the end, she'd simply planted herself on the floor next to the vending machine to bring her message of death to an exclusive audience of tourists with the pot munchies. When the jackhammer of paranoia finally subsided, a full day had passed. She awoke in her room at the hostel, realizing she was supposed to be at the Museé de l'Art Wallon in Liège, Belgium, patching the woeful holes in her knowledge of northern Flemish Renaissance art.

That was fifteen years ago, and she'd sworn never to touch drugs again. Now Anna casually slipped the shroom into her mouth as though she were covering a yawn. Taj turned toward the window. He coughed convincingly into his closed fist the way men do, and a moment later Anna noticed his jaw muscles working. For the next forty minutes, Anna pretended to read an article about a paternity suit involving some horrible reality-show star, all the while anxiously waiting to feel something. Wasn't that the irony of so-called recreational drugs? One took them in hopes of reaching a higher plane of enlightenment, then ended up sitting there, waiting and worrying that you imbibed too little, or too much, or had simply somehow done it wrong. Inevitably, she would have to make the humiliating admission that she'd somehow incorrectly followed the instructions when the instructions were simply: put this in you.

The best thing to do now, Anna decided, was to take a good, long pee. She stepped into the aisle and began her journey, during which nothing even remotely Hunter Thompsonesque took place. She entered the little stainless-steel privy. That word had suddenly arrived, unbidden, in her head: *privy*. Wasn't it British for bathroom? What about *water closet*? Was that also a British term for bathroom? Or was that French? Closets filled with water, now there was a crazy image! Closets full of waterfalls, geysers, tidal waves! She giggled at the ludicrousness of the very idea: a *water closet*. The door folded shut behind her and Anna was greeted by the universal soundtrack of airplane bathrooms the world over: a demonic sucking noise emanating from deep within the toilet bowl. She locked the door behind her and the light flipped on automatically. Ingenious! Click! Flip. Click! Flip. Click! Flip. Click! She sensed she would never cease to marvel at this particular feat of engineering, yet couldn't deny her bladder was calling. She sat down and did her business, then reached for the toilet paper. Her fingerprints, she noticed, left puckered little whorls on the tissue. *Like shriveled-up balloons or medical diagrams of cochlea or congealed soup scum*, Anna free-associated. She brought the roll up to her face for a closer look. Then came the impatient smack of someone's bare palm on metal and Anna realized she must *do* something with this toilet paper, dry herself, and return to her seat. She finished up, stuffing the roll of toilet paper under her shirt to bring back to Taj. Wait until he saw this!

Her journey back down the aisle was directed by Terry Gilliam. Even in the gloom of the main cabin, the upturned faces of economy-class passengers, held captive by Jennifer Aniston's sarong-wrapped thighs on their screens, stood out in sharp relief. She stopped at every row to smile at strangers who didn't smile back. Drawn to the hideously bright glow emanating from the galley kitchen, Anna made her way to the back of the plane, where she watched the stewardesses restock the beverage cart until they shooed her away. It was almost ten minutes before she arrived back at her seat to find Taj clicking through the channels on his monitor, wearing a beatific smile. Anna slid in next to him. The toilet paper fell to the floor and she didn't bother to pick it up. She watched the images stream across the screen, almost faster than perception, then turned to study Taj's face—the angry child's scribble of a unibrow, those uneven eyes, his mouth, Taj's mouth, slightly open, half smiling.

"You have really nice teeth," she blurted. At least it *felt* like blurting, but in fact, the words took an inordinately long time to leave her mouth. Was she still speaking?

"So do you," Taj said without turning around.

"I don't. My front teeth are all bent."

"Look at this crazy lady dancing!" Taj's eyes were still glued to the screen.

"My mom wanted me to get braces in high school but I said no. My incisors are terrible. Here, feel them," Anna said, baring her teeth.

Taj turned to look at her. "You are totally fucked up."

"*You're* fucked up. Here, feel my teeth and I'll feel yours." She pulled her lips back and opened her mouth.

"OK."

The air had somehow turned to Jell-O. She watched Taj's hand as it traversed distant galaxies before arriving in front of her face. He gripped her two front teeth between his thumb and forefinger. She pushed a finger between his lips and politely tapped on one of his teeth until he opened his mouth.

"Ur ight," Taj said, squeezing her front teeth lightly between his fingers. "Dey are crookt."

"Ee? An urs are fo fmooth and ftraight."

"Da hottom row's ewen worf!" he said, feeling around.

"I dow!"

The elderly couple across the aisle shot them a look of concern. Anna and Taj both nodded, attempting smiles without letting go of each other's teeth. They stayed that way for a while, silently running their fingers through each other's mouth in wonder until Anna, of course, started giggling. Soon they were both laughing hysterically. They dropped their hands to focus on laughing. By now, Anna's eyes were streaming. The woman in front of them pressed a disapproving eye to the crack between the seats.

"Can I poke your zit?" Taj asked.

"What zit?" Anna gasped.

"That one," he poked.

"No, don't!"

Taj reached forward and poked her zit again.

"I said *don't*!"

"But it makes you so happy!" he said, giving her another zit poke. Despite herself, Anna could only shake her head, helpless with laughter.

"See?" he said, poking.

"No," Anna wheezed, her voice a mere rush of air. "Don't."

And then just like that, without warning, she was no longer laughing; she was crying. Really crying.

"Hey," Taj said, still laughing, but laughing with worried eyes.

"Stop—" Anna sobbed. She couldn't get out another word. Why was Taj laughing at her?

"I can't stop." Taj laughed. "I'm sorry."

Everything was suddenly irrevocably wrong. She stared at Taj. *Idontknowyou, Idontknowyou, Idontknow—*

"Y-y-y-you—"

He took her face between his hands, his grin a sad clown's rictus. Anna kept crying. He kissed her. Was he kissing her to get her to stop crying or to stop himself from laughing? Anna didn't know. Their lips burbled against each other's. But she kissed him back and Taj kept kissing her. They stayed that way long enough for Anna to get a headache, the kind only horny teenagers get. They kissed until the stewardess announced they had hit turbulence so Anna and Taj would have to lower the armrest between them and buckle their seat belts. But once fastened, they leaned in and kept on kissing. Even though the armrest was digging hard into Anna's ribs.

Even after it almost started to hurt.

20

They awoke to the jarring *thwack* of dozens of plastic window shades rising and the pilot informing them they were now flying over Bakersfield, before dropping a parcel of useless facts into the intercom: the barometric pressure was just above 6 percent, it was −38 degrees outside, they were traveling at a wind speed of 444 miles per hour. Without the benefit of drugs, Anna came to with a horrible itching sensation behind her eyes and the feeling that a cat had thrown up in her mouth. Taj looked no better. He had produced a pair of sunglasses from his tote and was staring morosely out the window at the wing of the plane thoroughly obliterating their view.

"Hey," Anna said to the back of the seat facing her.

"Hey," Taj muttered starboard.

That was as much as either of them could manage. Soon the stewardess dropped off trays of rehydrated oatmeal, a bun, and fake cheese that no one wanted. Their landing and exodus from LAX passed in similarly cheerless style as they shuffled comatose through the landing line, then off to pick up Anna's suitcases, finally making their way to the cab stand only to confront shit weather: a lid of clouds sitting low in the sky and a dull rain. After an hour grinding their way through traffic—an almost physically impossibly slow journey during which nothing was said—they were at last deposited at their hotel, a converted piano factory in the subgentrified wilderness between Echo Park and Silver Lake. In trying to find them a place, Anna had kept confusing these names: Echo Lake, Silver Park. All places that sounded like they belonged on a map of Narnia.

The damp air followed them inside, into the enormous expanse of the hotel lobby. To the left of the check-in desk was a set of very modern square chairs and a molded plastic sofa, all of which looked about as comfortable as an enema. At the far end of the room, Anna glimpsed a computer carrel with one of those yacht-size Mac flatscreens floating atop it "for the convenience of our guests." She averted her eyes, finding that Taj had already collapsed into a chair, leaving Anna to deal with registration and a tedious one-way conversation with the chirpy concierge about the neighborhood's noteworthy lack of attractions and the miserable weather they could expect all week. When she was done, she went over to prod Taj awake, but was distracted by a plaque engraved with a quote that hung just above the sofa.

> I opened the door and they were in there. The clerks of the Federal Building. I noticed one girl, poor thing, only one arm. She'd be there forever. It was like being an old wino like me. Well, as the boys said, you had to work somewhere. So they accepted what there was. This was the wisdom of the slave.
>
> —CHARLES BUKOWSKI (1920–1994)

The Bukowski quote seemed highly out of place— sacrilegiously so—in a boutique hotel where the cheapest room was $250 per night. *Bukowski would roll over in his grave*, Anna thought. Eager to share this indignation with Taj and feeling more than a little anxious about their long silent spell, Anna nudged his foot. But when she pointed out the plaque, he shook his head, apparently too tired to read. Instead they followed a bellboy who was impossible to distinguish from the guests down an endless corridor and up two flights in the elevator to their room.

Their room had a soaring ceiling and contained the same modernist, uncomfortable furniture as the lobby. But to Anna its most salient characteristic was the queen-size bed, of which there was only one. It sat there like a giant unasked question. She had, of course, brought along certain necessities. Lingerie. Those superthin Japanese condoms. A slim plastic pouch filled with massage oils of varying flavors and densities. She had a feeling their relationship would fall on one side of the fence or the other during this trip, but it was hard to say which side. Would it help if Anna played the cipher, like Brie? If she adopted Lauren's cold hauteur? She knew men liked it best when women didn't seem to care, and yet Anna had to admit that this attitude secretly dismayed her, especially after watching Brie and Rishi. Rishi would forget to text her for a day, so she would casually ignore him for five. Like secret adversaries in a Kurosawa film, they would enter a state of virtual détente, changing their relationship status on Facebook from *It's complicated* to something even more nebulous, stealthily refreshing their OkCupid profile with a strategically withheld photo. Then that weekend they would meet up with some kickball friends at a bar for karaoke, careful not to speak to each other the entire night, only to go back to Rishi's apartment to have, as Brie liked to put it, "an ass-twisting sexathon." It was this dismal race to the bottom that passed for a normal relationship among Brie's generation. Anna, old-fashioned though she may have been, could not help wanting more. She didn't want to spend time vigorously affirming her low expectations. What she wanted was permission to care, for this phase of guessing and insecurity to end so that she could finally unleash her unrealistic, suppressed fantasies. But for that to happen, one of them would have to step forward and take responsibility for the relationship, and in this regard Anna felt mysteriously powerless. It was clear that Taj held the reins. It's vague, Anna thought, *would make for a better relationship catchphrase than* It's complicated. Vagueness was the scourge of their time. When Brie got pregnant, Anna remembered, she hadn't even bothered to formally break up with Rishi. It would have been like challenging a cloud of mist to a duel. What was there to break? And yet this state of being vague with someone, Anna had to admit, *was* complicated. Anna was already exhausted. Maybe just *It's exhausting*, then?

"Sleep," Taj said.

"I know, but we really shouldn't. It's only eleven-thirty."

"I know."

She, too, could feel the distant pulse of nausea that accompanies sleep deprivation and wanted nothing so much as to lie down. Then she remembered they had skipped their in-flight breakfast.

"We could eat something."

"Shower first," Taj muttered.

"OK," Anna said.

Taj sat up and swung his legs over the side of the bed. He stayed that way far too long, staring at the carpet, but eventually roused himself and staggered off to the bathroom.

Anna took the opportunity to lie down. She closed her eyes and immediately felt the urge never to get up. It had been so long since she'd traveled, Anna had forgotten these things: the sleepless first-day torpor, the enthusiasm-sucking ritual of waiting on line at museums or for dreary river cruises that always look better from the shore, not to mention the search for a satisfactory meal— all that desperate leapfrogging from one restaurant/café/bar to another, scarcely finishing one meal before plotting the next. Then again, she wasn't supposed to be having fun, was she? She was supposed to be overcoming her addiction. With that discomfiting thought, Anna opened her eyes only to confront Taj's lathered and naked silhouette. She hadn't noticed earlier but the bathroom wall was actually made of glass, shielded from the bedroom by a thin white curtain. Her eyes slipped down, almost of their own accord, to the vague bulge below his waist. She turned away quickly, hoping Taj hadn't seen her looking.

Taj emerged from the bathroom ten minutes later, wearing the same clothes as before but looking refreshed, his black hair sticking up in attractive little spikes.

"Good?" Anna said.

Taj nodded. "Better." He flipped open the leather binder on the bedside table that described the hotel's amenities. "There's a café on the first floor and a restaurant on the top floor."

"Restaurant," Anna said, relieved that they wouldn't have to drag themselves out to a bus stop, unfold some endless map, and stand on the street corner like a gift-wrapped present to a mugger.

"Also, it says here that they'll bring a goldfish to your room if you feel lonely."

"Weird."

"Yep."

"A real one?"

"In a bowl, I hope."

"Do you feel lonely?" Anna asked.

"No." Taj smiled. "But I wouldn't say no to a goldfish."

Feeling intrepid, Anna picked up the phone and dialed 0.

"Hello," she said. "I'm in room three-oh-seven and we'd like a goldfish."

"Oh," said the concierge. "We're under new management and don't do the goldfish thing anymore. We do have half-off drinks at the hotel bar from five to seven, though."

"That's OK," Anna said. She hung up and turned to Taj. "No goldfish," she said.

"Good," Taj said.

"But you wanted one."

"I wanted it and then as soon as you picked up the phone, I didn't want it. It would have been a drag. We'd have to feed it, maybe clean its bowl—"

"We'd be out somewhere, worrying—"

"Worrying *the fish* was lonely."

"You're right," Anna said, getting into it.

"Or what if it fucking died? That would become the symbol of our trip, the only thing we'd remember when we looked back."

"Our first pet."

"Who needs pointless obligations?"

Anna nodded, meaning it and not meaning it. On the one hand, yes, who needed a pointless goldfish? On the other, wouldn't it be nice to take care of someone else for a change? To have someone actually depend on her?

"Besides," Taj said, opening the door and making a gentlemanly motion for her to go first, "is there anything more depressing in the whole world than a goldfish alone in a tiny bowl?"

They made their way to the lift, a fashionably unfinished freight elevator, presumably used to haul pianos in the hotel's previous life. At the top floor, the doors opened to reveal a bar polished to a painful gleam. A hostess led them to a small table by the window and left them with their menus.

"So," Anna began, scanning the list of sandwiches, "what's our plan for today?"

"We should go to Silver Lake," Taj said.

"What's in Silver Lake?"

"Same exact stuff that's in Brooklyn."

"OK," Anna said, confused as to why they had left Brooklyn to go to Brooklyn.

"OK. I'm getting the quiche," Taj said.

"I'm getting the panini."

"Is it too early for drinking?"

"Well, it's half past noon here, but that's mid-afternoon back on the East Coast."

"Perfect! Then I'll have a Long Island iced tea."

"When in Rome—" Anna said, and they both laughed. *Almost like a couple*, she thought.

They continued their easy banter through lunch, and when they were done, Taj threw a couple of twenties and some change on the table.

"On me," he said.

As she thanked him, she couldn't help doing the math—now Taj owed her only thirty dollars, give or take a buck or two.

As promised, Silver Lake really was exactly like Williamsburg, only California-style: a carousel of boutiques chasing cafés, chasing art galleries, chasing bars, interrupted by vast stretches of boring parking lots for some mundane grocery or pharmacy, monuments to the dreary reality that there were still certain staples a person actually needed in order to sustain life. Anna wanted to walk around and do a bit of clothes shopping; Taj wanted to sit and have coffee. They passed a café named Minutia. Underneath the sign, a smaller sign read: BEST COFFEE IN SILVER LAKE.

"Would you care to join me for the best coffee in Silver Lake?" Taj asked.

"Do you think it's really the best?"

"OK, would you like to join me for the *allegedly* best coffee in Silver Lake?"

"The *self-professed* best coffee in Silver Lake?"

"The *averred* best?"

She wouldn't mind wittily trading synonyms with Taj like this for the rest of the day, Anna thought, the rest of her life, even, but instead said, "I'll walk around a bit and meet you here later."

They parted and Anna strolled around the corner. All the boutiques, Anna noticed, seem to arrange their almost-bare shelves around a minimum of merchandise, the truffles of the retail world. Two blocks up the street she paused in front of a shop whose window showcased designer clothes that all seemed to have been shredded, then recombined with canvas sacks and cascades of dirty shoelaces.

"Come in!" read the sign on the door. "We're closed!" *Closed or open*, Anna thought, *which is it?* She tried the door; it was open.

"We're closed," said the woman behind the front desk, annoyed. Then she added, "But you can look around for a minute if you want."

Anna quickly parsed the threadbare clothes on the racks: T-shirts with x-rayed cow heads and glittery skulls, burning buildings in fluorescent colors, a Rubik's cube, bits of soccer jerseys that had been torn up and randomly sewn together. She pulled a promising pair of pants dangling from a hanger toward her only to find they had only one leg. This, Anna decided, was her signal to leave. But she didn't have much luck elsewhere. Everywhere the clothes were all depressingly small and hilariously overpriced. She wandered into a few gift shops—the kind that sold coasters with photos of flesh wounds or charming seven-dollar greeting cards saying "Fuck Off!"—then wandered back out onto the street again. After a few more turns around the block, she made her way back to Minutia, where she found Taj reading the L.A. *Times* and munching on a biscotti.

"So how was the coffee?"

"Just OK," Taj said. "How were the clothes?"

"Douchey."

"Now we switch," Taj announced. He left her with the newspaper and went out for his stroll. What a lovely time they were having! Could it be, Anna wondered, that they had already reached that comfortable plateau where you don't have to speak to each other, or even *be together*, in order to enjoy each other's company? The man sitting next to her, a dreadlocked student type with an unopened philosophy book by his elbow, was pounding furiously away at a Blackberry with two fingers, double-fisting it as though he were unburdening his own personal *Ulysses*. With a measure of surprise, she found herself feeling sorry for him. She was here in Silver Lake with Taj, alive and busy knitting herself a

new life out of raw experience. A life where time wasn't measured in tweets tweeted or e-mail sent and social status remained
unquantified by friend requests. She was an aspiring filmmaker
sitting in a café, waiting for her boyfriend. OK, this was a stretch,
but by the loosest of definitions, plausible. And maybe it wasn't
so bad to be vague, to let Taj's boyfriendhood accrue softly and
invisibly, like plaque on her teeth. She would go with the spirit of
the times, she decided, and embrace vagueness. With that thought
propelling her out of her seat, she ordered a coffee that tasted no
different from the drip at the Korean bodega back home, then
leaned her head against the wall and promptly fell asleep.

It was Taj who shook her awake. He was holding a black
paper bag covered in cursive letters that were also black, and thus
indecipherable.

"Check this out," he said, holding up a T-shirt for her inspection. It was the x-rayed cow head Anna had seen earlier.

That shirt, Anna recalled, had cost $120, and the bag was half
full. She wasn't sure exactly what it meant that Taj was the kind of
person who could go off and casually drop so much money on
such a T-shirt, but surely it meant *something*?

"Let's walk," he said.

They walked up Sunset Boulevard, down Myra, and back up
Santa Monica. They didn't hold hands, but did do that thing
where they bumped into each other intentionally and jostled each
other with their elbows more than was absolutely necessary. They
walked farther, to a craft market set up in a strip-mall parking lot,
where Anna spent thirty bucks on a needlepoint with the words
so bored stitched in elaborate letters and surrounded by roses.
Taj declared Silver Lake's craft market no different from Brooklyn
Flea, and Anna had to agree. Eventually, they ended up at a dingy
and fluorescently lit curry shop, empty save for a quartet of unc-
tuous waiters. Ten years ago a scene in an important film had
been shot there and the walls were covered in framed, yellowed
newspaper clips eulogizing this event. They sat on the same side

of a red pleather booth and drank too many bottles of Singha and ordered too many appetizers in addition to their faux-chicken vindaloo, then got lost on their way back to the hotel.

By the time they'd returned to their room, it was past eight and Anna felt fine about going to sleep but Taj insisted on going swimming instead. There was supposed to be an amazing pool in the basement, he said, designed by some famous artist. So they grabbed their bath towels and took the shuddering elevator down three flights.

Finding herself alone in the ladies' changing room, a dim cube covered entirely in shimmering, mosaic tiles, Anna suddenly felt overcome by the guilt of undeserved luxury. The hotel, the restaurants, the *so bored* needlepoint, and now the heartbreakingly hot water flowing over her unemployed, abundantly fleshy body, opened up a new ache within her. Before she left, she'd received a text from Leslie to never mind about Brie's phone number, that she'd found her Tumblr and gotten in touch with her. She and Josh had already started couples therapy to get "copacetic" about the adoption thing. That same morning, Brie told her she planned to confront Pom, tell her she was done with interning and needed to start getting paid.

"What will you do if she says no?" Anna had asked.

"Temp." Brie had shrugged, leaving Anna impressed with the strength and certainty of this response. Back home, everyone was dealing with such grim, real-world problems. Pregnancy. Money. Couples therapy. Leslie and Brie were moving forward and shrinking their gaps, while look at her: here on a lark, browsing one-legged pants and drinking four-dollar coffees with a man from the Internet. She scrubbed harder, as though aggressive shampooing could serve as a form of absolution, giving herself a little talk. When she got back home, she would get a new job. A real job. She would work on Taj's film and her own film on nights and weekends, leaving no time for guilty showers. She would ask Leslie

"How are you?" and support Brie in her brave decision to become a single mother. She would learn how to love her mother and encourage Brandon to pursue his dreams just like Taj had encouraged hers. She would move through her days with clarity and purpose.

She stepped out of the shower, shivering in the sudden chill, and found herself staring at another brass plaque bolted to the wall. This one read:

I am fearful of something more than fear: it's something in the landscape surrounding the cities and smaller towns between here and the coast, something *out there* that feels so empty and it is not made of earth or muscle or fur; it's like a pocket of death but with no form other than the light one might cast upon its trail of fragments.
—DAVID WOJNAROWICZ (1954–1992)

What the fuck? Anna thought. It was ridiculous—this hipster hostelry desecrating the memory of subversive American artists by mindlessly plonking their quotes in a sea of expensive opalescent tile. Just like that, her resolutions were swept away by scorn, and this was the feeling she carried with her out to the pool, where she found Taj sitting with his long brown legs dangling over the edge. The pool was round and polished to an egg-like smoothness, with water the color of fresh wasabi.

"Did you have a weird quote in your bathroom?" Anna said. Immediately she regretted how loud and sharp her voice sounded. The room was an echo chamber.

"Nope."

"You won't believe—"

"I won't," Taj interjected. "Let's swim."

He slid into the water and Anna watched his back muscles flex as he reached the opposite end of the pool in five quick strokes.

She was wearing an oversize red-and-white T-shirt over her one-piece bathing suit. Looming above Taj at the lip of the pool, she feared she might look a bit like a milk carton. Quickly, she slid into the water after him.

"Oh! It's cold—"

"I know."

"What are we paying all this money for?"

"Not heat," Taj said. "Or goldfish. Come here."

"Look," she said, pointing to a quavering black spot on the pool floor. "Someone dropped a something. Should we get it?"

"So we're supposed to clean their pool now, too?"

Anna laughed and floated over to Taj. He offered his back to her.

"Hop on."

Anna hesitated—yes, he was taller, but she definitely weighed more.

"C'mon!"

Anna hopped, or rather clambered, onto Taj's back and he hooked his elbows behind the backs of her knees. She slipped her arms around his neck.

"See? You're light."

She was light! They bobbed through the deep end together, weightless and silent. Pressed against Taj, Anna felt herself warming up.

"This is nice," she ventured, bringing her face close to Taj's ear. She wanted to bite his earlobe, or lick the droplet of water that dangled from it. She could imagine sucking on it, the tiny ear hairs tickling her tongue like sea anemones. She opened her mouth, thinking it would be a good idea to breathe on his neck first, but at that moment Taj's knees buckled and she pitched forward. He had wandered a bit too far into the shallow end and let gravity take hold. But before she could even try to squirm out of his grasp, he swiveled back to the deep end, back to that special planet where Anna weighed nothing. And she leaned her head against his shoulder and closed her eyes, trying not to think, not to hope, not to wonder what Taj was thinking, just *being in the now*, with Taj's bare skin pressed against her cheek and the sound of water lapping against the stone tile.

Of course, after five more minutes of trawling back and forth from one side of the deep end to the other, the pool was about as interesting as the stone lining it. Three minutes after that, if they ever encountered another pool in their lives, even a biggish bath-tub, it would be too soon. Anna figured they could have lasted longer if they were drunk, but the Singha had worn off long ago, the pool was too small, and they'd both been up since six in the morning. She slid off Taj's back, her T-shirt tenting up around her, and the chilly water immediately rushed in to fill the gulf between them. Smelling strongly of chlorine, they headed back to the changing rooms, where Taj put on the same clothes he'd worn to JFK and Anna struggled not to let the plushness of her bath towel or the powerful rubber grip of the professional-grade hair dryer send her into another downward spiral of guilt. When they reconvened by the elevators, it was clear that whatever gauzy spell the water had cast over them had dissipated into bone-deep exhaustion. They both leaned against the wall and closed their eyes as they waited for the elevator. Anna didn't yet feel so tired that she didn't care what happened after they undressed and climbed into bed, but she was quickly approaching that point; the itch behind her eyes was enormous. The elevator pinged, and, fol-lowing Taj inside, she watched as he suddenly made a familiar grab for his ass cheek. He pulled out his cell phone and stared at the screen for a long moment, scrolling and reading. They both forgot to hit the button for their floor. The doors closed behind them and the elevator sat there, not moving.

"Holy shit!"

"What?" said Anna.

" '. . . late-submission waiver . . . very excited to receive your rough cut . . . ,' " Taj read.

"What submission—?"

" '. . . already shared it with the narrative shorts committee and we are delighted—' "

"You applied somewhere?"

"It's on," Taj yelled. "It's fucking on like Donkey Kong!"

"Yay!" Anna said. Then, after a reasonable pause, "What's on?"

"That festival I told you about. I'm in."

"But I thought—"

"I thought, too." Taj smiled. "I found a work-around."

"Wow," Anna said, hitting the button for their floor. "Looks like everyone's dream's coming true this week. When is it?"

But Taj didn't reply, he simply continued staring down at his phone as though he might deep-throat it or stuff it down the front of his pants or fling it joyously at the stupid, poverty-chic bare bulb hanging from a wire above them, engulfing them both in sparks. He looked so happy that Anna decided her gift to him would be silence. Just like the fifty bucks, she wouldn't mention what he'd said about never applying to a festival again and the jumped-up arrivistes and cockroaches. She would swallow all of these things and a lot of other things besides—ultimately they weren't important. Not important like kissing on the airplane was important, or the gentleness with which he ferried her through the water on his back. Nowhere near as important as including her in "all stages of production." Taj was thrumming like an electric wire. From the faraway look in his eyes, she could tell the events of the past day had already been left far behind. Her stomach lurched as the elevator swung upward, carrying them to their room.

Taj reached for her, not after they closed the door or climbed into bed and turned off the lights, but in the middle of the night, when Anna woke to realize she could not check her e-mail. Yet that does not explain how they ended up having sex in back of an ATM lobby on Del Mar Avenue at three a.m. They had both exhausted their usual scripts, pressed on into the virgin tundra beyond, until what began as a casual game of sexual onedownsmanship had landed them here, far from the hotel, in this miniature citadel of commerce. Still, no obvious methodology presented itself as they confronted the cold banks of molded plastic. Anna realized they would have to improvise. Worse, she discovered the word *cash* reminded her the electric bill was due and served only as a brake on the engines of desire. Lucky for her, there was no time for desire; neither the ATM lobby's architecture or ambience inspired lingering.

Taj placed his keys and cell phone on the ledge of a cash machine and Anna grabbed him from behind, working to get her hands past the crucial demarcation zone of his jeans zipper.

"Wait." He pushed her toward the opposite wall. "Here."

Anna shuffled back with him, an awkward two-step.

"No, better here," he said, glancing back at the ATM and shifting her rightward. "We wouldn't want . . ." He gestured to the mute eye of the security camera over the door.

The unexpected courtesy engendered a gush of warmth and wetness from Anna. He didn't want her dignity compromised, even by some unseen security guard. She pulled up his T-shirt and grabbed the hem of his boxers. Guiding him toward her, she couldn't help but think what kind of pinwheel they would form if filmed from above. He slipped a hand into her underwear and fiddled around in there for a moment as if searching for a light switch. Then, propping her up against the deposit-slip dispenser, he slid his jeans down halfway and made his deposit.

"Your transaction is complete," he whispered.

Anna laughed.

"I felt that," he said. They parted, though not as reluctantly as Anna had hoped, and he turned around to fetch the things he'd left on the ledge of the cash machine.

21

The hipsters didn't care. If anything, they thought it was funny. The door had beeped open while they were still fumbling with their clothes. The girl with the dreadlocks had a little dog that started barking. The guy wearing the Stetson said, "Whoa." Not even "Whoa!" Just "Whoa." And that was it. Anna and Taj had gone back to the hotel and slept an epic sleep, only rising at one p.m. to shamble into the cavernous elevator and descend to the hotel café.

"Coffee," Anna said to the waiter.

"Coffee," Taj seconded. "And where's the breakfast menu? This says 'lunch.' "

"We stopped serving breakfast at twelve-thirty, brah." The waiter looked so apologetic that for a second Anna thought he might offer them some pot instead.

"What happened to the customer being right?" Taj said. "Always."

"True that, true that," said the waiter with a game smile. "But, you know, the kitchen rotates its stuff so, all that breakfast stuff's—*phft!*—outta there. You should try the spesh, though. Seitan sunflower veggie burger. It comes with some wicked sauce."

But Taj was too gung ho for breakfast to go for the spesh. What was so hard about eggs cracked over a frying pan? It would take two seconds! He could go back there and do it himself! Later Anna would wonder whether *this* was the moment that things had truly started to suck. All she could remember was the feeling of wanting Taj to stop talking, only without her telling him so. *Please stop*, she thought at him, while pretending to examine the drinks menu. But it wasn't the waiter—who looked as though he could smilingly debate the impossibility of eggs all day—that cut off Taj's tirade. It was a woman's voice behind Anna's shoulder, accented in faint German.

"Zero?"

At the sound of this word, Anna found herself witnessing a total eclipse of Taj's ethnicity as his normally latte-colored skin turned white.

"I'll get you folks another chair," the waiter said, extricating himself smoothly as Taj rose and the woman Anna recognized as Simone Weil stepped forward to give him a hug. A real hug, Anna noted. Not a perfunctory squeeze-and-pat.

The waiter delivered Simone's chair, and Taj and Anna both reflexively ordered the Seitan sunflower burger.

"I'll have a Bloody," Simone said, omitting the Mary. Then, turning back to Taj, "You're in the festival?"

He gave her a why-else-would-I-be-here shrug as Anna struggled to absorb the news: that festival Taj was talking about must be *this* festival. And did he think his ravenous head-to-toe scan of Simone would go unnoticed?

Simone nodded approvingly. "Letting bygones be bygones. Very good. Well, tell me then, how did you get out of wearing their horrible fucking hipster shackle?" Simone laughed, fingering a green plastic wristband that Anna had just assumed was couture debris.

"It was a last-minute thing," Taj replied with studied nonchalance. "So, you're showing?"

"They're giving me an award," Simone said, as though they were giving her a schnitzel.

"Congrats. Where are you living now? Berlin?"

"London. I got a council flat." She said this in a way that was meant to explain a lot, and all Anna could do was nod. She kept thinking about how strange it was to sit across the table from someone she didn't know, but whose labia she could trace from memory on the napkin in front of her. Anna had read only as far as (what *Gawker* termed) Simone's "next stunt" on her Wikipedia page. After the furor over her video sex diaries, Weil had declared herself a "microprostitute" and set up camp at the Blum & Poe gallery for a three-week installation. For a nominal fee, Simone would hold her "clients' " hands, kiss them, stroke their hair, rub their back or tummy, or place a candy heart on their tongue. (Only these candy hearts said things like "Slave" and "I Suck" and now sold for $500 a bag on ArtAuction.com.) Clients were also allowed to rub or kiss certain parts of her own body that she had outlined in black Sharpie, Riot Grrrl–style, and labeled with things like "Shank," "Rib," and "Bottom Sirloin," intentionally giving her the appearance of raw meat ready for butchering. At night, when the gallery was closed but Simone remained, her act grew more risqué. Clients could pay via PayPal, collect their services via Skype. Here Simone might flash a boob, felate a fruit, sit on one of the objects arranged in the Bedouin tent that served as her boudoir. She would kiss and lick the screen or herself. Then, finally, in a scene memorialized by countless screenshots, she went all the way with herself for a payment of $2.87. The following morning, her first clients were the cops, who came to arrest her. Blum & Poe was charged with a class-D felony, for running a "prostitution tourism business," which everyone agreed was great for business. At that point, the art world collectively placed an "et cetera" at the end of Simone's résumé and she became an international art star. She was only twenty at the time, having ditched college as soon as the Gilman video debuted. And she was still young now, Anna saw.

It occurred to her that the new Simone Weil actually had a lot in common with the original. They were both hard workers, both grounded their work in untenable philosophies, both were self-obsessed. And now that she was meeting Simone 2.0 face-to-face, Anna saw another similarity: neither of them ate food. Simone was at least a head taller than Anna but still weighed less than a bicycle. She was draped in a knee-length gray shift with ragged seams that might have been sown by Inuit nomads or Sudanese refugees or the Rodarte sisters themselves, but would have looked good in anything; she had that kind of face, that lack of body. Her black hair was impossibly straight, guillotined at the shoulders, her eyes hazel and luminous in the way of Japanese anime dolls.

"And your friend . . . ?" Simone was saying. Her accent was barely there, a mere toss of confectioner's sugar on her otherwise perfect English.

"Anna," said Anna.

"Anna. You are showing in the festival?"

"Anna's here to work," Taj said, decisive by proxy. "She's making a video diary."

"How original!" Simone exclaimed. And after a brief shock Anna realized Simone wasn't trying to be mean—that's just how everything she said came out sounding.

"Well, as they say out here," Taj said, raising his glass, "it's 'execution dependent.' "

"Agreed," said Simone, and they shared a laugh that had obviously once served as currency in some long-forgotten country.

The waiter arrived with their order just as one of two identical iPhones lying on the table began to ring. Taj and Simone both reached for it at the same time.

"Hello?" Taj said, snagging it first. He handed Simone the phone. "Yours. We have the same ringtone!" He spoke with such wonder one would think it was an umbilical cord they'd shared. Anna might even have been jealous if Simone's lack of interest wasn't so apparent. Instead, she found herself wondering why, aside from that first meeting, Taj had never mentioned her.

"Well, it's the least offensive one, isn't it?" Simone said, sweeping up the phone and rising from the table in one smooth motion. "Allo . . . ?"

Anna turned back to Taj, who was busy ignoring the special sauce and squeezing mustard on his puck of seitan.

"Why didn't you tell me you were coming here for the festival?" Anna said, batting his shoulder in a wan attempt at playfulness.

"I told you I had work stuff to take care of in LA," Taj said, taking a bite of his burger. "Jesus, this tastes like a loofah."

"When were you going to tell me? What are you showing?"

"I don't know."

"Don't know what?"

"Both, OK? It doesn't matter. I don't want you to get distracted by this festival bullshit. Focus on your recovery. Have you started the video diary?"

"You know I haven't." They'd been together the whole time, hadn't they? "But when's your screening?"

"Never mind that," he said, spearing a truffle fry. "It's nothing that you haven't seen already. What you need is to get to work."

And as Anna considered which of these statements to pin her resentment on, Simone slid back into her seat, her arrival presaged by a whiff of mysterious perfume that smelled like fresh snow or old books or burning leaves. Anna took a swig of zero-calorie water. The glass was so thin she fought the sudden urge to bite down and crush it between her teeth.

"I have to go see about my installation. The projectionist says it's ready."

"We should have lunch later," Taj said, forgetting this wasn't breakfast.

"I have dinner with Deitch," Simone said, wistful and squinty. "I wish I wasn't so squeezed. But the festival . . . You know, we'll bump into each other a million times. It will get embarrassing, I promise."

"Drinks after?" said Taj, as if he hadn't noticed her artful evasion.

"Why don't you both come with me now?" Simone said. She

took a tiny bite of the celery staked in her drink. "The gallery is only three blocks from here."

"Great," said Taj. "Let me just change first." He rose abruptly from the table and Anna found herself suddenly alone with Simone and her untouched drink. Simone jiggled her foot. She flashed Anna a thin-lipped smile, but her eyes were elsewhere. Anna knew that look; it was the look of a woman who wanted to check her e-mail.

"I like your sneakers," Anna said.

"Spanish," said Simone, still jiggling.

"I was wondering, I've never heard that nickname you have for Taj . . ."

"Zero? He got that the first week in Herzog's workshop. You know about the workshop?"

"I didn't know Taj was—"

"It's how we found Zero. Me and Paul," Simone added.

"Really?" Anna said. Then, wondering whether these were things she was meant to keep to herself, "Taj told me he met Gilman jailbreaking his iPhone."

"Ha! Well, that's partly true." Simone laughed. "The film that got Zero into the workshop was about Foxconn, the factory in China where they make iPhones. They wouldn't let him film in there so he broke in and got arrested. He gave Gilman an iPhone 3G he'd brought back."

"Taj?" Anna said, unable to keep the incredulity from her voice. The closest she'd seen him get to politics was examining some Che Guevara drink coasters in a gift shop yesterday.

"I know, but that's how Zero was back then. Always in solidarity with the poor and trampled, blah, blah, blah. He was very intent on x-ing himself out of his films. Any whiff of that evil bourgeois entitlement. Goes back to college, I guess. He studied econ with some real lefties. And so, Zero, yes." She laughed again—a high trill with trace deposits of Arnold Schwarzenegger. "He's a different kind of artist now. You can say we brought him around."

"But why? Didn't people like his films?"

"Maybe not so many. I don't know. *I* did."

As Simone rooted around her bag for a moment, Anna's thoughts tetherballed wildly around the axis of these revelations. So many Tajes! A broken mirrorball of Tajes. Each seemed to cancel another out, reduce, indeed, to Zero.

"I'll tell you a little story," Simone said, in a way that implied she started a lot of little stories this way. "Growing up, I went to this tiny private high school in Berlin, an alternative school. The popular kids all smoked, *grufties* who bought their clothes in the Mitte and listened to Einstürzende Neubauten. They hung out by this one bench in a park across the street from the school and they always looked so cool, soaking in their little clouds of unearned darkness."

Anna's thoughts snagged, annoyed, on this phrase. How can you soak in a cloud? Who talked like this? Europeans, she guessed.

"Every year, a new class of freshmen would come in, so innocent and hopeful and scared," Simone continued. "The ambitious ones though, after a few weeks, they'd figure out how things worked and soon start hanging out by the bench themselves, bumming smokes. It was hard work standing out there in the cold, teaching themselves how to like these toxic things, but they did it anyway because they saw this was a blueprint for becoming popular. Within a couple of months, you couldn't recognize them. Their clothes, the way they talked. They became totally different people. And of course, the next year, they were always first to offer their Djarum Blacks to the new freshmen, continuing the cycle. I think that's what happened with Zero. Herzog was so supportive of what Paul and I were doing. Zero could see Nowism taking off right before his eyes and he didn't want to be left behind. Though sometimes I suspect his heart was never in it." She nodded at the waiter to take away her drink. "I can relate, though. I remember that feeling well. Sitting out there in the cold, choking on smoke. Who can blame him for wanting to be loved?"

Before Anna could even form a response, Taj returned wearing

his $125 x-rayed cow head and there was nothing to do but fol-
low them out into the drizzle in her sorry, slept-in T-shirt. The
dilapidated warehouses surrounding the hotel turned out to be a
cluster of high-end art galleries clinging strenuously to their pro-
letariat heritage. The blue-chip names were carefully hidden, engraved on tiny gold plates, while the huge, rusting signage of
long-displaced industries remained carefully preserved above the
doors. But Simone's gallery did not even reveal its name on the
call button inside the elevator, maintaining the illusion that they
intended to sell you a vacuum hose right up until the smoked-
glass entryway. The three of them passed into a chamber of polished concrete and exposed steel beams where an installation was
still in progress. Near the entrance, a pair of men stood examining a meat-themed mural.

"You can't ask what it's 'about,'" the skullcapped younger of
the two was saying. "I mean, whatever, like everything I make, this
series is kind of a dumb joke. I was playing with the idea of, you
know, a 'sausage party,' right? Because making sausage is a kind
of cooking that combines these really brutal elements—slaughter,
metal grinders, squeezing, compaction, animal blood, enclosure
in intestines . . ."

The other man, a collector type, leaned in to admire some
phallic-looking columns on a Pantheon that looked as though it
had been carved from steak.

". . . the mid-digestive shit channels of mammals. And I fucking love sausage! How do I deal with that, you know?" Here Skull-
cap paused to add a daub of penis-colored paint to the Pantheon.
"But mostly I just wanted to play around with color, which is
something I don't normally do."

The man nodded gravely. Anna glanced over at Simone, who
was wearing a wry smile.

"Well, he's got one thing right," she said, sotto voce. "It *is* a
total sausage fest around here." Anna looked around and noticed
it was true: all the artists in the room were men. Simone motioned

them past the muralist toward a series of aerial photographs. "Ah, shooting shit from the window of an airplane." She sighed, moving on to a neighboring painting. "Nice work if you can get it."

"Agreed. And I wonder when whoever did *this* knew it was done," Taj snorted, indicating the painting. "When he came on it?"

"Really? I find this piece tremendously moving." Simone said, turning to Anna. "What do you think?"

Anna flushed at finding herself the unexpected center of attention. Whose side to take? She took an inadvertent step back, felt a mysterious tug at her head.

"It's definitely a challenging piece," Anna hedged, trying to extract her hair from the mesh sculpture behind her without attracting attention. But this milquetoast statement was the cue ball that broke the trio apart, setting them separately adrift throughout the gallery. Anna wandered past a confusing row of flat-panel screens and tangled headphones to arrive at another wall of photographs: depressed people in nice homes, blurry-looking snapshots, something underwater. There was a caption somewhere to the left that explained what it was all supposed to mean, why these images weren't just a camera going off in someone's backpack by accident, but Anna was too lazy to read it.

A few minutes later, they regrouped in the narrow hallway leading to Simone's installation. Taj went first, holding the heavy black curtain open for them. She followed Simone inside and the instant the curtain swung back it became so dark Anna lost all sense of the room's volume. They could have been standing in a swimming pool basin for all she knew. Somewhere far above them a projector whirred, but the screen remained black.

Anna blinked into the darkness, wondering what to expect. Something that upped the ante on Simone's carnal, lo-fi, autobiographical fare, she supposed. Perhaps a film narrated by her vagina? As Anna waited for Simone's vagina, blown up to IMAX proportions, to wrap itself around her face like a giant squid, she began to ruminate on the shelf life of an art star's vagina. She'd once read an interview with Madonna where she complained how after she turned forty, any mention of her name was immediately followed by her age, as if to underscore her unfuckability. There probably comes some later point when a star's age starts getting mentioned *before* her name, Anna mused, and a point after that where they just omit the name and add an exclamation point after the age. In any case, what would happen to the artistic valuation of Simone's snatch as the years passed? Would her audience mature with her? Or, like the bag-headed lothario in Gilman's *Age of Consent*, would they simply strike out for younger and tighter turf?

It was about then that Anna realized the movie hadn't started and they were all just standing in the dark listening to the whir of a projector. Had there been a malfunction? Should she say something and risk looking like an idiot? In the end, Anna decided against it. Where were Taj and Simone? The projector was so loud she couldn't hear them moving. She wondered if there was a bench somewhere nearby, stretched a tentative toe forward but encountered no resistance.

How much time passed before Anna realized this *was* the piece? A minute? Ten? She didn't know, but at some point she noticed the sound of the projector was subtly changing pitches, shifting into higher and lower gears. Of course this revelation only presented new challenges. Did the piece have an "end" and was she expected to wait for it? Was she allowed to sit down on the floor? To speak? She stood there for what felt like a gerbil's lifetime, by turns itchy, bored, and angry, wondering how long she would have to keep sucking on this bouillon cube of narcissism. Then came a new sound—the stuttering end of a film reel—and the black curtain parted. A warm yoke of light spilled across the room from the hallway. Simone was beckoning for them to follow her.

"Wow," Taj said, once they were back in the hall.

Anna felt an anticipatory smile tugging at the corner of her mouth. If Taj thought the Romanians were dull, what would he think of this? The Romanians' films, true, took place in real time, or some slower facsimile thereof, but hey! at least there were people, plots, dialogue. Watching a tofu loaf brown through an oven window, watching gym socks circle in a dryer, watching a *fucking scab harden* was still more interesting than pretending to listen to a projector while watching nothing at all.

"Wow?" Simone said.

"Well, you know, it's not exactly your demo . . ." Taj trailed off.

"What's my demo?" Simone asked. Her voice was neither angry nor coy—merely curious.

Perhaps deciding that "anyone interested in seeing your pink parts" was either too insulting or too broad a demo, Taj suddenly changed tacks.

"You know who it reminds me of?"

Simone cocked her head.

"Michael Snow."

"You remember!" Simone exclaimed. For the first time, she seemed to regard him with real interest.

"You forget that I remember a lot of things." Taj dropped his voice a register, put on a new face. "Like this: 'I'm a flaneur. That's what I do. I just flaaaan around.'" He began to do an odd little dance in the corridor, waving his arms—flanning around, apparently—and quoting someone they both knew, to Simone's obvious delight. Then he whirled and grabbed Simone brusquely by the shoulders, drilling her with an intense stare.

"What are you doing?" Simone said, her smile simultaneously managing to convey affection and *fuck you*.

"I just shot a film of you. Up here," Taj continued, in the same deep voice, tapping his temple. "I call it Mental Cinematography."

"Oh my God!" Simone broke down laughing. "Herzog. We were *such* idiots."

"Yup."

"We were young!" Simone said. And Anna couldn't help thinking this was generous, since Simone was so much younger than Taj.

"Not Paul," Taj said, an edge to his voice.

"Not Paul," she conceded.

Why couldn't the spongy sculptural installation lining the hallway wall just silently absorb her, Anna wondered? How long would she have to stand here, witness to Taj and Simone's courtship dance, with this stupid waiting-to-be-clued-in look stuck to her face?

"Seriously, though," Simone said, sobering. "What did you think?" She seemed almost vulnerable. "You know, about the piece?"

"Gerda," he said, as serious as Anna had ever heard him. "I loved it."

Her heart felt like a juggling pin that Taj had just dropped. Anna had assumed they would end up at Minutia later, making fun of Simone, had even already begun coming up with witty analogies for the film in her head; a roller coaster of boredom, the Matterhorn of monotony . . . But now Taj took a step closer to Simone, put a hand on her back, right between where the wings would sprout. He was clearly just about to say something else—something warm and sincere and potentially life-altering—when the frigid blonde from the front desk hurried up to them.

"Ms. Weil. I'm sorry to interrupt. That journalist—"

"Already?"

"I told him—"

"Ech. Sorry, guys," Simone said, sloughing off Taj's arm. "Have to run."

"Simone—" Taj began.

"Thanks for the Bloody. I owe you!" The curator was already unhooking a velvet rope, leading Simone away through the area marked PRIVATE.

"Later let's—"

"Yes, see you later!" she called back with a wave, leaving Taj and Anna to watch her vanish between the twin parentheses of their raised hands.

They took the elevator down and emerged to find the sky had turned a nauseating gray and the air had the sharp smell of a freshly struck match. It began to rain.

"Shit!" Taj yelled, pulling his cow head over his real head. They ran as the rain thudded on the car hoods around them. Anna hurried after him, past a man carrying what had been a bouquet of paper flowers but now resembled a wad of used Kleenex on a stick. Back at their hotel room, Anna lay on the bed with too many pillows watching Taj towel his head dry. Throughout lunch and the trip to the gallery, Anna had left Simone's revelations about Taj to simmer on some mental back burner. Now all the prattle had burned away, leaving only the clarified truth: Simone was a total ice bitch. Obviously, Taj had loved her, or did love her, and that had fucked him up. How could it not? She was a fruit-fellating microprostitute who had lured them into a dark shaft and subjected them to an art-based version of waterboarding. Who does that? Who thinks it's OK to stick people in a black box, where time can be measured only by bladder accretion, to wonder what's wrong with *themselves* that they can't appreciate a motherfucking drone?

A psychopath, that's who.

Connected, she suddenly thought, *feel free to talk now*.

"I just want you to know I know."

"Hm?" Taj rubbed his ears with the towel as if he hadn't heard.

"Simone told me all about the Zero thing."

"Oh." Taj shrugged. "Have you seen my power cord?" He began wandering around the room, scanning outlets.

"You were in that class with Herzog," Anna continued, thrown off by how not thrown off Taj seemed.

"I know."

"Why didn't you tell me?"

"It's a long story." He lifted the bedspread and plucked his cable from a three-prong. "I don't really feel like getting into it right now."

Anna felt her face prickling. How come people like Brie and Taj could so easily shut down a conversation with one of those Teflon phrases? Did it even matter to anyone what *she* felt like doing? She scooched over to where Taj was sitting on the bed, determined to be the anti-Simone.

"Taj," she said, placing a strategic hand on his arm. "Are you OK?"

He looked up from wrapping his power cord and threw her a sharp glance. "What?"

"I just know it's been a long time since you've seen Simone, and you seem kind of—"

"Anna, you're getting clingy, and it's weirding me out." Abruptly, he got up and reached for a clean T-shirt.

She tried not to be hurt by Taj's dismissal. And while she failed at that, Taj changed into dry clothes. Suddenly he was standing by the door with a laptop bag swinging from his shoulder. Now she saw he was wearing another T-shirt from the shop. The one with the glittery skull.

"Where are you going?" she said, alarmed.

"To find a coffee shop. I've got a ton of editing to do."

"What editing? Taj, I want to—"

But he cut her off. "Have you even started your video diary?"

"No, but—"

"No buts. Get your mind off things and get to work. Work, Anna. It's the most important thing."

"OK," she said, feeling like Taj was the most important thing. The door slammed and Anna stared at the digital clock on the stand across the bed. Everything was unraveling. It was like one of those time-lapse films of fruit rotting. First things were perfect, then kind of mushy, until finally what remained was just—the door opened again, and as if in a dream, there was Taj. Two strides and he was again beside her. On the bed.

"As soon as I left, I realized I was being a dick," he said. The most beautiful words, Anna couldn't help but think, that he'd ever said to her. Taj picked up her hand and began to massage its underside with his thumb. Each stroke felt like a sexual telegram to all points south. She secretly thrilled at the prospect that maybe now they could make up with a proper ass-twisting sexathon.

"You must think I'm such a Pol Pot, shipping you off to LA, telling you to do this video diary."

"No—"

"It's only because I think you have so much potential. You know, next year, I bet *you'll* be the one showing here."

"But I haven't done anything!"

"I said you have a lot of potential," Taj continued, "not a lot of accomplishments. That's why the video diary is so important." To tell the truth, the idea of making a video diary only made Anna feel tired, but for Taj's sake she nodded with heartfelt affirmation.

"I know. I've been lazy."

"You're not lazy. You know what your real problem is?"

She shook her head. "That I'm not Simone?" She hadn't meant to say it, but there it was. And why not? Why not mix things up with a little honesty? Surely they both knew that men like Taj never looked at a woman like Anna the way they looked at someone like Simone. Or that girl at the carnival. They never did weird little dances in hallways to make her laugh or ran off to change their shirts just to ensure her approval. But men like Taj also didn't sit around massaging the inside of her hand either, and right now Taj was doing just that. So how long could she go on pretending it was OK for him to openly lust for other women right in front of her? Regardless of whether their relationship could be classified as "complicated" or "vague" it was still, undeniably, *something*. Wasn't it?

"Exactly," Taj said, and Anna looked up at him, surprised. But from his expression it was clear he'd misunderstood. "No one knows who the fuck you are, Anna. Fame, that's what you need. Not a lot—I'm not saying get grubby here—but even a little would do wonders for your self-esteem."

"I don't know—" Anna began, but Taj cut her off again.

"Take your relationship with your mom. A couple newspaper clippings, a little item in your college alumni mag? She'll forget all about that stuff she's always harping on BAM! like *that*." Taj let go of her hand and snapped his fingers. Anna laughed.

"I'm serious," he said. "All you have to do is hop on the fame bus to happiness."

"Could I just maybe take a fame scooter to mild satisfaction?"

Now it was Taj's turn to laugh and Anna saw her opening. She picked up his hand again. This was it, she realized. The part in the rom-com when the sunny alt-nineties music is cued—something by Matthew Sweet or the Lemonheads that says it's OK to be unlovable but also be loved—and the undernourished antiheroes the audience has been rooting for all along fall into each other. She leaned hard against him, signaling that what was on offer here was the entirety of her and not just this one hand. But he merely leaned in the same direction, as though they were two trees bent by the same unseen wind. For a long moment they stayed that way, looking for all the world like twin forward slashes in a URL. Then he gave her hand a pat meant to convey *I am definitely not going to fuck you* and rose from the bed.

"Tape something for your diary by dinner, promise?"

"Promise," Anna exhaled.

"Cool. I'll meet you downstairs at six."

This time when he shut the door behind him, he didn't come back. Anna slumped against the pillows and looked at the clock again: it had been almost thirty-seven hours since she last checked her e-mail.

22

Anna sat down in a chair in front of the AVCCAM and the issue of what to do with that flab of fat that disappears when you stand instantly manifested itself. She stared at the blinking red light, feeling the same way she did when staring at the (1) in her in-box and waiting for it to change to (2). It's not like she was Simone, engineering her life so as to maximize nudity and scandal. What was there to say, really? But if she didn't say something, she wouldn't even be able to tell Taj she'd tried. *I tried.* That could be her gravestone epitaph.

"I don't know what to say," she said to the AVCCAM, thinking only of her stomach, its folds. Then an idea came to her. This was supposed to be a diary about her Internet addiction, after all.

"Tiny bubbles of discontent surround me," she said, "because I'm as lonely as a shark in the deep blue ocean."

But the words just hung awkwardly in the air and nothing new suggested itself. Thinking of Simone again, she decided to take her shirt off to see if that might help. Going topless didn't seem to help at all. After floundering for another hopeless minute or two, she went over to the camera to review the footage, then set the camera back down, disgusted. Hadn't she and Taj decided they didn't believe in titillation without the plus? Now look at her: only six minutes into her diary and she was already taking the easy way out, choosing boobs over content. Time for a break, she decided. She flopped on the bed and picked up the remote control. Did watching TV violate the terms of her parole? *Soon this question of what does and does not constitute the Internet would be moot*, Anna thought. *Soon everything will be one endless continuum: airwaves, brainwaves, microwaves.*

She clicked listlessly through the channels—a curling match, C-SPAN, the closed-circuit ravings of some imam—and settled on a laugh-track sitcom. For fifteen minutes, she watched the actors lurch to and fro, displaying an almost preternatural lack of humor. She thought of Simone and imagined replacing the soundtrack's bursts of stale laughter with bouts of hysterical weeping or angry catcalls. Imagined changing everyone's face to an ominous black dot. She had to stop thinking about Simone. She had to stop lying here. The day was slipping away from her.

Outside! She would go outside, offer her starved neuroreceptors some much-needed vitamin D, carpe her diem. She grabbed the camera, pressed it to her eye, and filmed her awkward, camera-encumbered egress, her procession down the piano-wide hall, the trip down the elevator, none of it interesting. She breezed through the lobby, past the concierge and the cluster of cold-eyed trendocrati perched on the uncomfortable furniture, stopping only when another of those horrible little plaques caught her eye. This one was by the front door. Anna zoomed in.

There's really only one not-so-fine line. Everyone is so proud of their own insignificant little boundaries. Scrupulously they vow, *I would never do that!* And perhaps they wouldn't. More likely, they'll never have to. Anyway, that's them, that's fine.

—JOHN O'BRIEN (1960–1994)

Then it was outside onto the still-wet sidewalk, where a hipster was smoking a cigar on the curb, just like a cartoon hipster. The rain had ended but the sky was still luminous and gray. She turned right, away from Simone's gallery, and began to walk. In

Brooklyn it was possible to feel nostalgic for six months ago—the deli-turned-fetish-shoe-store, the shuttered gallery, the dog run paved over to make way for a bocce court—she could tell this was the same kind of place. A landscape of permanent transition. Suddenly she felt herself strangely at home. At the stop sign at the end of the block someone had stenciled *dithering* under the word *stop*. Not dithering, she turned boldly left, panning over the cracked sidewalk, planets of crushed black gum, a starburst of ambitious crabgrass. She remembered that she was forgetting to speak. But what to say when her only thoughts were of herself and Taj? Taj and Simone? Taj and Taj? She forced herself to concentrate, to cut through the static of the day's events and isolate the brutal, PowerPoint essentials of what it was that she was feeling, as though commanded to do so by Chad Brohaurt himself. She had to admit: a cold tapeworm of doubt was winding its way through her gut. She was afraid of where this whole thing with Taj was going:

- Emotionally
- Creatively
- Financially

She squatted down to document a dead pigeon on the sidewalk. Was her fatal flaw really a fame deficit, as Taj had suggested? Somehow she thought not. Maybe her fatal flaw was that she started things the wrong way. In such a way that made them unlikely to continue. Or was it that she gave too much, like the fortune-teller had said, leaving nothing to the imagination? Maybe this was what made women like Simone so attractive to Taj, and men like Taj so attractive to her: this quality of unknowability. But how to make herself unknowable? Mysterious? Elusive? The answer was itself elusive. She could find someone to teach her how to blog, but who would teach her to be less knowable? Especially with memories of their ATM tussle pinging her nipples erect every other second? The physical hunger alone was enough to make Anna lay everything out on the table: her bank statements, her Pap smear results, her Gmail password. She suddenly regretted not bringing that *Fatal Flaw* book along with her. Maybe she could hire Lab Coat's expensive consulting firm to anonymously poll Taj, see if she could confirm her hypothesis about her lack of elusiveness?

But for now she continued down the street, filming, the breeze warmed by the occasional gust of exhaust. Everywhere she looked, Anna saw metaphors. A pool floatie in a moss-limed pool. She was a pool floatie. Floating on what? A pool of metaphors. Skaters falling off their skateboards in an endless loop. An umbrella, broken and abandoned in the gutter. She glanced inside a café, each table occupied by a solitary coffee drinker. They looked like little islands of loneliness in a greater archipelago of sorrow and self-doubt. Then life began pulling her back inside. The promise of food, Taj, rest. Anna went back to her room at the hotel. She picked up the phone to call Leslie or Brandon, only to realize she didn't know anyone's cell phone number by heart, and decided to flush away the day's toxicity with a little self-makeover instead. She tweezed her eyebrows and gave herself a rice-bamboo derm-abrasion facial. That done, she carefully applied a set of Crest White Strips to her crooked incisors and lay down on the bed-spread to rest.

At 5:30 she went down to the mostly empty hotel bar, where happy hour was under way. Taking a seat at the bar, she ordered an optimistic Bloody and looked around. Throughout the room, hipsters were slumped singly or in pairs over their drinks, prod-ding unappetizing appetizers. An Elliott Smith song was playing—the jaunty sound of suicide—but not loud enough to mask the death rattles of caipirinhas. In all honestly, it looked more like sad hour to her.

"Anyone sitting here?"

Anna turned around to find the cartoon hipster she'd seen smoking a cigar outside earlier hovering by the seat next to hers. She moved her purse and he sat down.

"You must be Fucked," he said, nonchalant. "I'm Tim."

"*What?*" She had taken exactly one suck of her Bloody—she was hardly even buzzed.

"Fucked? You know, the fest? Sorry, I saw you here earlier with Zero and Simone and just assumed—"

"Oh, right. *The fest*," Anna said, recovering. "Ha."

"It's weird to see Zero at Gilman's fest, you know, after all that stuff," he said, motioning for the barkeep. "Especially so chummy with Simone. Did you see her new piece? I heard she attached a microphone to a speculum."

This was *Gilman's* festival?

"So what's their deal, anyways?" Tim continued, sotto voce. "I mean, Zero and Simone."

"You tell me," Anna said. Thinking fast, she offered a half-truth. "We just met yesterday."

"Fucked threw you together, huh?" He chuckled. "The fest has a crazy way of doing that. Last year I ended up at karaoke with Laurel Nakadate."

Anna nodded as if she knew who that was and for the next half-hour Tim filled her in, starting with the Herzog seminar that reunited Simone and Gilman after the "James Franco" affair (it turned out the world of po-mo, mumblecorish, DIY art film involved the same twelve people traveling the same Möbius strip of festivals, fairs, and workshops) and the now-famous tweet—purchased for a record sum by an undisclosed Middle Eastern buyer—heralding the birth of Nowism. There was the fertile period of manic productivity, followed by the fallow season of personal recrimination and scandal. Zero loved Simone, loved her to the point of self-harm, but Simone loved Gilman, whose tongue was firmly adhered to a roulette wheel of Hollywood starlets. A great toing-and-froing ensued. Simone fled the country. Zero followed her around the globe. Gilman didn't give a shit; by then he'd discovered Buddha and blow. Zero zeroed in on Simone in Berlin, where for a few months she alternately tolerated and indulged him before leaving him for good—for Marina Abramović, according to some blogs. Anna listened and ate the complimentary nuts until there was nothing but salt left in the bowl. The bar was already filling up with a different kind of crowd. But just as she thought Tim was done, he pulled out his iPhone and began diddling it.

"The reason I can't believe he's here, though, is this. Have you seen this?" He handed her the phone. She glanced at the screen and shook her head. It was a YouTube video called *From Zero to Sixty in Less Than Two Minutes*, by P. Gildaddy.

"Gilman premiered it at the first Fucked Fest." Tim chuckled. "Rumor is he stole Zero's Moleskine diary—though he swears Zero gave it to him—and had some homeless guy narrate it. Check it out. It's hella wicked."

The homeless man did look "hella wicked." Cinematically toothless and wild of hair, his skin tanned and windburned to a luggage-like consistency, he held the Moleskine far away from his face, hinting at a tragic lack of prescription lenses, and began to read in a cracked voice.

"'Acceptance from Yale Art came today. I let Simone burn it, but not before pissing on it first.'

"'Sometimes I just feel powerful. POWERFUL! Like *Rarrrr-www*, superhero-roar powerful. Why can't a person feel powerful?'

"'I've decided I'm only going to date hot girls. There's no point in wasting life on the non-hot.'

"'Idea: calculate the Gini coefficient of inequality for the art world, comparing it to Brazil, Africa, other third world countries. *Fucking brill*. Marry economics background with art, Gilman says people love that shit. Simone says, especially when you're brown. (Or, better: the Gini coefficient of jealousy?)'"

The bum was skipping around. Flipping pages. Pausing to let out the occasional tubercular cough. Many of the entries were appallingly egomaniacal, others, like "standing serenely in a sea of wooden swords," simply made no sense. All of it sounded grotesque coming from the vagrant's mouth even though Anna had to admit he was a surprisingly good reader. For a second she wondered if this was another of Gilman's tricks and the beggar was really an Oberlin grad. But she was jolted out of these thoughts by a familiar phrase.

"'Things are getting blurry,'" the hobo read, scratching the back of his neck. "'Nothing ever feels right when it's supposed to.'" *Things are getting blurry.* Hadn't it been Brie who'd said that? Could she have been quoting Taj? Or was "blurry" just the way people felt now, Anna wondered.

"'People shouldn't ask, What happened? A better question, What didn't happen?'

"'Gilman, Simone, I feel like they're on some definite road and I'm just manning the tollbooth.'"

The bum flipped to the last page. "'I'm a comer. Got to remember that. The Young Turk. Keep telling yourself. Rising star, rising star.'" The homeless man stared straight at the camera as he'd obviously been instructed to do. Then he began to laugh—a wet, horseradishy, ugly sound Anna wished would stop as soon as it started—before closing the book.

"'Fuck you, world,'" he snorted. "'I'm a fucking comer.'"

The movie had ended but Anna kept staring at the screen.

"So what's your thing?" Tim was asking her, plucking the phone from her limp hand. "Film? Performance?"

"I'm offline," Anna murmured, her thoughts still faraway. Spotting Taj across the room, she slipped off her stool.

"Interesting." Tim nodded.

She began to thread her way through the crowd. *Poor Taj!* Finally, it was all starting to make sense: Gilman had fucked him. Fucked him at his own fest, no less. Simone had never loved him.

Both had surpassed him. *Café Schadenfreude, indeed.* Tears actually sprang to her eyes at the humanity of it. And so now she knew what it was—aside from their dual interest in China—that she and Taj had in common: they were *real people.* People who tried things and failed. People who occasionally changed their minds and, OK, names and personas, to forge new and uncharted paths. Brave people who took that plunge, even when their Life Maps ended up full of winding roads that didn't lead to any strategic destination. People whose maps were still sketched on napkins, even. Vulnerable to gusts of opportunism, insecurity, lust, and sheer boredom.

"You look different," Taj said.

Anna had arrived at the hostess station, eyes moist with sympathy.

"I did my eyebrows."

"They look nice."

"Thank you," Anna said. The compliment spread through her like a gulp of Sriracha. They slid into a booth. "How was your day?"

"Productive," Taj said with unexpected gusto. "How about you? How was your shoot?"

"Good," Anna said, still trying to shake off the image of the homeless man, the grotesque echo of his laugh. "I walked around a lot."

"Get anything good?"

"Tons of interesting stuff." Not exactly true, but Brandon had told her there were plug-ins for everything in Final Cut Pro. Even interestingness.

"Awesome," Taj said.

Normally, Anna suspected she radiated a vibe of quiet desperation. But with the discomfiting disclosures mounting on Taj's side of the ledger, she found herself experiencing an unfamiliar surge of confidence. Everything was going to turn around for them tonight, she could feel it.

"And how are you feeling, you know, about the Internet? It's been like two days."

In truth, the Internet, its absence, ached like a phantom limb. Unable to play her usual games of call-and-response with Google, she didn't feel saved at all. She felt stranded. Stranded on a Luddite island here in the heart of Silver Lake. But before she could come up with a suitable lie, Taj pulled up a butt cheek and took out his cell phone.

"Shit, I'm buzzing," he said. Then, to the phone, "Hello? What? No." He held the phone back from his ear and stared at it for a second. "Jesus, I've had it off all day, I was—OK, no problem. Where? In ten." Just as quickly, he hung up and stood.

"Simone," he said to Anna. "We swapped phones at lunch by accident. This is hers. I'm gonna run and meet her at the gallery. Order something for me."

"When will you be back?"

"Soon."

"But—"

"How about just bring it upstairs?" Taj said, giving her a meaningful look that made her pulse quicken.

"I'm so glad you said that, Taj, because I want to talk tonight." She grabbed his hand. She would never blame him for wanting to be loved. "*Really* talk."

"I do, too." He smiled. Then he picked up his bag and was gone.

Even though it wasn't on the menu, Anna requested a custom omelette: three eggs, leeks, goat cheese, hollandaise sauce, sprigs of cilantro—the works. The very thing Taj had wanted that morning before Simone surprised them, and the kitchen miraculously obliged. She had them box it up and took it upstairs. And because she did not yet know Taj was never coming back, she turned the heat up to 78 degrees and changed into a negligee she'd bought on sale at Agent Provocateur three years ago but had never found an occasion to wear. She lit the fancy-looking scented candle on the nightstand labeled "Moonlit Pearls," which smelled like a

Christmas-tree air freshener, arranged all the lubes and travel-size bottles of massage oil that she'd brought with her in order of size, then put the Japanese condoms within easy reaching distance.

An hour passed without Taj, then another. She kept the cell phone he'd given her on the pillow next to her head as she surfed the channels. It grew late. She watched infotainers interview we-lebrities on channels she didn't know existed, until soon even these negligible entertainments melted into static and test patterns. At one point there was a sound in the hall. A fumbling followed by a hopeful *floosh!* and Anna flew to the door. But instead of Taj, she found only a dumb flyer about some party in the lobby tomorrow. It was past three a.m. when she finally fell asleep clutching a bottle of Kama Sutra Intensifying Gel in one hand as though it were some kind of talisman.

She woke up the next morning in her lingerie, the room too warm, to the soundtrack of a morning talk-show host getting exercised over massive loss of life in some forgotten glove compartment of the globe. Taj's side of the bed remained untouched; the antique cell phone lay next to her head. She checked it for messages. Finding none, she tried calling Taj for the hundredth time. Her call went straight to voice mail. She rolled over onto his pillow, inhaling the smell of his stale spit while contemplating the door. What would she say if he were to walk through it right now? What was the etiquette for being abandoned in a hotel in Los Angeles?

She decided to order breakfast in. Twenty minutes later, pancakes, home fries, sliced fruit, a reassuring mug of coffee arrived nicely arranged on a tray outside her door. She brought the tray in and settled into an uncomfortable Lucite chair. She took a sip of coffee, so hot that it burned her tongue. The metanarrative was already taking shape, the way in which this latest failure both informed and reflected her prior failures. It wasn't too late to turn this trip into a vacation, Anna told herself, though in truth all she wanted was a vacation from herself. To crawl into the gap between bed and wall and assume the form of an orphaned sock or dull penny.

An almost physical sense of pain flashed through her as she considered what Leslie would think if she could see her now, followed by the thought, *Well, what* would *Leslie do?* She wouldn't just sit here wedged into this unholy chair, feeling sorry for herself. She would walk down to Simone's gallery to confront Taj, sort out the tedious business of the money he owed her, and put herself on a plane back to New York. When she'd first lost her job, her mother had given her a book: *Chicken Soup for the Unemployed Soul*. And Leslie had quite memorably mocked it. "Fuck chicken soup, Anna," she'd said. "What you need is *Viagra for the Unemployed Soul*. Stop wallowing and remember: the more decisions you make, the more your life is your own."

Anna finished eating and got dressed. Leslie was right. Even though much had been lost, she could still decide to salvage her dignity. *Dignity.* The word made Anna wince as she considered Taj's untouched omelette in the minifridge, the pitiful arrangement of lubricants still sitting on the night table. She was out of the chair and out the door, propelling herself down the hall to the freight elevator, where an OUT OF SERVICE sign was posted. She wound her way through the hallways until she found a distant stairwell. The heavy fire door at the bottom of the stairs warned ALARM WILL SOUND IF OPENED, but what choice did she have? She had to find Taj and put an end to this, even though the thought of facing a single day without the promise of his calls and mysterious directives induced a buzzing panic. Bracing herself, she threw a shoulder against the metal bar and was instantly engulfed in sound. Not a fire alarm, but rather ear-searing indie rock and the roar of a crowd shouting to be heard above it. The place was so humid, it felt like stepping inside someone's mouth.

A woman with a half-shorn head suddenly appeared at Anna's elbow.

"Everyone gets a bunny!" she shouted, thrusting a bunny at her.

"Gratis!" yelled another man with a handlebar mustache, shoving a flute of prosecco into her free hand.

The bunny thrummed against Anna's chest. Reluctantly, she began to move. The room seemed to be populated entirely by refugees from Brie's kickball team. Girls who sold arm warmers made from kneesocks on Etsy, guys who developed apps that controlled toy keyboards remotely, amateur taxidermists with iceboxes full of freeze-dried pets. Everywhere she looked, beautiful people were holding drinks and clutching bunnies, conducting conversations in air quotes, all looking past one another as they talked, scanning the crowd for other people to talk to.

What kind of gathering was this? And why were they all drinking at eleven on a Wednesday morning? Then she saw something that emptied her head of all these questions—across the room, glowing like the sword of Excalibur: the giant Apple monitor. Now she began making her way deliberately through the crowd, emptying her flute of prosecco without thinking, only to have another magically appear in her hand. A man to her right was shouting "Why vinyl?" while poking a similar-looking man in the chest. "Because vinyl gets you laid." It was so crowded Anna felt as though she were running a marathon in warm Jell-O but kept moving, reassuring the bunny that it was going to be OK notwithstanding the Odd Future song pulsating the walls, the guy on the sofa holding a joystick not apparently connected to anything, the girl yelling "Eeeee!" and dumping an entire bottle of Ketel One into a punch bowl. *These people, deep inside, they are normal*, she told the bunny, *just like you and me. They are only acting this way because* . . . well, for example, the girl with the jewfro loudly discussing the recent placement of her IUD and its future implications for butt sex was not simply a tasteless and scary person. No! She was a person with diverse skills and personal attributes. Someone with pets and hobbies—then suddenly Anna's way was blocked by a woman laughing, head thrown so far back it looked as though she were about to dip into camel pose. For a second Anna forgot all about Taj and her dignity; she couldn't help wishing that she were that drunk and that happy.

"Do you have any questions?" a woman with a clipboard was asking. It took Anna a moment to realize that she was talking to her.

"Excuse me?" the woman repeated loudly, pen poised. "Any questions?"

"*Any* question?" Anna repeated. The woman nodded. "OK, what's my fatal flaw?" she yelled. The bunny's nose was a wet exclamation mark against her neck. Her head was buzzing.

"What?" said the woman, shaking her head.

"My fatal flaw?" Anna yelled, louder this time. But the woman only laughed and disappeared into the crowd with her clipboard, leaving Anna no choice but to keep going. When she arrived at the other end of the room, she was relieved to find the computer carrel miraculously unoccupied. As she slid into place the room seemed to right itself, the clamor of the crowd retreating to some interior conch shell.

"Silver Lake," she typed, "Fucked Fest."

Immediately, up swam a top result for "F'd Fest."

As Anna waited for the flash intro to load, she reflexively opened two new tabs for Gmail and Facebook. Her hopes lifted as they always did when typing in her password, only to be crushed almost immediately by the poverty of her in-box, the paucity of shout-outs on Facebook. No irksome platitudes from Leslie? Not even a desultory weight-loss tip from her mother? She had already been gone for two days. Didn't anyone even miss her? The bunny was wriggling assertively against Anna's chest.

She clicked back to the festival home page, and began to scan the schedule. Strangely she could find no mention of either Taj or Zero as she moused her way down through the list of panelists and participants. When she reached the bottom of the page, her eye drifted over to the "About Us" sidebar: "When Paul Gilman's now legendary 3-minute masterpiece, *Minority Queers, Majority Rears*, failed to get into Sundance, he said to himself, 'That's fucked.' Welcome, kids, to F'd Fest."

Then there was a hand on her shoulder and she flushed with sudden shame. Taj! He had caught her in the act, a bulimic binge-ing at a digital buffet. But wait, why should she be the one to cower—she, of the custom omelette!—when he was the one who had run off with another woman, leaving her to sleep alone among a pharmacy's worth of unopened lubricants?

"Where's Taj?" came a familiar voice. Anna looked up from the screen to find not Taj but Lauren, resplendent in a black Brooklyn Industries sweatshirt with her hair pulled back from her flawless face. Since that day at the carnival, Anna had carefully nurtured her dislike of Lauren, letting it flower into something more malevolent. All the while, she couldn't help but acknowl-edge to herself that the only basis for this animus was Lauren's perceived dislike of her. Turning to address her now, she found it hard to affect the proper hauteur while holding a bunny.

"What are you doing here?" she managed.

"He was supposed to be at my screening last night," Lauren continued, ignoring her. "Where is he?"

Only now did Anna remember; that day on the roof, Taj had mentioned that Lauren had a short in the festival, hadn't he?

"I called his phone yesterday and some woman answered."

"That was Simone—"

"He's with Simone?" Lauren said. Something in her face collapsed.

"No," Anna said, a hint of sedition in her voice. "He's with *me*."

Lauren stared at her, clearly making some internal calculation. When she spoke again, it was in a clear and authoritative voice.

"And he's *my* husband," Lauren said, "so what the fuck is he doing with her?"

For a second Anna could hear nothing save for a loud buzzing in her ears. Then the bungee cords around her heart loosened and she plunged.

"Th-that's not possible."

"We're together. We're married."

"He came here with me."

"I know that."

"We . . . we have a thing."

"There's a name for that thing," Lauren said coldly. "It's called going for the Gugg."

Husband. Husband. Husband. The word was a taser to the brain. She had just gotten used to this idea of Simone, and now here was Lauren, *Taj's wife*. Moreover, Lauren, *Taj's wife*, somehow knew they were here together? Knew, or so it seemed, they had slept together? Anna had initially feared their tryst might have been a pity fuck. Now, if Lauren was to be believed, it was actually a Gugg fuck. But what did fucking her have to do with the Gugg? It's not like they gave Guggs for that. At least not so far as Anna knew.

"Where are they?" said Lauren.

"I don't know," Anna admitted. "He went to meet her last night and never came back. When's his screening?"

"What screening?" Lauren snapped. "He isn't screening."

"He told Simone he was showing at the festival."

"Not possible," said Lauren, dismissive. "It's *Gilman's* fest." Lauren spoke as though Taj's whole history with Gilman was a threadbare doormat laid at the foot of the Internet.

"He did, though," Anna pressed. "He applied earlier but he didn't get in. Then the other night he got a message from someone at the last minute saying his film had been accepted."

Anna watched the realizations crest upon Lauren's face in waves.

"What the fuck . . ." Lauren trailed off. Her eyes dropped to the monitor, where the F'd Fest website was still quivering.

Suddenly she shunted Anna out of the way and began scrolling furiously. Anna could only sit there mute, feeling as though all her blood had just been replaced with antifreeze. The bunny tried to squirm out of her hands, but she was drunk and miserable and didn't want to put the bunny down even though this was clearly what the bunny wanted.

Lauren straightened up, her eyes zooming in on something. "Shit," she said, rising. "It's today and it's starting soon."

Without waiting for a response, she headed for the door. Anna followed, doing her best to squeeze through the Lauren-size channel left in her wake. When they reached the front entrance, a man wearing a skirt plucked the bunny from her hands, placing it in a basket with all the other bunnies. Anna followed Lauren out to the curb in front of the hotel, where a cab was always waiting. She gave the cabbie an address, then turned toward the window and immediately began chewing all the flesh from her fingers. A signal, Anna assumed, that she did not want to talk. Anna turned toward her own window. She missed the bunny, the warm throb of life against her collarbone.

The car began to move, streets and buildings sliding away from them. The sun was out today, glazing everything with an unnatural Technicolor glow. Palm trees hung over Sunset Boulevard like miniature explosions. Nothing seemed real anymore, least of all her own life. She remembered the man with the ruined paper flowers running down the street yesterday and wondered if maybe all of Echo Lake was just an elaborate stage set. Cardboard streetlamps and manhole covers and fire hydrants. Papier-mâché traffic signals swinging, piñata-like, from paper masts. All waiting for one big storm to wash them away. Was that why her shoes made no sound on the steps leading up to the theater? All of a sudden, a too-solid doorknob was in her hand.

Whoever had been checking wristbands had evidently left their post. They passed easily through the double doors and into a chamber aromatic with designer soaps and spendy perfumes.

These were the people from the bunny party, plus twenty years. A great mass of Urban Outfitterites who'd been herded into J. Crewian pastures. Anna remained glued to the doorframe, watching them move purposefully through the room—meeting, greeting, consolidating their positions on various grids of power. *It's* them, Anna thought. The self-appointed gatekeepers. The jumped-up arrivistes. Visigoths who had sacked their fatal flaws like Rome, emerged flawless. You could stick a fork in them, they were done. At least, that's how they looked to Anna. But what the hell did she know? These were obviously not her people.

Anna watched Lauren dart forward into the crowd. A second later, Taj emerged from the other side of the room. Seeing Anna by the door, he threw an arm in her direction. He'd clearly just been talking with the man standing next to him, but they stopped talking as they watched Anna approach.

"Anna! I was just telling Jaime about you," Taj said. "Jaime works for *New York* magazine." Jaime nodded to confirm this was true.

"Taj," Anna said, not giving a shit about Jaime, "you're *married*."

"Yes, I know." Taj's laugh was directed first at Jaime, then at Anna. And he sounded so natural as he said this, so unguarded and free of guile, that Anna couldn't help but doubt herself all over again. Had Taj already told her and she'd somehow managed to forget? Or was the fact of their ringless union so obvious to everyone that no one condescended to mention it to her? Taj placed a hand on the small of her back, guiding her forward. His touch sent an inadvertent current through her, and out of this regrettable wave of moisture tumbled a new thought: *What if it's all somehow OK?* Her, Taj, Lauren, Simone. Theoretically, she knew such things existed. There were even websites. She'd heard of them: AffairsClub, MarriedDateLink, AdultFriendFinder, GetItOn.com. What if the massive misunderstanding had been on her end alone and the skull on Taj's chest was some universal bat signal employed by swingers the world over? A signal she'd failed to recognize? She clung to the driftwood of this improbable notion as they floated down the aisle together. Every few seconds Taj would stop, accepting hellos and congratulations with a quick bow of the head, like garlands. The lights had begun to dim in stages. There was an anticipatory murmur throughout the room, a great holstering and unholstering of cell phones being set to vibrate. As they neared the front row, Taj leaned down, speaking quietly into her ear so that only Anna could hear.

"I'll explain everything," he said.

"But when?" *There's no time*, Anna thought, *and so many people.*

"Now." Taj's hand slipped from her back and Anna looked around to find that he was no longer behind her. She swayed woozily. The last of the lights winked off and she was alone in the aisle, the apparent loser in a spontaneous game of musical chairs. The screen went white. Around the room designer glasses glinted as everyone turned eagerly toward the front. A title card shimmied to the surface.

The Society for Advancement of Poetry presents . . .

There it was, Taj's work-around. He'd used SAP as his Trojan horse, wrapped himself in the sad hopes of poets yearning to be tweeted. The words faded but the big, bright square remained. She felt uncomfortable spotlit here in the aisle, the white light gilding her upturned face, but stood rooted to the carpet, spellbound along with everyone else. Who would be the first to appear, she wondered. Mr. Leung and his implausible lottery win? Lamba and Tweety? Or some other dream-seeker that Anna hadn't met? But anticipation quickly turned to dread as her own face—big, dumb, hopeful—filled the screen. She was nodding to a tinny voice proclaiming, ". . . anything could be a camera. You know, *this* could be a camera. Or this." Cut to Anna with her glittering green glasses, pleasuring herself on Chat Roulette as a two-by-two-inch bald head looked on with malevolent lust. Anna dancing in slow motion in a Lynchian music video backed by the dissonant samba players, lurid in her red unisuit. Anna making out with Taj—a shadowy figure viewed only from the back—on the roof, under the Tilt-A-Whirl, in the ATM. How was it possible? Who had filmed this? *How?* She stood rooted to the red tongue of carpet, forgetting and then remembering where she was, what was happening, the motor of consciousness refusing to catch. Then a soundless image, blurred to the point of being Impressionistic, of Taj and Anna bobbing across the pool together shot from below. Her voice dubbed in, saying, "Tiny bubbles of discontent surround me, because I'm as lonely as a shark in the ocean." And she remembered, *the tiny black box*. That thing at the bottom of the pool.

The vignettes were lashed together with silent interstitials: Anna wandering Frodo-like though the darkening carnival. Fruit dying in a bowl. The abandoned pool floatie. Kids falling off skateboards and getting up and falling off and getting up. The inner folds of the fortune-teller's wrinkles. Footage Taj must have snagged, last-minute, from the memory card in her camera. Snippets of decontextualized conversations and bits of text triggered firecrackers of memory:

"Where am I supposed to look?"

Stranger: would like to have fun too?

"Yeah, yeah, right there . . ."

"I can tell you're a good person, and it's not a good time for you."

Stranger: you have a pretty smile

"But it makes you so happy!"

You: Thanks

There was Anna staring out the window of the van, melancholy, as the trashy exurban landscape unspooled and loud eighties music played. Her AVCCAM trembling over the close-up of the John O'Brien quote: "Everyone is so proud of their own insignificant little boundaries. Scrupulously they vow, *I would never do that!*"

Only she would, of course. She did. She had. Her dream *had* come true: real life had turned into Gmail. Only the whole world was blind cc'd on her message to Taj, the dream that started out so full of romance and promise. Now there was no undoing it. No command-Z. She could not shut it down and she could not turn away; she was on-screen, sitting on a chair and blinking at the camera. She was pulling her shirt off and telling herself she didn't know what to say. Then Anna did something she didn't remember—she took a paper bag and pulled it over her head. An homage, it seemed, to *Age of Consent*.

As the full weight of what had happened—what continued to happen—came raining down on her, the deciders were already deciding, rising to their feet in a standing O. Somewhere in the front row, Taj rose, too, the skull on his chest shining hard. Anna tore her eyes away from the hideous doppelganger on-screen. She volte-faced, almost colliding with Jaime. He smiled an almost loving smile and raised his camera. The flash showered her like a bucket of bleach, scouring her eyes, her skin. She threw an arm up over her face, too late. The onlookers lining the aisle had turned to see what was happening. A wave of surprise and recognition rippled through the crowd. One by one, they raised their cell phones like flutes of champagne, looking not at her, but at their screens. At the hundreds of miniature Annas running away, up the aisle, out of the frame.

He was the last person she saw before racing from the room, standing inconspicuously at the back. He did not turn at her approach. His face was definitely older, pouchier. He had grown a thick beard, probably to distract from the balding pate. Still, it was undeniably *him*. And as Paul Gilman rose to his feet, as he brought his hands together in rapturous applause, never taking his eyes off the other Anna, the one on-screen, she could see that there were tears streaming down his face.

23

Bouvet is a glacier-covered speck of land of nineteen square miles that lies halfway between Cape Town and Queen Maud Land in the South Atlantic Ocean. It is the most remote island on Earth. In Norwegian its name is Bouvetøya, the little slash through the second *o* emphasizing its stark remove, the nullification of life itself. Brandon had sent Anna the link to Bouvet's Wikipedia page, subject line, "You could always move here . . ." And even though Anna didn't trust Brandon, sensed he saw a movie in all this, she clicked on it anyway. Of course she clicked on it. "The center of the island is an ice-filled crater of an inactive volcano," Anna read. "Bouvet Island has no ports or harbors and is therefore difficult to approach. The easiest way to access the island is with a helicopter from a ship. In 1964, an abandoned lifeboat was discovered there although its origin has never been determined . . ." Viewed from above, the island looked like an ad for Swarovski crystal: all pincushions of ice. There was no telephone service on Bouvet, no postal distribution or access to the Internet. The only evidence of human life was an unmanned weather station.

Anna made a photo of Bouvet Island her screensaver.

She was sitting in front of her laptop at the kitchen table surrounded by the molted skins of microwaved burritos. There were a few other things going on in the room—the window had developed an annoying rattle every time the wind blew, the plant on the table might have died but looked so realistically embalmed she was loath to remove it—yet her attention remained on the screen, where six tabs were opened to sites hosting what she'd come to think of as *her* video, *The Ballad of Anna K.* YouTube, *New York* magazine, *Gawker*, *The Observer*, *Vice*, and, of course, *Squeee!*, which she was now perusing.

When she first got home, she hadn't been able to so much as open a browser. It felt as though she'd been exiled from the one country she'd ever called home. But where else could she go? So she'd asked Brie to google *The Ballad of Anna K.* for her while she sat across the table repeating, "Is it bad? Tell me it isn't bad . . ."

"Not *too* bad," Brie said. And even though Anna could hear the lie in her voice, she still felt grateful.

Of course, nothing could prepare her for the brutality of the comments section. The first time she saw herself referred to as a "fat cunt" the rush of blood was so intense it blocked out all sound. The words beat a timpani in her head. *Fat. Cunt. Fat. Cunt.* She'd shut down the computer and retreated to the couch, where she let the horror of Taj's betrayal grope her brain like a dirty old guy at the back of a bus. A man fitted with an array of "nanny" cams procured from the Sharper Image catalog and the back pages of spy magazines—cameras hidden in pens and key chains, in chunky glasses and no-brand baseball caps, in his very own dick for all she knew—had turned her life into an unwitting reality show. He had enlisted his friends, his wife, *Anna herself* to create a film so brutally intimate that no one could believe she hadn't knowingly taken part in it herself. How does one recover from that? She felt as though she were living through a transitive version of Kafka's *Metamorphosis*, waking up one morning only to discover that Taj was a cockroach. In this, she had Brie's whole-hearted agreement. "Total ego rape," Brie had called it, wrapping Anna in the blue Vellux slanket she'd unironically purchased from a Montel Williams infomercial. "I can't believe he cared more

about a hypothetical goldfish—its hypothetical fucking loneliness—
than he did about you, a real fucking person."

Brie's solidarity came as a surprise, filling Anna with a bottom-
less gratitude. For it was Brie who souped her, Brie who put her to
bed when she arrived back in Sunset Park, scraped raw and ready
for the pot. In fact, Anna knew that if it weren't for Brie she never
would have been ready for the comments section again the next day.

The following morning Anna found the names hurt less.
Two weeks later, they didn't hurt at all. "Attention-seeking fame
whore." "Talentless self-mythologizer." "Wallowing narcissist."
She scrolled through today's epithets with a total absence of feeling. This is what she did now. It was her job. Whenever she left the
computer, she found herself flitting in and out of reality, falling off
little cliffs of memory into deep gorges of self-pity. But so long as
she could sit here, with her tabs open and her search terms saved
on Twitter, following comment threads as they ground down into
ever dustier and more obscure cattle trails, the center would continue to hold.

She finished reading today's *Squeee!* comments and switched
over to *Vice*.

NormanMailerLives
Is anyone bored? I'm really bored. The same sexually explicit, messy, quirk-centeric, diaristic crap smeared on an
Internet cracker. There's no growth here, nothing to learn,
no one transcends anything. I resent sites like Squeee!
publishing this stuff and shoehorning it into our consciousness. You're turning us all into a bunch of voyeurs and
gossips, with one eye pressed up to the hole in the bathroom stall. (As I hit "unsubscribe.")
   CleverURLsSuck
   It's wrong to view the "Ballad of Anna K." as the unfil-
   tered vlog-vomit of a confession junkie. This is a raw

and moving portrayal in the tradition of Mary Gaitskill and Sadie Benning. Long live the anti-ingenue! I cried.

JacquelinHandy

Except, sorry Clever, this has nothing to do with privileging the female gaze. Anna K. says she didn't make this video, which means it has more in common with surveillance footage from your local bodega than Anais Nin.

HeroinHeroine

How do we really know who made what? Whether it's even nonfiction? Why should we believe Anna K. when she says she didn't know? Why should we believe Taj/Zero that this was "found" footage? Maybe it's all just a joke on us.

FuckADuck

The only reason anyone does anything is to get famous, even if they don't know it yet, LOL. Plus, could anyone be so dumb?

NotAHater

Anna was Taj/Zero's collaborator and muse, natch. They were in it together. The manufactured controversy just a PR move. My theory.

SquidNapkin

Simone Weil rip-off.

Masshole

Simone Weil is a Tracey Emin rip-off.

Toasty4Eva

The road to Simone Weil leads through Tracey Emin's vagina.

ASeriousFilmBuff

The only reason anyone cares about Simone is Gilman. That guy so much as blows a fart in your direction and you're the new It Girl.

>> **Toasty4Eva**
>> Nowism = Thenism.
>>> **Burp**
>>> Why is everyone so angry?
> **NotAHater**
> "The Ballad of Anna K." touches on something universal.
> Just the fact that we are all here, talking about it, *feeling*
> something together.
>> **CrazyLikeZelda**
>> Ich bin Anna K.
>>> **LollyCats**
>>> That's retarded.

Obviously NotAHater was Taj, but it didn't matter; he never responded to Anna's entreaties in the comments sections. He existed only on the Internet. Brie had made Anna promise not to call him, to turn back at the threshold of that final humiliation. Of course, Anna went ahead and did it anyway. There was nothing else she could do—she couldn't help it and couldn't stop. She left messages of excruciating specificity about the hotel bill, including the charges she'd incurred for the overpriced nuts he'd taken from the minibar (as though the $1,746.30 she would gain by taking him to small claims court could ever plug the hole in her heart). Meanwhile, she couldn't help replaying the events of the past weeks over and over, trying to isolate the exact moment she doomed herself. But like a VHS tape recorded over too many times, the facts had gone blurry; it was impossible to untangle the narrative from the metanarrative. She even half-managed to convince herself Taj was right; she really *had* known all along she was being filmed, really *was* his collaborator and muse. Especially because the movie itself—she had to admit—wasn't bad. Not the "Michelangelo of nut sack" perhaps, not Paul Gilman, but still, it had its own odd shuffling magic.

Ultimately it didn't make a whit of difference what Anna

thought; *The Ballad of Anna K.* had taken on a life of its own. The consensus was formed in aggregate, gang-pressed through the unsolicited opinions of anonymous thousands. Half-truths morphed into whole untruths, until finally the truth was just abandoned, thrown joyfully in the air and left to dangle from the wires above some anonymous street like a dirty pair of Keds. People would believe what they wanted to believe, felt it was their right.

"It is what it is," FuckADuck wrote, quoting Gilman. A comment that earned ninety-one likes.

She must have fallen asleep at the table. The solar-powered flower was bobbing up and down, which meant it was morning.

"Where's my computer?" Anna said.

She blinked up at Brie sitting across from her, calmly spooning her yogurt, and pain shot through her neck. Wait—Brie was never up this early. Then Anna remembered: Pom had given her the promotion. Getting paid real money probably meant working real hours.

"It's gone," Brie said. "I took it."

"Ha-ha. Not funny."

"No." Brie nodded in agreement. "But we really have to dial down the level of dysfunction around here."

"I *need* my computer." Anna scanned the room for a telltale glint of silver. She could hear the hysteria edging into her voice.

"Mm."

"I *do*," Anna lied. "I'm expecting an important e-mail today." She imagined today's comment threads silently unspooling on a half-dozen sites somewhere far out of reach, reproducing and metastasizing like some malignant tumor. Her throat tightened; the panic was real now.

"Like from your friend? The one who wants to buy my baby?"

Anna blanched. Had Leslie called her? She'd forgotten about that whole thing.

"No," she said, quickly. "A job."

"Oh well." Brie shrugged. "Sucks to be you." And Anna fought the urge to reach across the table and slap her face.

"I'm being serious."

"You *do* realize that no one cares about this shit except online?"

Anna stared at her. What did that even *mean*?

"Yeah," Anna said, "no one except everyone."

Brie stood up and tossed her Fage container in the trash. She had started to show, wore her blouses untucked now. "It's so gross not being able to eat anything but white foods," she sighed. "If I ever see another saltine, I'll kill myself."

"I need my computer back." Like Anna was supposed to give a shit about Brie's morning sickness, her fucking cracker preferences?

"I threw it out, Anna. I threw it in the Gowanus Canal." Brie smiled her maddening smile.

"You didn't—"

"It made a cute little bubbling sound when it went down." She walked over to the door. Anna couldn't let her leave.

"Brie, I mean it—" Anna tried getting to her feet but sank back suddenly into her chair—both legs were asleep.

"Blub, blub, blub," said Brie.

"Brie." Anna began to cry. A fat tear rolled past the corner of her mouth. "Please?" This last word but a husky whisper.

"I have to go, Anna," Brie said, not without sadness. "Bye."

The door clicked quietly shut behind her.

Outside everything looked different, as though she were viewing the world through a cheap-ass Zi8 at full zoom. Too jittery and close, too real and too sad. The clouds hung low over the buildings; it felt like a lid on her brain. Anna walked down Fifty-Sixth Street, wending her way past her former selves, her would-be selves, the occasional real, live Mexican person, conscious of a sense of downward social mobility. How much money did she have left? A few hundred dollars? And that was *after* selling the AVCCAM to Brandon. The plane tickets to LA and hotel fees had nearly cleaned her out. Even the CanadianPharmaPharm people ripped her off; her phentemine had never arrived.

Brandon told her she was crazy not to "use this as an opportunity." An opportunity for what? she'd asked. *FAME! MONEY!* He'd typed back. *1107 comments on Gawker? There are formulas for monetizing shit like that. Views. Comments. Clicks. Eyeballs. You need to brand yourself. Engage with your public. Can I just remind you that your roommate is practically a publicist? Why not get her to do something useful for once in her life?*

But Anna couldn't do it. Couldn't even start the new Twitter account—AnnaBallad—Brandon had suggested. Because it would mean becoming *her*, wouldn't it? Accepting she was now "Anna K.," not Anna Krestler. Slipping out of her skin and taking up permanent residence in this new, shadowy zone, a place full of "friends" who found one another "pinteresting" and occasionally made arrangements to meet up and shoot one another in the face. OK, this was probably just paranoia stemming from those links her mother wouldn't stop sending—more craigslist murders—but it didn't sound like taking the "fame bus to happiness" either.

Still, she realized certain decisions about her life had to be made. Brie was moving out soon. She'd overheard her talking to her parents on the phone. They'd come around, evidently, were helping her buy a place in Bed-Stuy. The news hurt Anna more than she'd ever expected. It was silly to think that she and Brie would share an apartment forever, and yet she had no other plan, did she, than to round out her thirties watching Brie flounder from one internship to another, feeling vaguely superior? But now Brie was going off to have a baby, leaving her alone.

For a second, Anna pictured what that would be like. Her

laptop carefully positioned on the kitchen table's coveted sweet spot, where it could be viewed from couch, sink, or stove, and she, rotating around it like a lonely lighthouse beam. Walking to the refrigerator, glancing back. Touching the mouse pad gently. Scrolling. Moving over to the counter. Checking over her shoulder. Straining to see the parenthetical count next to the word *inbox*. Heating a box of something on high for thirty seconds, but failing to wait thirty seconds before refreshing. Loading. Reloading. Clicking. Breaking away, finally. Down the dark hall and to her bedroom. But only for a moment before drifting back again, remembering something else she forgot to search. That last gnawing thing . . .

No, she couldn't allow that to happen, Anna thought, and she felt another rush of anger toward Brie. Not for hiding her computer—for getting pregnant. For getting a promotion. For buying an apartment. No one should be allowed to do those things unless she was doing them, too, especially not someone a decade younger. Someone from the generation everyone had written off as hopeless, clueless, stuck. She raised a hand to her pounding head and imagined the bad feelings circulating, infecting her chi. Dimly, she recognized the truth—that Brie was only trying to help—and all she needed was for everyone, everything to just *stop* and give her a chance to catch up.

Instead Anna stopped and caught a reflection of herself in the window of a parked car: her hair was still plastered to her forehead from falling asleep on the table, her face puffy and snack-cheese white. She looked exactly the way she felt, disembodied as a jellyfish. She started walking again. Without even realizing where she was heading, she had arrived at the threshold of Lucky Star Nails. She looked through the window at the bank of manicure stations. A woman padded down the aisle like some exotic bird, white tufts of cotton blooming between her painted toes. Sure it was expensive, but according to *Oprah* and the other estro-mags,

wasn't this exactly the kind of pick-me-up Anna deserved? Besides, her "landing strip" probably looked more like the airport
parking lot by now.

Anna went inside and took a seat on the bench by the register
while she waited for Wendi to finish a manicure. Surrounded by the
familiar toxic smells, the soothing whir of the foot dryers, she felt
her pulse begin to slow. Wendi finished with the woman and nodded for Anna to follow her into the back room, a drab vestibule
where two massage tables were separated by a vinyl shower curtain.
Anna took off her pants and lay down on the crinkly paper, feeling,
as always, a bit like deli meat. She pinched the top of her panties
together without being told. The wall facing her was bare save for
a mirror with a few gift-wrapping bows stuck to it, a festive touch
that managed to suck the remaining cheer from the room.

"How are you?" Wendi said, dipping a popsicle stick in a vat
of hot wax. It emerged trailing pink, taffy-like strands. She blew
on it—more a bored exhalation—and, without waiting for Anna's
response, set upon her crotch like an eighth plague. Despite the
pain, Anna found herself telling Wendi everything. Not that Wendi
understood; her English was bad, reserved mostly for berating the
management of Lucky Star Nails, her conception of the Internet
vague. Wendi was afraid Anna was crying because she was tearing
her labia off, but Anna assured her this wasn't true. She was crying
because her life was a total craptastrophy, to use Brie's term.

"You need wax more often." Wendi tsked. "You feel better."

Anna nodded. It was true; she already felt better. Lighter.
Cleaner. Maybe Wendi was right. After all, those women who
waxed regularly—with their pencil skirts, silk blouses, pearl-drop
earrings—women like that never had *her* kinds of problems. A
man like Taj would certainly never make it past the first wall of
their defenses. Perhaps their meticulously groomed faces, nails,
and crotches formed a kind of humiliation-deflecting armor. What
had Brandon said when he sent that stupid movie idea about the
girl with the designer dress? *A mask doesn't hide, instead it reveals*

the true essence, because we are what we pretend to be. Was that the answer? To look more like those women? Like Leslie?

"You want between buttocks, too?" Wendi said, indicating for Anna to flip over onto her stomach.

The thought of her friend sent a current of shame coursing through her. There was no hiding from Leslie; Leslie had a Google alert on her. And yet that's exactly what she'd been doing for weeks now, wasn't it? Hiding from Leslie. From her silence, Anna could only assume Leslie was too horrified to make the first move. She was waiting for Anna to crawl back penitent, the prodigal friend. But how could she face Leslie when even on a good day her powerful mix of good posture and orthodontics threatened to overwhelm her, send her tobogganing straight down a mountain of regret for lives not lived?

Turning her head to the side, she found herself facing another wall, bare save for a framed certificate hanging askew from a single nail. She strained to read the loopy font, before realizing it was Wendi's esthiology certificate from the Aveda Institute. She felt a hot stab as Wendi buttered her left ass cheek, then the reassuring pressure of her firm hand on a strip of gauze and *scrrk!* Anna gasped, but not from the sting. It was the action-reaction simplicity of it that left her starry-eyed. She had been trying so hard to ignore the pain that she'd failed to see the beauty of it. *Waxing*. In a way, it had become the most exotic of things: a job that could be described in a few short, simple words, utterly free of qualification. What do you do for a living? *I remove unwanted hair*.

She mouthed it to herself: *I remove unwanted hair*.

She looked around the room. It was practically a monastic cell. There was no Internet. No computers at all. It was like going back in time. From the look of the glam poster of a Chinese pop star on this new wall, it could be 1987, when things were convenient but not oppressively so. When you had to look things up in books and places up on maps and wait after sweeping your finger around a rotary dial for the *chk-chk-chk* sound to fade. All those forced pauses had seemed so inconvenient at the time, but the lost fermatas and lungas, they gave you just enough time, didn't they, to change your mind. To save yourself.

Yes, she could imagine herself passing the days here with Wendi, learning how to wax and how to be Chinese. And hadn't Brandon spent an entire PCH lunch extolling the "manscaping boom," the growing demand for back-, sack-, and crack-stripping skills? Maybe her clients would tell her everything the way she told Wendi everything. Because wasn't Wendi, like Leslie, a life coach of sorts? A hair coach, at least?

"This one gonna hurt," Wendi warned as she pulled back an arm's-length strip of gauze with a mighty rip. And it did hurt. Felt just like sitting down on a leaf blower, in fact. But it was a purifying pain, and when she was done, Anna tipped Wendi extra without regret.

The door tinkled and she merged seamlessly into the foot traffic streaming up Fifth Avenue. The flag above McDonald's was snapping hard in the wind and Anna felt a sting of color in her cheeks. She walked past a Vietnamese restaurant and a Mexican restaurant and a shop selling quinceañera supplies. A man on the corner had spread out a blanket and was selling DVDs that were probably pirated, but so what? So what! People were buying them and they looked happy. The mango lady waved from behind her stall and, on a whim, Anna stopped. With a few expert whacks, the woman transformed the mango into an orchid. She dipped it in salt and gave it a squirt of lime juice from a plastic bottle as Anna handed over her dollar. She bit into it. The mango was amazingly ripe. Hot and cold at the same time, bitter yet sweet. *They should call this fucking* life *on a stick*, Anna thought, letting mango juice drip brazenly down her chin. She pulled out her cell to call Leslie. She knew it was too soon—that she was probably just jacked up on a cocktail of mango juice and hope, high on the feeling of the wind whistling jauntily between her Formica-smooth thighs—but the need to testify was too great.

She had a shining picture of herself asking Leslie, *How are you? How is Dora? What happened with Brie? Is everything OK?* And if Leslie brought up Taj, Anna would agree to everything—Taj's perfidity, her stupidity, Leslie's lucidity—all the idities. Leslie would tell her to look at it another way; that Taj had given this new chapter of her life a Genesis. And Anna would take the opportunity to lay out her vision in a clear and purposeful tone. She would demonstrate a newfound maturity and restore Leslie's faith in her powers of judgment. Because a goal without a plan is just a wish, but she *had* a plan. She would find that long-unread e-mail from her mother, subject line: Offer. She would click on it, zeroing out the balance on her in-box. She would hit reply and compose a message. A message consisting of exactly one word.

Yes.

Acknowledgments

Thanks to:

My parents and my late grandmother, Irina Simon. Joshua Knobe, without whom this book would not exist, our daughter, Zoe, and Bruce and Kath Knobe.

The wonderful and long-suffering women of FSG: Kathy Daneman, Charlotte Strick, and Gabriella Doob. John McGhee, I've never met you, but you sure as hell know your way around a semicolon. And especially Eric Chinski, for believing in me.

Merrilee Heifetz, Sarah Nagel, and Jean Garnett at Writers House.

Benjamin Coonley, Andrei Konst, Amanda & Neil, Bob Gourley, Maria Sonevytsky, and Marlo Poras, for your friendship and support. Galina Kuleshova, the best nanny on Earth. Anna Moschovakis, thank you for the CARBS. (Also, thank you, carbs. I love you.)

And to the guys at Southside Coffee, who nicely let me sit there for a year or two nursing a cup of coffee while secretly writing a book. Your coffee is truly the best in the universe.